C000160813

A Butt of Heads

Book two in the Robot vs Dragons trilogy

Stay in touch!

Author's newsletter:
spacejock.com.au/ML.html

facebook.com/halspacejock
twitter.com/spacejock

Works by Simon Haynes

All of Simon's novels* are self-contained, with a beginning, a middle and a proper ending. They're not sequels, they don't end on a cliffhanger, and you can start or end your journey with any book in the series.
Robot vs Dragons series excepted!

The Hal Spacejock series for teens/adults

Set in the distant future, where humanity spans the galaxy and robots are second-class citizens. Includes a large dose of humour!

Hal Spacejock 1: A robot named Clunk
Hal Spacejock 2: Second Course
Hal Spacejock 3: Just Desserts
Hal Spacejock 4: No Free Lunch
Hal Spacejock 5: Baker's Dough
Hal Spacejock 6: Safe Art
Hal Spacejock 7: Big Bang
Hal Spacejock 8: Double Trouble
Hal Spacejock 9: Max Damage
Hal Spacejock 10: Cold Boots (2019)

Also available:
Omnibus One, containing Hal books 1-3
Omnibus Two, containing Hal books 4-6
Omnibus Three, containing Hal books 7-9
Hal Spacejock: Visit, a short story
Hal Spacejock: Framed, a short story
Hal Spacejock: Albion, a novella

The Robot vs Dragons Trilogy.
High fantasy meets low humour!
Each set of three books should be read in order.

1. A Portion of Dragon and Chips
2. A Butt of Heads
3. A Pair of Nuts on the Throne
4. TBA (2019)

The Harriet Walsh series.

Set in the same universe as Hal Spacejock. Good clean fun, written with wry humour. No cliffhangers between novels!

Harriet Walsh 1: Peace Force
Harriet Walsh 2: Alpha Minor
Harriet Walsh 3: Sierra Bravo
Harriet Walsh 4: Storm Force (2019)
Also Available:
Omnibus One, containing books 1-3

The Hal Junior series

Written for all ages, these books are set aboard a space station in the Hal Spacejock universe, only ten years later.

1. Hal Junior: The Secret Signal
2. Hal Junior: The Missing Case
3. Hal Junior: The Gyris Mission
4. Hal Junior: The Comet Caper

Also Available:
Omnibus One, containing books 1-3

The Secret War series.
Gritty space opera for adult readers.

1. Raiders (2019)
2. Frontier (2019)
3. Deadlock (2019)

Collect One-Two - a collection of shorts by Simon Haynes

All titles available in ebook and paperback. Visit spacejock.com.au for details.

Dedicated to my loyal fans. You're awesome!

Bowman Press

v 1.02

This edition published 2018 by Bowman Press

Text © Simon Haynes 2018
Cover art © Bowman Press 2018
Stock cover images copyright depositphotos.com

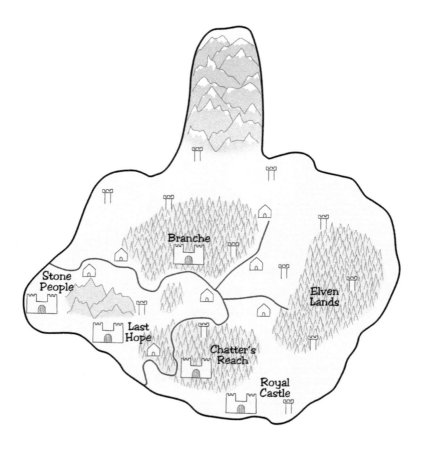

Old Kingdom Map Makers ... pointing the way since 564 A.F.

Warning! Spoilers!

This novel follows directly after A Portion of Dragon and Chips, and I thought it would be a great idea to include a very brief recap of where the various characters ended up. If you've only just finished reading A Portion of Dragon and Chips, or have an excellent memory, feel free to skip this section.

If you haven't read the first novel yet, stop now because A Butt of Heads is book two in the trilogy.

At the end of the previous novel ...

... Clunk, Millie, Father M and Hurm had just arrived in the city of Last Hope, where Clunk helped to put out a raging fire. Hurm is on a quest to become Queen Therstie Mollister's new champion, and must return with a baby dragon. Clunk needs a dragon for an aerial survey of the Old Kingdom, Millie is sticking with Clunk, and Father M is just after the cash reward a baby dragon will bring in.

... Queen Therstie is entertaining Prince Feine Grayne of the Barks at her palace. He arrived with news of Tyniwon Mollister, her half-brother, and in response she sent a brave knight to fetch Tyniwon home.

... Sur Loyne, who's not really that brave, enrolled the unwitting knights Sur Kah and Sur Pryze in his quest. Together they are riding to the city of Branche, in Bark. Unfortunately they lost their money and most of their gear in the Great Tavern Robbery.

... Having just killed the King of the Barks in a terrible face-moulding incident, Tyniwon is fleeing towards Elven lands with his master, Wiltred the metalworker.

But wait, there's more!

Lord Varnish, the Spymaster, is plotting Queen Therstie's demise.

...So is Lord Chylde, her uncle.

...So was Tiera, of the Grey Mountain people, but she decided not to go through with it.

...Captain Spadell, who wanted Tiera to kill the queen, is now plotting Tiera's demise instead.

...Under Captain Spadell's orders, Pentonville and Islington are searching for Tiera in order to kill her.

...Tiera is fleeing Mollister lands to save her life. She's accompanied by a suspiciously normal farm boy, Thonn, who happens to gain magic power when he's exposed to perlstone. They were heading to Last Hope, but changed their plans to throw off pursuit, and are now heading north towards the Bark Kingdom instead. Neither of them are currently planning to kill anyone ... but stay tuned.

...Runt was heading out to sea, powering towards the horizon aboard a tiny wooden boat towed by a humongous sea snake, which will probably kill him.

...And finally, Lord Greyfinger, the sneaky, conniving cad, is *still* dead.

The gigantic sea serpent had come out of nowhere, passing so close beneath Runt's little rowing boat that it almost tipped the craft onto its beam ends. That wasn't the worst of it, though, for the knot at the end of the mooring rope had lodged itself between two of the serpent's huge scales, and then all hell really had broken loose. The rope tightened with a *twang*, the boat leapt forward as though fired from a catapult, and the sudden jerk almost tossed Runt over the stern.

Now the boat was throwing out a huge, curling bow wave as it sliced through the sea, towed towards the horizon by the unwitting sea serpent.

Runt scrambled to the bow and poked his head over the side for a better look. The sight was not promising, for the creature was many times larger than his boat, with huge, glittering scales and a lithe, powerful body. Fortunately, the serpent didn't seem to be aware of him, or the boat, and thus he wasn't in any immediate danger.

Runt glanced around for inspiration, but the sea was empty in every direction. The land of his birth had disappeared over the horizon, and the sea serpent was showing no signs of slowing down.

Then, cursing his stupidity, he remembered the sword at his

belt. The boat's mooring rope was stretched taut ahead of him. All he had to do was chop through the thing! He had a sack of provisions on board, and the ocean currents would eventually carry him ashore. After all, things washed up on the beach all the time.

Runt drew his sword and grabbed hold of the rope ... just as the sea serpent decided to dive for the ocean depths.

'Whoa! *Spit!*' exclaimed Runt, as the rope suddenly angled downwards, dragging the fore end of the boat under water. Fortunately, he was still holding the rope, but he was flung bodily into the air and lost his grip on the sword. He landed with a splash, and as he opened his eyes he saw the sword spiralling away into the depths.

The water was clear, shot through with rising bubbles, and Runt held his breath as he scrabbled at his belt for his dagger. The sea serpent's tail was so close he could reach out and touch it ... if he were completely mad.

Instead, his fingers closed on the hilt of his knife, and seconds later he was sawing at the rope like a maniac.

The rope parted, the serpent swam off with a flick of its powerful tail, and the wooden boat stopped sinking. Runt was still clinging to the remains of the mooring rope, and he hung on for all he was worth as the boat rose towards the surface. His head emerged from the waves, and he took a deep breath of salt-laden air before momentum plunged him underwater again. He could see the boat above him, capsized, the waterlogged sack of provisions still jammed under one seat. Slowly, he pulled on the rope, until he broke the surface again. He was at the bow, and the wet hull loomed over him like an oversized turtle shell.

Runt realised he only had one chance. He must right the boat, or he'd die. His fingers would weaken, and once he let go of the rope he'd follow his sword into the ocean depths.

It was easier said than done. The boat was heavy, waterlogged, and there was nothing to brace against. Every time he tried to push one side up, he'd be forced down into the water, desperately clinging to the rope for survival. And each time he kicked his way to the surface, he imagined what kind of tasty morsel he looked like to the creatures of the deep. The sea serpent, a passing shark, carnivorous jellyfish ... his imagination ran riot with the horrible deaths in store for him.

Then he had an idea. Instead of pushing one side of the boat upwards, why not use his weight to pull the other side down? The net result would be the same, after all. The wooden planks comprising the hull were rough and worn, and his fingers found purchase. Slowly, he climbed upwards, expecting the boat to right itself at any second.

Instead, he found himself sitting athwart the keel, legs splayed. It was uncomfortable, to say the least, but he was no longer in danger of drowning.

Runt scanned the horizon, hoping the little boat had returned to shore while he'd been fighting for survival, but there was nothing in sight. The salt water had left him thirsty, and his stomach growled as he remembered the ham and the jug of fresh milk in the sack of provisions, but he was not yet desperate enough to try reaching it. After all, it was directly beneath him, and he'd have to go back into the water and make his way under the hull to reach the sack.

Runt checked the horizon again, shielding his eyes from the afternoon sun, and his heart leapt as he spotted a white smudge. Was that land? Snowy mountaintops, perhaps? He rubbed his eyes and stared again, trying to make out details. The smudge looked square, like a pocket handkerchief, and as he watched it, it slowly grew bigger. He wasn't aware of any square mountains, not even in the wildest sort of tales, and when the vision got closer he realised his mistake. The square was a sail, and coming into view beneath it was the prow of a huge sailing ship.

The Old Kingdom didn't have such vessels, not since the sea serpents turned up to infest the coastline centuries earlier, and Runt could only stare as the ship got closer. It was sailing directly towards him, and he could see faces above the rails. Some of the crew were pointing, and Runt saw a flash of light as the sun caught the lens of a spyglass. Half-heartedly, he raised a hand in greeting.

As the ship got closer he realised there wasn't just one sail driving it along . . . it carried many of them, billowing from three huge masts in a row. He'd only seen the one because the ship had been heading directly towards him.

There was a shouted command, a whistle of pipes, and the sails were furled expertly, leaving only a couple for steerage. Runt could see dozens of men high in the rigging, working furiously to bring the flapping fabric under control, and even as he watched the ship turned gracefully in its own length, until the few remaining sails acted as a brake. When the ship came to a halt, they too were stowed.

'Why, it's a child!' said a voice. 'What's the little fellow doing out here all alone?'

'You down there!' shouted another voice. 'Was your ship wrecked?'

'A sea serpent dragged me out to sea,' Runt called back.

There was a round of laughter. 'He jests, even in the face of danger. What a stout little fellow.'

A rope ladder was deployed, the end splashing into the sea nearby. Runt eyed the ladder, and his gaze travelled all the way up the side of the ship to the faces far, far above. It looked as high as a wooden cliff, and the rungs were almost two feet apart. But before he could gather up his courage to tackle the climb, a sailor came flying down the rope ladder, his hands and bare feet guiding him unerringly. When he reached the bottom, he stared at Runt in surprise. 'You are no child!' he said.

'I'm Runt. Nice to meet you.'

'Well met, little man.'

'Not so much of the little,' said Runt acidly. 'That is, if you want to keep both ears.'

The sailor grinned. 'That's the spirit. Now, let's get you aboard before the captain sails off without the pair of us.'

'Hurm starving.'

Father M was hungry too, but he wasn't one to show weakness around minor party members. The previous night they'd been treated to a feast in their honour, but alas the city of Last Hope was not prosperous, and the days of taxpayer-funded tables groaning with roast meats, side dishes and tankards of ale were a distant memory.

Instead, as their reward for saving the city from a firestorm, they'd been offered a modest platter of cheese and crackers washed down with lashings of fresh water. The water was essential, because the crackers were very dry indeed, and as for the cheese ... well, Father M wasn't even sure it had finished aging, for it resembled lumpy milk and tasted like something squirted from an entirely different part of the cow. He wasn't sure whether the little green bits were chives or chewed blades of grass, so he stuck to the crackers and tightened his belt.

But now it was a new day, and his stomach was grumbling. Father M opened his eyes, and he brightened a little when he realised the merchant stalls would be open for business. He could buy himself a real breakfast ... or better still, he could send Hurm to fetch it for him.

Father M sat up on the rough wooden bed, wincing at his aches and pains. He was just stretching his arms when he heard footsteps, and a moment later Clunk looked in.

'I have a message from the mayor,' said the robot. 'He says we can use this house indefinitely.'

'They were very grateful I helped put their fire out.'

Clunk ignored the sudden distortion of the facts. He was the one who'd put the huge fire out when they first arrived in Last Hope, but he wasn't about to quibble over minor details. 'It wasn't about the fire. They're keen to keep me around and make use of my skills.' He hesitated. 'Rampaging dragons have been driving residents away, which is why half the houses are empty. They've asked me to come up with a new slogan for their promotional material.'

'How about 'Come to Last Hope, where you probably won't get eaten'?' said Father M sourly. 'Don't forget to include a drawing of the local cheese, to really drive the point home.' He dug around in his robes until he found a small silver tin, and after inhaling half the contents his outlook brightened considerably. 'Did you tell him we'd take him up on his offer once we return from the rocky wastes with our dragon?'

'I didn't mention that part, no.'

Father M eyed the metal man, trying to read his expression. He prided himself on being a body language expert, and could usually read other people as though they were mere books.

6

Unfortunately, Clunk's pages were as difficult to pry open as those of a teenage boy's porno mag. 'What's the issue?' he asked, and instantly regretted the turn of phrase.

'Through subtle questioning, I learned that the townsfolk do not want adventurers stirring up the local dragons. Apparently this leads to revenge attacks, and so venturing into the rocky wastes is ... discouraged.'

Father M gave the robot a knowing smile. 'If it's a question of buying a dragon-hunting license, I'm sure we can gather enough funds.'

'A license?'

'You obviously don't know these types like I do. They can't tax fresh air, but everything else is fair game. Why, they'd put a tax on water from the stream, should such a thing be possible.'

'This is not a question of licensing.'

'So how do they discourage adventurers, if it's not via this license nonsense?'

'They hang them, displaying their bodies on hooks near the southern wall.'

Father M swallowed. 'They ... '

'Hang them,' finished Clunk. 'Of course, hanging wouldn't have any effect on me, but they would probably devise a suitable alternative.'

'Then the solution is simple,' said Father M, with the air of someone used to outwitting mere bureaucrats. 'We will buy provisions and depart to the south, before heading west the moment we are out of sight of the city.'

'Most people would consider that a wise idea,' said Clunk, with the air of one who didn't. 'Unfortunately, there's a line of watchtowers to the west of here. Each tower has a complement of archers and an early warning system. Originally, the towers were built to warn the city of incoming dragons, but they're just as effective at barring adventurers from the rocky wastes.'

'By Zephyr's hairy chest, this is indeed a problem!' exclaimed Father M. 'How does one pass such a barrier without attracting arrows?'

'I was going to suggest we pass them at night,' said Clunk.

'Yes, I was just about to recommend such a course. It's obvious to a trained mind such as my own.'

'Except they have patrols. And the patrols have attack dogs.'

Father M pursed his lips, and he decided to hold back any plans he might come up with until he had all the facts. Actually, he couldn't think of any plans, save raising an army and storming the towers, and that would be rather expensive in both coin and lives. A day or two earlier Runt had suggested creating a fake dragon by sewing bat wings to a lizard, and now Father M realised it wasn't so foolish after all. It might hold together just long enough to convince the queen it was a baby dragon, and then they could collect their reward and get the hell out of there before it started chasing mice.

However, the metal man wasn't finished yet. The robot had a faraway look in his eyes, as though he were coming up with a devilish plan, and Father M was pretty sure it wouldn't involve needles, surgical thread and unwilling reptiles.

'Silk,' said the robot. 'That is the answer.'

'I'd agree with you, but I'm not sure what the question is.'

'You must purchase all the silk in the city. Bring it here with all the fine thread you can find. Rope, too. We'll need a lot of rope.'

'You want me to run errands like a grocer's boy? Why not Hurm?' The moment he spoke, Father M knew why not. Hurm couldn't count past three, and the first wily shopkeeper he met would take all their money for a mere scrap of silk. Plus

...breakfast. 'Very well, I shall attend to the matter. Hurm can fetch and carry.'

'You'll need to work quickly,' said Clunk. 'The other fabric merchants will raise their prices if they smell a shortage.'

'You said *all* the silk, but exactly how much do you need?'

Clunk did a quick mental calculation. 'One thousand, three hundred and forty-two yards of fabric, assuming a width of one yard.' He actually tried to say metres, but his internal translation routines supplied the local version of the measurement. After a few more calculations he reeled off the rest of his requirements, making sure Father M noted them down correctly.

'A wheeled wagon? Enough rope to hang three quarters of the population? Small metal rings? To what end do you need such items?' asked Father M. 'Are we to wear silken disguises to avoid the guards at the watchtowers? For if so, there will be enough to disguise a very large army, but I will have to buy silks in the most subtle colours.'

'Colour is irrelevant,' said Clunk. 'Anything will do.'

Still mystified, Father M fetched Hurm and left on his errand. Meanwhile, Clunk refined his plans in his head, adapting designs and specifications until he had something which could be put together with the materials available to him. Once he had what he needed, he woke Millie, and together they set about clearing enough floor space for the construction of his project.

2

Thonn and Tiera made good time on the north road. They walked in silence, taking cover whenever they heard horses, and generally keeping to themselves. Once they reached Branche, the Bark capital, they were hoping they could find a safe place to sleep before making plans for the future.

'Hide!' muttered Tiera, as she heard hooves coming up behind them. They left the road just in time, crouching behind a large bush just as three men trotted up on horseback. From their clothes and weapons, the men looked more like itinerant knights than the city guard Tiera knew were pursuing her, but for all she knew the word was out everywhere. Spadell might have put a bounty on her head, and if he had, she wouldn't be safe anywhere.

Then she felt Thonn's grip on her arm, and she turned to see him staring at the knights with a look of intense hatred. She was puzzled by his reaction, but when she studied the men she saw what had angered Thonn so much . . . the lead rider was Sur Loyne, the queen's champion. The very coward who had almost beaten Thonn to death in the Chatter's Reach prison several days earlier.

Well, that sealed it. If the queen's champion was on her tail, Spadell must have given her up. With a sinking feeling Tiera realised she'd be running for the rest of her life.

'We must kill him,' hissed Thonn.

'Not now,' whispered Tiera. She too had a bone to pick with the knight, but the last thing she wanted was for the angry young farm boy to run into the road and die in some pointless duel. So, they hid until the horses vanished into the distance, and then Tiera and Thonn emerged from the bushes, pulling leaves and twigs from their hair.

'Will this change our plans?' Thonn asked her.

He spoke calmly, and Tiera was grateful. Yes, Sur Loyne was a coward and a bully, but they had bigger things to worry about. 'We'll keep going for now. When he reaches Branche they'll tell him they've never heard of us, and then he'll ride back to Mollister lands.'

Thonn was silent, and Tiera knew he was thinking of his revenge. 'Let him go,' she said gently. 'He has wronged so many, his early death is all but assured. There's no need to put yourself in harm's way.'

Thonn nodded, but she could see he wasn't convinced. So, they walked on in silence, keeping a wary eye out for the returning horsemen.

Tiera had estimated a day's walk to reach the border, and night was falling when they came across a small settlement straddling the road. A signpost announced that the Bark kingdom was five leagues ahead, and Tiera decided it was a good opportunity to replenish their supplies. The first stall they encountered sold cloaks, priced from two shillings each. Tiera shook her head at the seller, who spread his hands as he saw her reaction. 'You're going to need them in Bark lands,' he said.

'We'll manage.'

11

'Trust me, you won't.' The man indicated Tiera's weapons. 'You'll want a cloak to hide those.'

'If anyone tries to take my sword I'll run them through.'

'That's not–'

'Give up,' said Tiera. 'A cloak is sixpence in Chatter's Reach, and even that's too much.'

The seller shrugged. 'Suit yourselves, but don't come crying to me later.'

They bought a few supplies from the other merchants lining the road, then left the settlement behind as they continued up the north road towards the border. A league or two further on they came across another stall, this one selling cloaks for five shillings each.

'Five shillings!' muttered Tiera. 'I thought two shillings was a rip-off, but five is insane.'

Thonn glanced over his shoulder. 'Perhaps we should go back to the settlement and get the cheaper ones.'

'We-don't-need-cloaks,' growled Tiera, through clenched teeth. Despite her assertion, even she could see that other travellers on the North road were all wearing the long, black garments. By now, though, she was adamant none of the stall holders would be getting their hands on her money.

An hour later they reached a marker post indicating one league to Bark territory. Beside the road was yet another vendor, this one with cloaks for ten shillings each.

'I really think we need cloaks,' murmured Thonn.

With a thunderous expression, Tiera approached the seller. 'Do you think we're fools?' she demanded.

'No, I think you're brave,' said the seller, as she took in Tiera's outfit. 'If you take that sword into Bark lands, you'll be arrested on sight. A cloak is your only chance, unless you want to sell me your weapon.'

Tiera considered the offer. The sword was a piece of junk, and she still had her stiletto, concealed in the sleeve holster. 'Two cloaks for the sword?' she said at last.

'No, but I'll give you a couple of capes.'

'What's the difference?'

The seller held one up. It was forest green, and unlike the full-sized cloak it was barely long enough to reach her waist.

'Fine, whatever,' snapped Tiera. She handed over the sword in its scabbard, and accepted two capes in return. She slung hers over one shoulder, while Thonn donned his and tied up the little ribbon at the front. 'Happy now?' Tiera asked him, as they continued on their way. Quite frankly, she thought Thonn looked ridiculous, with his top half covered by the cape, and his bare legs sticking out of his loincloth below. Still angry, she strode for the border at a punishing pace, hoping to walk off her bad temper.

They finally reached the border, which looked exactly like the rest of the road apart from a signpost advising that all visitors bringing metal into Bark lands would be put to death. Tiera pursed her lips as she studied the sign, and then she looked down at her boots with their polished brass buckles. A cloak would have hidden the buckles, but the cape ... well, the cape was patently useless.

'You're gonna need a bigger coat,' remarked Thonn.

Islington reined in his horse, bringing the mount to a halt. There was a settlement ahead, with a jetty protruding into the river, and he could see several children playing in the dirt. It was an unlikely hiding place for their quarry, one Tiera of the Grey Mountain people, but he was fed up with searching the woods and there was always the chance of a good meal and a tankard of ale.

'Looks harmless enough,' said Pentonville. 'How do you want to handle this? Are we looking for an escaped prisoner, or shall we tell them Tiera's our long-lost sister?'

'There's no love for bounty hunters in these parts,' said Islington. 'Let's go with the missing sister routine.'

Pentonville nodded, and they spurred their horses onwards. As they approached the settlement they reined in once more, dismounting so as to seem less threatening. Since their mounts were laden with all manner of murderous weapons the gesture was probably pointless, but they had to try nonetheless.

'Village ahoy!' shouted Islington.

The reaction was swift. The children took one look at them, screamed in terror and vanished into the nearest house.

'Good start,' muttered Pentonville. 'You just scared the spit out of their brats.'

'What would you have me do, remove my armour and approach the village naked?'

'If that was your alternative, I'm glad you merely shouted at them.'

Islington noticed they were being observed, and he raised a gloved hand in greeting. 'We mean you no harm,' he shouted. 'We're looking for our sister, that's all.'

'There are no sisters here,' shouted the woman. 'We don't have none!'

'Not that sort of sister. I refer to a blood relative named Tiera.'

The woman studied him, then Pentonville. She was still hiding in the doorway, so it was hard to determine her expression, but the next words out of her mouth were pretty clear. 'Never heard of 'er. Now go away before you scare me crops.'

The two men exchanged a glance. 'Er, are you certain?' called Islington. 'She's about this tall, dark hair, handy with the knife.'

'Like I said, she was never 'ere.'

'Very well, I appreciate your help in the matter. Some might lie to us, given the size of the reward we're offering.'

The woman vanished, and they heard a muttered conversation with someone inside the hut. Then she reappeared. 'Tiera, you say? What's it worth to you?'

Islington hid a smile. 'Two silver shillings for information, and another for your best ale, and a round of provisions.'

'Make it five shillings, and you got yourself a deal.'

'Four, and not a penny more.'

'All right, all right,' grumbled the woman. 'Tie up your horses, and I'll fetch you a tankard each. Bread and cheese also, and ham cured only last week.'

The two men secured their horses to a tree, then entered the modest hut. There was a blazing fire and a small table, and as they took their seats the woman laid out a decent meal in front of them. There was an old man seated by the fire, his white whiskers so long they drooped over his chest.

'Tiera was here yesterday,' said the woman. 'My daughter hired her to take care of some bandits.'

'Why would you pay for such a thing?' demanded Pentonville. 'The city guard is duty-bound to take care of such matters.'

The old man snorted. 'The city guard don't do spit,' he rumbled. 'Those ninnies wouldn't venture into these parts without they were two dozen strong, and even then they'd

15

trip over a root and drown in the piffing river before they did any good.'

'The guard is a noble body of men–' began Pentonville, irked by the man's tone. Islington silenced him with a swift kick.

'Noble, my stick,' growled the old man. 'Bunch of sword-waving pansies, the lot of 'em. Less backbone than a jellyfish, and stink twice as bad.'

'Why don't you say what you really think?' muttered Pentonville, looking hurt.

'Shush now,' said the woman. 'You'll be here all night if he gets onto his hobby horse.'

'Leaving the merits of the city guard aside,' said Islington, ignoring the old man's snort of derision, 'we really do need to find my sister.'

The woman nodded. 'She was travelling with a farm boy and a halfling, the first time I saw her. When she came back, the halfling had vanished.'

'They do that. It's their forest training.'

'And their short stature,' added Pentonville.

Islington remembered the lad they'd met in the woods the previous day, tending to a mule. 'Tell me about the boy.'

'A very polite young man, he was. Dunno how he stayed warm, wearing nothing but that loincloth, but that's youth for you. Full of vigour.'

Islington cursed under his breath. Had they but questioned the lad further when they encountered him the night before, they might have captured Tiera and saved themselves hours in the saddle. As for the halfling, who knew where the little fellow might have ended up? Then a thought occurred to him, and it wasn't a pleasant one. They'd been tracking a lone assassin, and odds of two against one had seemed like a decent advantage. Now it was three against two in Tiera's favour, and Islington didn't like that idea at all. 'The halfling ... was he a joyous fellow, much given to japes in the manner of a court jester?'

The woman shook her head. 'He was a vicious little spit. Sooner cut your throat than shake your hand, if you know what I mean. A dark soul, that one, you mark my words. Why, I wouldn't send ten men against a little monster like that, not if I wanted to see any of them alive by daybreak. Shivers he gave us, like the hand of death over–'

'Yes, yes, thank you. I get the picture.' Islington drained his mug and casually put five shillings on the table. The four they'd agreed on, and one extra to ensure he got the truth. 'Did they say where they were heading?'

The woman eyed the coins greedily. 'West, I think, to the city of Last Hope. The crossroads is nearby, just over the next hill.'

'Are you certain?'

'Yes, I've seen it many times.'

'No, not the crossroads. Are you sure that's where Tiera went?'

'Yes, yes. West it was.'

Islington stood, and he and Pentonville accepted a sack of provisions before heading outside to their horses. 'What do you think?' murmured Islington, once they were out of earshot.

'She'd have said anything for the money.'

Islington spat in the bushes. 'It's a long road to Last Hope, with little reward at the end. Why not go home, and tell the captain we killed this Tiera in his name?'

'What if she shows up again?'

'Then we apologise, and tell him we killed the wrong person. It happens.' Islington shrugged. 'By now she'll be using a new name, she's probably altered her appearance, and to all intents and purposes, she's dead.'

'It *is* a long road to Last Hope,' said Pentonville slowly. 'Perhaps we should rest in the inn for one night, then return to Chatter's Reach in the morning. An extra day's delay will lend credence to our story.'

'Then that's the plan,' said Islington, and he dug into the sack to tear off a knob of crusty bread.

3

Warning! Metal is forbidden in the Bark Kingdom, and any found carrying such will be put to death.

Sur Loyne snorted at the weathered sign. He was a Mollister knight, the Queen's champion, and he was engaged in official business. If any of the locals wanted his sword they'd have to climb over the bodies of Sur Kah and Sur Pryze to wrench it from his cold, dead fingers. Anyway, his horse's tack had brass fixings, and if he removed them his saddle would fall off.

'Backward peasants,' he muttered under his breath, and he urged his horse onwards with his metal spurs. Moments later he realised he could only hear one set of hooves, and when he glanced back he saw Sur Kah and Sur Pryze dismounting at the border. 'What the hell are you doing?'

Sur Kah gestured at the sign.

'That doesn't apply to us, you fool!' shouted Sur Loyne. 'We're practically royalty around these parts.'

'Between 783 and 785 they used a wooden saw to execute three princes,' said Sur Kah, as ready with the dates as he was unready with a sword.

'It took two years to cut their heads off?' asked Sur Loyne in disbelief.

'No, there were three separate trials over two years. One of the princes returned from the wars with a gold earring, and the other two refused to hand him over to the courts. So, as you can see—'

'You fool!' cried Sur Loyne, now thoroughly incensed. 'Could you not have regurgitated some of these facts before we set off on our mission?'

'I thought you knew,' said Sur Kah, with a sniff. 'It's common knowledge amongst educated men.'

Sur Loyne ignored the insult, and glanced at his surroundings. The road passed through a narrow ravine ahead, a classic ambush site if ever he saw one, and he suddenly felt exposed on the Bark side of the border. Spurring his horse, he rode back to the signpost at speed. 'What do you suggest? There's metal in just about everything we own.'

'We could paint our swords brown,' said Sur Pryze. 'If we did so, they would look like wood.'

'They would still ring hollow, like your head,' growled Sur Loyne. Brown swords, indeed! 'Why, we could paint them blue and pretend they were made from water ... except we have no paint.'

'I was only trying to help,' muttered Sur Pryze.

The three knights sat in their saddles, contemplating the problem while their horses cropped grass beside the road. There were puddles from recent rainfall, and as Sur Loyne studied his incredibly handsome face reflected in one, he hit upon the solution. 'I have it!' he exclaimed. 'We will coat our equipment with mud, so it takes on the appearance of wood.'

The other two exchanged a glance. They had no intention of getting executed for breaking local laws, but if things turned south so would they ... leaving Sur Loyne to face the music. This much was agreed upon in silence, with meaningful looks that Sur Loyne mistook for expressions of wonder at his sheer genius.

The knights dismounted and found a flattish stick each, and they spent the next ten minutes applying mud to every shiny metal part on their horses' tack, and to the buckles on their own boots. Most time of all was spent dabbing mud on the tiny metal rivets holding the harnesses together.

'What about our swords?' asked Sur Pryze.

'They're in the scabbards. Who's going to know?'

'But if we're forced to draw them?'

'When I run people through with my sword, their last thought isn't 'Oh, I wonder what that's made of?" said Sur Loyne darkly. 'Instead, it's usually 'Woe is me, for I have been bested by the most famous knight in the land'.' Then he realised they might be forced to remove their swords if they encountered King Larch, and he backtracked slightly. 'If necessary, we will remove our belts with our swords still sheathed. Now let us ride on, for I tire of your endless questions.'

They were all 'tired', for they'd stopped at a tavern along the way, where they'd managed to down four or five pints each before the awkward subject of payment came up. In the end, Sur Loyne presented the barkeep with a valuable ring which had been handed down from one family patriarch to the next for generations ... Sur Kah's family patriarchs, that is.

Now, after several attempts at getting their feet in the stirrups, a couple of head-first tumbles off the other sides of their horses, and much stomping around and unintelligible cursing, they mounted up and rode for the ravine, where they kept a wary, if somewhat bleary, eye out for signs of ambush.

It was suspiciously quiet between the steep rocky walls, but they emerged unscathed from the far end, and Sur Loyne

21

immediately picked up the pace. He wanted to collect Tyniwon as soon as possible, before the inhabitants of this backward land had a chance to put his metal to the test.

Wiltred and Tyniwon were heading east, cutting through a heavily wooded valley between two hills. From his knowledge of the area, Wiltred knew that the woods thinned out ahead, opening on broad, featureless marshlands. There would be a path of sorts, but frequent flooding and clouds of biting insects would make the going tough. Not for the last time, he sighed as he pictured his new workshop, and his tools, and the bright, metal-making future which had been cruelly snatched from his grasp.

'Leave me alone, you oaf!'

Wiltred raised his hand, and Tyniwon stopped. The shout came from a girl, or a child, and the source was just ahead, through the trees. Slowly, they crept forward, using the undergrowth for cover.

'I said leave me alone! I don't have anything you want!'

'You got everything I want,' replied a rough voice. 'I know you been to market, girly. Now give it.'

Wiltred raised his head for a peek, and he spotted a slender woman in a hooded cloak, her forearm gripped in the meaty paw of a burly ruffian. The girl looked more annoyed than frightened, and as she tried to back away Wiltred saw a purse of coin at her belt. The man saw it too, and made a grab for it.

'Oh no you don't!' shouted the young woman, twisting in

his grip. 'My family worked themselves to the bone for that coin, and I'm not giving it up that easily.'

'Is that so?' The man drew a dagger, smiling cruelly. 'Let's see you fighting after I've slit your throat.'

Before Wiltred could react, Tyniwon burst from the bushes like a charging bull. His boots thundered on the turf, and a second later his seven foot of muscle cannoned into the rogue. The man went flying one way, the girl went flying the other, and the dagger flew straight up in the air. As it came down again, turning slowly end-over-end, Tyniwon plucked it from mid-air before turning to offer the shocked girl his hand.

She regained her feet as the rogue fled into the bushes, leaving a path of broken twigs and shredded leaves. 'Why sir, I do believe you saved my life.'

Tyniwon reddened, and bowed deeply. 'It was my honour,' he said.

'Look out, it's another one!' shouted the girl, and Tyniwon spun on the spot, dagger at the ready.

Wiltred had just stepped from the bushes, and he stuck his hands up quickly before Tyniwon got a rush of blood to the head and knifed him. 'Relax, my dear, for we travel together.'

'Then you too are well-met, sir.'

Up close, he saw the girl had exquisite features, with high cheekbones and lively eyes of the purest violet. Curls of shining gold hair peeped out from under the hooded cloak she wore, and Wiltred smiled to himself as he took in her appearance, because it was obvious Tyniwon was already smitten. Despite his many and varied experiences with women, the giant was tongue-tied and blushing like a bridegroom on his wedding night. 'What are you doing out here, all alone?' Wiltred asked the girl.

'I was on my way home from selling produce at the market.' She put her hand out. 'I am Allyance of the river people.'

'Well met, Allyance. I am Wiltred of Tharn, and this is Tyniwon of, er, other places.'

They shook hands, and Wiltred was shocked at her strong grip. Upon seeing her slender hand, he'd been worried Tyniwon would crush it in his huge mitt, but instead it was the giant who winced.

'Oh, have you heard about poor king Larch?' Allyance asked them. 'I got out of the city just as the fuss erupted.'

'We've heard,' said Wiltred. 'Shocking news indeed.'

'There was a deathly pall over the city.'

That was probably the king going up the chimney, thought Wiltred, but he wisely said nothing.

'Where are you both going?' Allyance asked them.

'Oh, we're just out for a walk.'

The girl eyed their bulging packs and hiking boots. 'If you say so.'

'It's a very long walk.'

'And where exactly are you walking to?'

Wiltred hesitated. He didn't want to reveal his escape route, but they were obviously heading towards the marshlands so it was hardly a state secret. 'We intend to visit the eastern reaches.'

'You head for Elven lands?'

'N-no, not that far.'

'Good. It would be unwise in the extreme.' Allyance paused. 'Might I travel with you for the time being? My house lies in that direction, through the woods, and I would feel safer with company.'

Wiltred realised the girl would be useful cover. If word went out to hunt them down, the guards would be looking for two men, not two men and a peasant girl. Then he eyed Tyniwon's seven-foot frame, and sighed. They might travel with a dozen peasant girls, and the towering giant would still stick out like a sore thumb. Still, it was better than nothing. 'Of course you can, my dear. We can while away the journey with tales and merry japes.'

'Knock knock.'

Wiltred smiled, for her style of humour was famous in Bark lands. 'Who's there?'

'Supter.'

'Supter who?'

'Supter who to let me in.'

Wiltred's smiled faltered, and he realised that while the style of humour might be famous, the content was a little lacking.

Tyniwon cleared his throat. 'I could tell you about the time I met a king.'

'Knock knock,' said Wiltred hurriedly, before the big dolt could land them in trouble.

'Who's there?' said Tyniwon, getting into the spirit of the thing.

'He.'

'He who?'

'He who keeps his mouth shut is very wise indeed.'

And with his words ringing in their ears, they set off through the woods, heading east towards the marshlands ... but not too far east, lest they reach the lands of the Elves.

4

Moving swiftly, the sailor attached ropes to each end of Runt's rowboat, reaching underwater to tie them off, then signalled to the faces peering down from above. There was a cry of 'heave, you lubbers, heave!' and the little boat began to roll over in the water, forcing Runt and the sailor to clamber around the hull, over the side and into the soaking wet interior.

Then, righted once more, it shot into the sky, the sailor fending off from the warship's nice clean lines with a wooden pole.

Hi ho, pull him up
Yank that fishy from the sea!
Yes lads, haul him in
We'll have that fishy for our tea!

They rose in time with the singing until the little boat was level with the entry port at the ship's midpoint, where a pair of sailors dragged them inboard with boat hooks. Runt expected to see the captain and senior officers lined up to receive him, but that wasn't the naval way. Instead, the officers were on the quarterdeck at the stern, feigning disinterest until an underling could approach them with a report. There was no way they were going to stand around like excited schoolkids if Runt turned out to be a common sailor.

The little boat had barely thumped down on the clean white decking when there was a bellowed order from the quarterdeck. Overhead, sails dropped from the yardarms, and the warship's rigging creaked as the ship got under way. Nearby, Runt saw half a dozen men casting fishing lines into the sea, no doubt to help feed the ship's company. They were using corks tied to their lines, with a bent pin to hold the bait, and Runt smiled to himself as he thought of the massive sea serpent. Those men were going to need a bigger float.

A young officer in a faded uniform stepped forward to give Runt a quick inspection. He was wearing an impressive tricorne hat with a shiny badge of crossed swords, and his lively dark eyes took in the halfling's waterlogged clothing, the dagger at his belt, and the empty scabbard for his sword. 'Well, you don't look like a Methusian spy,' he said at last. 'Come below. I'll find you some dry clothes, and in return you can tell me your story.'

'What . . . what ship is this?' asked Runt. 'Who are you people? Where do you come from? What's a Methusian?'

'Easy on the questions there, lest I change my initial impression.' The officer relieved Runt of his dagger then gestured towards an open hatch, where a set of wooden steps led to the lower decks. 'I'm midshipman Berry, of the Stalyan navy. What is your name?'

'Runt.' There seemed little point in lying, and in any case Runt was too dazed to make anything up. To the inhabitants of the Old Kingdom, their land was the entire world. It had always been so, but this powerful warship now proved otherwise, and Runt was having trouble dealing with the implications. Berry's accent was foreign, the ship was a mobile fortress, and the level of technology around him was astounding. As they went below, Berry removed his hat and tucked it under one arm, keeping his head bent to avoid the low beams. Meanwhile, Runt trotted along beside him, looking around in astonishment. The deck contained twin rows of hulking great tubes on fat wooden trolleys, each tube at least ten feet long and seemingly cast from a single piece of metal. They were as thick as wine barrels at their widest point, and next to each one was a row of iron balls, each the size of Runt's head. There were implements, too. Long rods with sponges on the end, rammers, and others he couldn't even begin to see the use of. 'Wh-what are those things on the trolleys?' he said, as Berry led him to the stern of the ship.

'Those are our teeth.' Berry slapped the breech of one of the cannon as he passed it by. 'Without our guns, the *Intrepid* would be little more than a floating holiday home.'

Runt realised the metal balls were meant to be fired from the huge guns, and he swallowed. 'How far do they shoot those things?'

Berry gave him a calculating glance. 'If you're a Methusian spy, you're not a very good one, for their cannon are the equal of ours.'

'I've never heard of these Methusians.' Runt gestured, encompassing the cannon, the deck, and the thick wooden bulkheads. 'I've never seen guns like these, I've never heard of a ship which can navigate the oceans, and I've never–'

'Then you have led a sheltered life indeed, for the war has raged for decades.'

'Which war is that?'

Berry laughed. 'Very funny.' He pushed through a curtain, and motioned Runt towards one of two wooden benches flanking a table. A lantern hung from the ceiling, swinging gently in concert with the ship's motion, and the candlelight threw long shadows on the walls. Runt could see patches of new wood, repairs maybe, and he wondered what it would be like to sail aboard such a ship when the enemy were hurling those giant metal balls at it. Surely they would go right through the thick hull, cutting men down with flailing splinters of wood? He shuddered at the thought, and resolved to make his escape as soon as he could, for he had a better chance of survival against the sea serpents.

Berry lifted the bench seat and took out a heavy boat cloak, and once Runt was wrapped in the thick fabric, Berry took his seat. Then he took out Runt's dagger and stuck the point into the wooden tabletop, leaving the knife quivering between them. 'Interesting weapon,' he said. 'I've seen the like in history books.'

To Runt, the knife was cutting edge, so to speak, and he was getting tired of the officer's condescension. 'To you it might be an antique, but the men and women I've killed with it didn't seem to care.'

Berry eyed him thoughtfully. 'A fearsome warrior indeed, to take women's lives.'

'They were trying to take mine at the time,' said Runt, without elaborating.

'Right, enough of the idle chatter. I've been charged with obtaining your story, and it had better ring true or the captain will have you thrown overboard.'

'As long as you put me back in my boat, I'd be grateful.'

Berry smiled, and shook his head. 'We're avoiding the Methusian fleet, so as to strike at their transports without hindrance. If they were to pick you up, they'd soon learn of our presence. No, I'm afraid you're along for the mission.'

'How long will that take?'

'Months.' Berry shrugged. 'Perhaps a year or more, if we find suitable provisions.'

Runt gaped at the young officer. In the back of his mind he'd been hoping the ship would sail to the Old Kingdom and drop him off, but now it seemed he was going to war with the rest of the ship's crew.

Over the next ten or fifteen minutes Runt poured out his life story, or as much of it as he thought the midshipman would believe. Leaving out the stabbings, and the arrests, and the drunken debauchery so beloved of his kind, Runt finally ended on the sorry tale of how he managed to get swept out to sea.

'You're in pretty good condition for someone who's spent days in a boat.'

'Er, yes.' So far, Runt had omitted all mention of the Old Kingdom, for it had dawned on him that the land of his birth would be no match for such a powerful ship. He could picture half a dozen such vessels pounding the cities he knew and loved into gravel with huge cannonballs, the inhabitants slain or enslaved. No, better to keep quiet about the Old Kingdom, and pretend he'd floated away from Methusian lands ... wherever they were.

He was about to find out, for Berry left him alone for a few moments, and when the midshipman returned he was carrying a big roll of paper which turned out to be a map. He laid it on the table and secured the corners with empty beer mugs. 'Tell me now, from where do you hail? I must know, for the captain himself will surely question me.'

Runt stared at the huge, detailed map, which was covered in landmasses and vast oceans. There were borders within the landmasses, indicating whole countries, as well as cities, castles, dockyards and more. Alas, there was no sign of any familiar places.

The midshipman smiled at his expression. 'Not a seafarer, eh?' He indicated an expanse of empty ocean. 'We are sailing in this area.'

Runt noticed a smudge on the map near Berry's well-chewed thumbnail, and when he looked closer he realised it was a tiny, insignificant island, hundreds of leagues from anywhere. He was familiar with the coast of the Old Kingdom, and this blotch was a fair approximation. But where were the settlements and cities? Where were the rocky wastes, and the Elven kingdom, and the towering mountains? And why was the Old Kingdom so small?

Berry saw his interest in the island, and his expression changed. 'No!'

'What?' Runt looked up, and realised the midshipman was staring at him in horror. Indeed, Berry looked like he'd seen a ghost. 'What's the problem?'

'Y-you hail from the Cursed Island?'

Runt thought quickly. From the tone of Berry's voice, admitting he was from this Cursed Island, whatever it was, would probably lead to him being pitched overboard without ceremony. If he was lucky, they'd throw the boat in after him. If he was unlucky, they'd throw it into the sea *at* him, and it would land on his head. 'No, of course not. Cursed Island? Me? Who'd believe such nonsense!'

Berry relaxed. 'That's fortunate indeed, for the crew would have torn you limb from limb and scattered your parts to the four winds.'

Ping! Correct answer, thought Runt. He eyed the blotch on the map again. Obviously someone had got the scale wrong, for if they were right then the Old Kingdom was nothing more than a misplaced apostrophe on some illiterate shopkeeper's poster. Why, the scale of it! He scanned the vast continents, and could only shake his head in amusement. He'd heard of kings directing that their own countries be displayed more prominently, to encourage national pride, but with this map things had clearly got out of hand. 'So, this place here,' he said, indicating a coastline at random. 'How long to cross from one side to the other?'

'Six days, with a good wind.'

Runt smiled. Six days? It was about the same in the Old Kingdom, and yet the land mass was drawn ten times larger than the insignificant spec representing his home. The he realised something. 'What do you mean, with a good wind?'

'That's the sailing time, of course. On foot you'd be looking at several weeks.'

Runt swallowed. It was as though he'd lived in a cupboard his entire life, only to be shown the outdoors. The Old Kingdom really was an insignificant speck. Then he had another thought, a much more selfish one. With a ship such as this he could rule the Old Kingdom ... or at least, the bits of it around the edges within cannon shot. With a trained army as well, he could even rule the middle bits. The Mollisters, the Barks, the Elves, the Stone People and those other two kingdoms he could never recall the name of thanks to their inadequate tourism budgets ... all would bow to him. An invasion by sea! What could possibly go wrong?

The midshipman stood up, and Runt realised the questioning was finished. 'Is there any chance you can drop me off at a friendly port?' he asked Berry. 'I have family, and companions, and–'

'There aren't any friendly ports in these parts. Not friendly to us, at least.'

'Is there anyone I can talk to? To plead my case?'

The midshipman hesitated, then shook his head. 'My orders are to sign you to the ship's company. You obviously have your wits about you, so you'll train with the young midshipmen. If you fail at that, we'll sign you on as a landsman. And if you fail at that too, you're fish bait.'

Runt swallowed.

'Look,' said Berry, taking pity on him. 'It's not going to be that bad. We probably won't sight another warship for weeks, so there's plenty of time for you to learn your place. If there's any fighting you can hide in the bilges. You'll be safe enough down there ... unless we sink.'

Runt heard footsteps approaching, and the midshipman sprang to attention as he spotted the newcomer. It was a tall man with an elaborate uniform, and he barely spared Runt a glance. 'Well?' barked the man.

'He doesn't appear to be a spy, sir. In fact, he doesn't appear to be much of anything. An unwanted child who grew up alone, living off the land wherever he could. It was only by the merest accident that–'

'Yes, yes, spare me the heart-rending tale. Can he be pressed into service or not?'

'Aye, sir.'

'Then he should report to the sailing master, for the afternoon's navigation class is about to begin.'

The midshipman nodded, and as the officer departed, Berry lowered his voice to a conspiratorial whisper. Although, with the constant sound of waves along the hull, cries from the deck, and the wind whistling through the rigging, there was barely any need. 'That was the third lieutenant. He would have made First by now, had he not lost a prize in a storm. You'd do well to keep on his good side, for he does not suffer fools.'

5

After Father M left with Hurm to collect the silk, rope and other materials, Clunk turned to the next part of his project. Earlier that day he'd sewn hundreds of yards of water pipe by hand, and while that had been completed relatively quickly, this job was going to need a whole new level of automation. There was nothing else for it ... he was going to have to build a crude sewing machine.

'I need you to speak with each blacksmith in the city in turn,' Clunk told Millie, all the while drawing diagrams on sheets of parchment. 'Each should be given one page, no more, and if they don't seem confident in their skills I want you to walk away.'

Millie eyed the diagrams. 'What are they making?'

'Irrelevant. The important question is ... can they make it, and how quickly can they do so?' Clunk drew a circle, added a pair of equidistant holes, then sketched a side view with the thickness of the part measured in fractions of an inch. He was trying to keep everything as simple as possible, for the blacksmiths would be more used to hammering out horseshoes than forging the sort of delicate components he required. Then he noticed Millie's look of curiosity, and relented. 'These parts will be used to build a sewing machine.

It will enable me to join large pieces of fabric quickly and efficiently.'

'But the fabric ... what is that for? Is it to be a large bag, to store a dragon in?'

'I'm sorry, but there's no time to explain. I will go into more detail later.'

Millie left with his diagrams and a handful of money, and Clunk set off on a quest of his own. He needed woodworking tools, and within half an hour he'd bought a hand saw, a hammer and a crude pair of pliers. There were one or two other items as well, and, to cap his shopping trip off, he bought a couple of wooden planks to make the body of his sewing machine.

On the way back to their temporary quarters he encountered Father M and Hurm, who were pushing a handcart laden with rolls of fabric. Clunk inspected a loose end and nodded. 'Thank you. This is excellent.'

'I should hope so,' muttered Father M. 'Do you have any idea how much this cost?'

When they got home, Father M went to make a pot of tea while Hurm unloaded the cart. Clunk set to work on his planks, cutting out the shapes he needed with precise strokes of the saw. Every few moments there was a ground-shaking thud as Hurm dumped another roll of fabric nearby, until there was an impressive stack. When he was finished, Clunk beckoned him over and handed him a screwdriver. 'I want you to remove three internal doors. We're going to make a cutting bench.'

Hurm inspected the flat-bladed screwdriver, then shrugged and approached the nearest door. Instead of carefully removing the screws from the hinges, he grabbed the door and tugged, wrenching it clear with a splinter of breaking wood.

'No, not like that!' said Clunk quickly. 'Use the screwdriver!'

Hurm strode to the next door, jammed the screwdriver into the gap between door and frame, and levered the door off its hinges.

Clunk decided to leave him to it, instead concentrating on making three pairs of trestles. When he was done, he got Hurm to bring the doors over one by one, and when they laid them on the trestles they formed a huge, rectangular bench which half-filled the room.

'That hand cart you brought back ... ' began Clunk.

Hurm looked at him.

'I want you to remove the wheels and handles. Just save the carriage part. Understood?'

'Yes.' Hurm brandished the screwdriver. 'Hurm work.'

'Off you go then. And be careful not to break it.'

Seconds later he heard the sound of splintering wood, and he hoped the big man was following his instructions. Then Father M came in, sipping a hot mug of tea, and his eyebrows rose as he saw the doors. 'What are you doing?'

'It's a cutting bench,' said Clunk. 'We'll need plenty of room to measure out fabric.'

'I've gone along with this so far, but it's time you explained what you're doing.'

Clunk shook his head. 'The design is far beyond your comprehension. It will take too long to explain, and even if I did so, you won't believe it will work.'

'Will it get us a dragon?'

'It will certainly help.'

'Then you can save your explanations until later,' said Father M, and he took another sip of his tea.

Clunk took a roll of fabric and pulled several yards free, smoothing them on the bench. Then he took up a sharp blade, and after a few swift strokes he had two large panels.

'They're not square,' remarked Father M. 'One end is narrower than the other.'

'That's intentional,' said Clunk.

Father M sipped his tea. 'I say the same thing whenever I make a mistake.'

'It's not a mistake.' Clunk cut two more panels, and his lips thinned as he heard Father M tutting behind him. 'They're supposed to be like this!' protested Clunk.

'Sure they are. I mean, near enough is good enough, am I right?'

Clunk rounded on him. 'I'm building a huge sphere, you imbecile. If I cut all the pieces square it'll just make a cylinder, and that won't ...' his voice tailed off as he saw Father M's satisfied smirk, and Clunk realised he'd been goaded into revealing more than he meant to. 'You, sir, are a tricky one,' he said, in grudging admiration. It wasn't often a human got the better of him, and he resolved to be more alert around Father M in future.

'What can I do to help?' said Father M, pouring oil on Clunk's troubled waters. 'Can I cut some of those panels?'

'No, there are many different sizes, and it will take much longer if I have to draw the shapes for you.' Clunk hesitated. 'You can fetch me some glue, though.'

Father M frowned. 'That sounds like a job befitting Hurm.'

There was a splintering of wood from outside.

'He's busy,' said Clunk.

'Oh very well. How much glue do you need?'

'Half a barrel, if you can get it.'

Father M's eyebrows rose. 'Let us hope the local butchers have been rendering all their off-cuts.'

After he left, Clunk was alone for almost an hour, the silence broken only by the swish of his blade through the fabric and the splintering of wood from outside. Millie returned first, her face smudged with soot from the blacksmiths' fires. She eyed the growing pile of fabric panels without question, and watched as Clunk cut several more. When she realised he wasn't going to pause, she cleared her throat. 'I found three blacksmiths who could do the work. There was another one, but he said it would take a week so I left him off.'

'Thank you,' said Clunk. 'How long did they say?'

'At first they said tomorrow morning, but when I offered them more money they put aside their other work. You should have all the parts later this eve.'

'That is excellent news. Thank you.'

'I saw Hurm outside smashing up that handcart, but where's the wizard?'

'Fetching glue,' said Clunk, as he cut two more panels. He'd used up the first roll, and was now working with a new one of a muddy brown colour.

Millie came closer. 'Won't you tell me what you're making? I swear I'll burst if you don't.'

Clunk decided to confide in Millie while the others were absent. 'This is a balloon, and it's designed to carry us through the air.'

'If you're going to make fun of me ...' began Millie, an annoyed look on her face.

'It's the truth. This balloon will carry us over the watch towers. With luck, it will take us deep into the rocky wastes.'

Millie laughed, but stopped when she realised he was serious. There was an audible gulp, and she eyed the rolls of silk with a mix of fascination and fear. To her credit, it was mostly fascination. 'But ... how will it fly?'

'We will fill the balloon with hot air, which will cause it to rise.' Clunk saw disbelief written on her face, and explained further. 'Picture a blazing hot campfire. Do you recall how the sparks fly upwards into the night sky?'

'Of course.'

'A hot air balloon employs the same principle.'

'But how do you come down again?'

'That's inevitable, once the air inside the envelope cools. If you want to come down sooner, you just let the air out.'

Millie eyed the fabric panels he was cutting. 'I can scarcely believe this ... device of yours will fly.'

Me neither, Clunk almost replied, but he held his tongue. Truth was, he was working from theories and estimates, and there was no guarantee this entire project wouldn't end in a giant fireball on a mountainside. It was one of the reasons he hadn't told Father M, because he suspected the wizard would have refused to help.

As though summoned by magic, Father M returned at that moment. His face was pale, and he kept it averted from the small wooden barrel he carried at arm's length. As he entered the house, he was preceded by a pungent smell.

'Why, that is truly foul!' protested Millie.

After catching a whiff, Clunk suspended his olfactory process. 'Perhaps you could store that outside until I need it?'

Father M did so, and when he came back there was a bit more colour in his cheeks. 'I trust we won't be exposed to that stench for long.'

'It will smell better once it dries,' said Clunk. 'Now, can one of you check on Hurm? It's been some time since I last heard the sound of breaking wood, and–'

'I'll go,' said Millie.

'Remind him to leave the carriage part intact, along with its wooden seats.'

Father M watched her go, then approached the cutting bench. 'For the past hour I've been turning over every possibility in my mind, and I believe I know what you're building.'

'Oh yes?' said Clunk warily. He'd designed the balloon for the weight of four people, and if Father M backed out now he'd be forced to alter his plans. Either that, or he'd need a lot more ballast.

'Yes, it's clearly a type of bladder, which you will fasten to a wooden frame so that we might navigate the ocean. Come now, it's the only explanation.'

'I'm certainly building a mode of transport,' admitted Clunk.

'I knew it!' Father M clapped him on the shoulder, then winced and rubbed his smarting fingers. 'You are a stout fellow indeed. This lightweight boat will help to avoid the attention of those marauding sea serpents, of that I am sure. Genius, pure genius!'

Clunk smiled to himself, and went on with his cutting. Father M could think whatever he liked, as long as he helped build the thing. There would doubtless be more questions when it came time to carry the 'boat' up to the roof for its maiden voyage, but he'd deal with those later.

6

After a comfortable night in the riverside tavern, Pentonville and Islington enjoyed a leisurely breakfast before heading out to meet the local arms dealer. Their sergeant had equipped them with several valuable weapons when they'd embarked on their quest to find Tiera, and now that they were heading home again they had no intention of returning their stash. No, far better to sell them and claim they'd been stolen.

The arms dealer operated out of a nearby farm, where he kept a barn crammed with all manner of weapons. A wooden sign next to the entrance declared there was 'Something for everyone', and the statement was patently accurate. From cute sets of armour for children, to ballistas and giant catapults for dragon slayings and the odd spot of city wall breaching, the range of stock was truly impressive.

The arms dealer was a squat, elderly man with a long grey beard and an even longer grey ponytail. He sported a chainmail vest which appeared to have fused to the leather jerkin he wore underneath it, and he had a pair of hide trousers made from dragonskin. He looked up from a big ledger as the two city guards dismounted, then stood up and casually shouldered a huge war hammer. There didn't appear to be any bodyguards, but the man seemed more than capable of looking after himself. 'How can I help you, gentlemen?'

'Are you a dw–' began Pentonville.

'–one of the stone people?' interrupted Islington quickly, for the warhammer looked like it could crush them both with a single blow.

'Indeed I am, if it's any business of yours.'

'I thought your kind was into mining?'

'No, we're into gold.'

Islington studied the dwarf with interest, for it was said they could rip up a fair-sized back yard and pave it with neat flagstones in a single day. And, truth be told, the only thing they liked better than working with stone was getting paid for the work afterwards. Branching out into the weapons business was unusual, but he supposed the profits made it highly lucrative. 'Do you sell many of those?' asked Islington, nodding towards one of the ballistas. The giant crossbow was bolted to a carriage, and the barbed bolts were taller than he was.

The dwarf eyed him thoughtfully, shifting the warhammer to his other shoulder. 'What are you, tax inspectors?'

'N-no, just curious.'

'Curiosity doesn't pay the bills,' said the dwarf. 'Now out with it, why are you here?'

'We have weapons to sell.'

The dwarf snorted. 'You and every other deserter fleeing the city guard. I'll save you the time, for there's no demand for your lousy swords, and even less for your poxy armour.'

'We're not talking about guard weapons,' said Pentonville. 'This stuff is special.'

'All right, let's have a look then.'

Pentonville fetched the horses, and the dwarf's eyes gleamed as he saw the elven bow, and the curved swords, and the

43

daggers with their pommels of pure perlstone. He recovered quickly, though, and shook his head sadly. 'Sorry, lads. I'm up to here with fancy weapons.'

'What do you mean?' said Pentonville.

'It's like I said. People don't go for the detailed stuff these days. Too ornate, know what I mean?'

'So how much will you give us?'

The dwarf sucked air through his teeth. 'Well, you've caught me in a generous mood, so I'll say five shillings the lot. Shake hands on it, for it's a fair price.'

'Five shillings! Why, this bow alone–'

'Who uses bows these days? Crossbows are all the rage, believe me. More stopping power, and much easier to carry. Now if you were to bring me an elven crossbow, why then the sky's the limit.'

'But these daggers! That's gold around the handle, and the gems–'

'Worthless. The gold is just foil, and those aren't gems, they're pebbles.'

Pentonville opened his mouth to protest, but Islington silenced him. He'd seen the greedy look in the dwarf's eyes when the arms dealer handled one of the daggers, and he realised they were being played. 'Pentonville, leave it. We'll be back in the city within hours, and the merchants will surely offer a better price.'

Pentonville looked like he was going to argue, but Islington slowly closed one eye. 'Yes, you're right,' said his fellow guard. 'After all, they were selling basic swords for ten times their worth, so these weapons will fetch a pretty penny there.'

The two guards turned away and prepared to mount up. Islington held his breath, and his patience was rewarded.

'All right, gents,' said the dwarf. 'There's no need to haul those weapons all the way to Chatter's Reach, for I will make this one-time offer of ten shillings, and I swear that's final.'

It took half an hour and five more 'final offers' before all parties were satisfied, and after exchanging their weapons for cash, the two guards mounted up and set off for home. Islington decided to keep one of the daggers, just in case he could sell it for a higher price elsewhere.

They arrived in Chatter's Reach several hours later. The guards on the gate didn't recognise them at first, being out of uniform and all, but once they sorted out their identities they were ushered off to a meeting with Captain Spadell.

'Done already?' he remarked, without looking up from his paperwork.

'Yessir,' said Islington smartly.

'That assassin won't be troubling any more nobles,' added Pentonville.

'Excellent news. Well done, both of you.' Spadell stood up, and came around his desk to face them. 'Did she offer any excuses for her actions, after you captured her?'

'There wasn't much capturing involved.' Islington drew his thumb across his throat. 'Done nice and quick, it was. No fuss.'

'Very well. Take the rest of the day off and report for duty in the morning.'

Islington and Pentonville exchanged a glance. They'd expected a grilling, and they were surprised their story had been accepted without question.

When Islington and Pentonville told him they'd killed Tiera, Spadell felt a stab of guilt tinged with an even bigger feeling of regret. Guilt that he'd ordered her death, and regret because of her ready smile and her lively, intelligent eyes. An assassin she might have been, but he'd admired Tiera and he was truly sorry she was dead.

There'd also been a sneaking feeling of relief though, relief that Tiera could no longer reveal that Spadell had asked her to kill Queen Therstie. Had Lord Varnish learned of that little matter, Spadell would be lying dead also.

But then he realised Pentonville and Islington were lying through their teeth. They'd no more killed Tiera than he'd killed Queen Therstie by his own hand. Again, he experienced mixed feelings, only this time it was guilt that he'd failed Lord Varnish and overwhelming relief that Tiera was still alive.

After the two guards left his office, he dwelt on the matter for a moment, and he resolved to draft a report from Pentonville and Islington. In it, they'd vow that Tiera was indeed dead, and if she showed up again later he'd use the document to protect himself from Lord Varnish. He decided not to trouble the men for their signatures ... first, because he wasn't sure they could write, and second because it would be far less trouble to forge their names.

'Make way for the Lord's Messenger! Make way there!'

Spadell sighed. Even here, in his very own office, there was no respite from officialdom. He stood, just as the door opened and an oily little man slinked in. The Lord's Messenger was a creepy fellow, dressed all in black, and his slicked-back hair and obsequious manner set Spadell's teeth on edge. 'Yes? What is it?' demanded Spadell. 'Can't you see I'm busy?'

'No man is busy when Lord Chylde calls,' said the messenger, in a dry, lifeless voice. 'His Lordship requests your presence immediately.'

'I'll be right there. I just have some paperwork which–'

'This instant!'

Spadell had no choice but to obey, and he followed the unpleasant little man to Chylde's quarters. 'My Lord,' said Spadell, with the briefest of bows.

Despite the entreaties of the messenger, and the apparent urgency of the meeting, Chylde dismissed the oily little man and then took his sweet time pouring a goblet of wine. When he was finally happy, he sat down and swirled his wine gently, firelight reflecting off the polished brass goblet. 'Let's not waste time, Spadell. I want Sur Roybot back, and you're going to find him for me.'

'Are you referring to the metal man, my Lord?'

'Of course I am. He was secured in your cells, was he not?'

'He was, but he broke his irons as though they were made from paper, and the door he shattered as though it were nothing but straw.'

'Yes, I heard. A lamentable lapse on your part.'

'My Lord, I was called to the High Chancellor's tower at the time, to investigate his murder. All my guards were busy hunting his killer.'

'A lapse nonetheless, and one you must correct with all haste.'

Spadell suppressed a sigh. He'd only just fixed the Tiera problem, sort of, and now he was supposed to scour the Old Kingdom for the metal man. Still, he thought, at least Sur Roybot would be easier to find than an assassin ... and it wasn't like he'd be the one combing every square inch of the land. 'Yes, my Lord. Indeed, I have two men admirably suited to the task.'

'Only two?'

'Send any more, and I cannot guarantee your safety. There have been too many deaths in the city already.'

'Two sounds like the ideal number,' said Lord Chylde quickly, and he drained his goblet. 'Well? See to it man, and do not tarry!'

The interview clearly over, Spadell bowed again and left his Lord's chambers. On the way to his office he encountered a guard, and he sent the man to fetch Pentonville and Islington.

When they showed up, the two of them looked nervous. Spadell wanted them compliant and willing to help, so he didn't get right to the point. 'About that assassin, Tiera,' he began, and he suppressed a smile as the guards blanched. They were obviously worried their ruse had been uncovered, and he left an uncomfortably long silence so they could think about exactly how much trouble they might be in. Then, when he judged they were ready, he continued. 'You two did such a fine job that Lord Chylde himself wants you to carry out an even more important mission.'

Pentonville and Islington were so relieved they weren't being charged and executed on the spot, that it took a while for the rest of their captain's words to sink in. 'Another mission, sir? But you ... you gave us the rest of the day off.'

'What I gave, your Lord has just taken away again,' said Spadell pleasantly. 'You recall the metal man, of course?'

The men nodded. How could they forget, when they had found the creature in the first place?

'Well, Lord Chylde wants him back again, and he's asked me to put my best men on the job.'

'A-and why are we here, sir?' asked Pentonville.

'He means us, you fool,' muttered Islington.

'Correct,' said Spadell. 'After your resounding success with Tiera, I could think of no better pair to send out into the kingdom on this vital task. So, congratulations, the both of you. Take up your arms and secure supplies, for you leave immediately.'

'Oh *spit*,' growled Islington, as they left the captain's office.

'What is it?' Pentonville asked him.

'We've only got to buy our fudding weapons back off that arms dealer, that's what.'

'That's all you're worried about? You realise it could take months to find this Roybot character, and ...' Pentonville lowered his voice, '... it's not like we can lie about the outcome this time, is it? There aren't too many metal men in the Old Kingdom, are there?'

'Indeed there are not.'

'So that means we've really got to do our job. And what about my wife and daughter?' demanded Pentonville plaintively. 'I'm going to miss my home comforts!'

Islington was also going to miss the comforts of Pentonville's wife, but he wisely said nothing. 'Well, let us retrieve our horses and obtain supplies, for the metal man will not find himself.'

'Mother-fudding Lords and their mother-fudding orders,' growled Pentonville. 'What happened to the easy life, when all we had to do was stand guard on an empty beach?'

Islington clapped him on the shoulder. 'Come now, it won't be that bad. We only need one weapon each, and there'll be plenty of money left over. Think of it as an adventure! Why, we might even gain promotion if we succeed.'

'Yes, and we'll gain unmarked graves if we fail,' said Pentonville morosely.

And, on that happy thought, they went to find their horses. Again.

7

Allyance was as good as her word, for her parents' farm was indeed just over the next hill. The modest fields were neat and well-tended, and were surrounded by wooden fences to protect the crops. Wiltred could see carrots, cabbages, lettuce and more, all growing lush and healthy in even rows. There was even a cow in a separate field, a strong-looking animal with a clear eye and a gentle disposition.

'I'm impressed,' he said to Allyance. 'This must be the best-kept farm in the kingdom.'

She smiled at him. 'I thank you, sir. My family is hard-working, and this place means everything to them.'

As they passed through a gate he couldn't help noticing it opened smoothly on metal hinges, and he paused to admire the handiwork.

'Oh!' said Allyance, and she put a hand to her mouth. 'You won't report this, will you? My parents were immigrants, you see, and they're wedded to the old ways.'

'Of course I won't tell,' said Wiltred. 'Why, the king himself recently commissioned a workshop so that I might forge metal for his use.'

'Really?'

'Indeed. The kingdom is finally modernising.' Or would

be, he thought, if Tyniwon hadn't set it back decades by accidentally killing the king. Who knew what terrible despot might replace the free-thinking monarch, and what new laws they might bring in? Then Wiltred looked closer, for the metal had a curious green tinge. 'Now that's an unusual alloy,' he said, lost in thought. Never had he seen its equal, but he'd heard rumours. 'If I'm not mistaken, that's–'

'Oh look, my parents come to greet us. Mother! Father! These gentlemen saved me from a thief in the forest.'

Allyance's parents were a tall, willowy couple, and they wore the same hooded cloaks as their daughter. The man was welcoming, and he shook Wiltred and Tyniwon's hands eagerly, thanking them for their help. His wife, Allyance's mother, was another matter. She held back, regarding the newcomers with suspicion.

'I am Treeborne,' said the man, in a deep voice. 'This is my partner, Willowmere. Originally we were of the river people, but we have now settled here in the Bark kingdom.'

'It's a pleasure to meet you,' said Wiltred, bowing low. 'I am Wiltred, and this is Tyniwon.'

'They're metal-workers!' exclaimed Allyance.

At this, her mother breathed a sigh of relief. 'Then you are most welcome here, both of you. I apologise for my earlier reserve, for I thought you signalled an end to our peaceful lives.'

'I was admiring your hinges,' said Wiltred. 'That's a curious metal indeed, for it brings to mind tales of another land. A land far to the east of this place. I refer, of course, to the land of the E–'

'Won't you come inside?' said Willowmere quickly, as she scanned the nearby forest. 'Talking about such matters out here troubles me greatly.'

They entered the cottage, where Wiltred's senses were assailed by the plethora of metal objects on display. Next to the fireplace, an iron poker and matching tongs. Above the metal grate in the fireplace, a row of copper pans, their bottoms blackened from use. There were metal knives and forks, metal fasteners on the windows, even metal nails holding the furniture together. By the time he sat down at the table, his head was spinning.

Tyniwon, a Mollister, was less interested in the hardware. Indeed, he was far more interested in Allyance, and she in turn cast frequent admiring glances at the strapping young man.

'Let me fetch you a bowl of stew,' said Treeborne. 'Meanwhile, recount for us how you protected my daughter.'

'It was nothing,' said Wiltred. 'Allyance was being accosted in the woods. Some foul fellow roaming the wilds, it was, and he was intent on her earnings, and perhaps even her virtue. My companion, Tyniwon, put the fellow down with an impressive body check, and thus were the undesirable outcomes avoided.'

'Then we owe you a debt of gratitude,' said Willowmere. 'We don't have much, but you shall see a reward.'

'As I said, it was nothing. Anyone would have done the same.'

'Of course, it is fortunate you are wise to the ways of metal,' continued Willowmere. 'For if I had suspected you would turn us in to the king's guard, you would even now be buried in the midst of our compost heap.'

At that moment a cloud obscured the sun, and Wiltred swallowed in the sudden gloom. The tall strangers seemed to grow in the half-light, their violet eyes intense and, frankly, incredibly scary.

Then the sun came out again, and a bowl of stew was placed

in front of him. Wiltred took up a metal spoon, and was about to tuck into the delicious food when he paused. If they wanted to add him and Tyniwon to their compost pile ...

'Relax,' said Treeborne. 'Killing with poisons is the coward's way. A nice sharp sword ... that's more my style.' Taking up his own spoon, he dipped it into Wiltred's bowl and tasted the stew. 'Hmm. Could use a little more salt.'

Wiltred smiled weakly, and decided to trust these curious strangers. He found the stew very much to his liking, salt or not, and he finished the bowl in record time. Treeborne refilled it, and Wiltred ate until he was stuffed.

When they'd all finished, Treeborne cleared the bowls while Willowmere filled tiny steel cups from a stone flagon. The liquid was dark, and it glistened in the sunshine. 'A toast,' she said. 'To welcome guests, and the stories they bring.'

Everyone raised their cups, and Wiltred knocked back the thimbleful of drink in a single gulp. Immediately, his throat began to burn, and tears ran down his cheeks. The room revolved around him, and the next thing he knew he was lying on the floor, his cheek pressed to the cold stone. There was a babble of voices, the words reverberating in his ears, and seconds later he lost consciousness.

Runt's lessons with Mr Tinch, the sailing master, were not going that well. First, there were two other midshipmen, both of them young lads of high birth who resented his intrusion into their carefully ordered lives. Their career paths had already been mapped out, barring unexpected death or maiming, and they saw Runt as another step in the ladder ... one which they intended to grind under their heels as they climbed ahead of him.

One of the midshipmen, Dallow, was a pasty-faced lad, about thirteen and big for his age. The other, Cormley, was a rat of a fellow, perhaps a year or two older.

Every time Runt tried to take a sighting with the big spyglass, one of them would jog his elbow. Whenever he went to write down his observations, one of them would nudge the ledger. By the time he finished, the book was a mess.

'Ha-hmm,' said Tinch, as he observed Runt's results. 'Congratulations, sir, for you have placed us two miles from the Methusian capital.'

'Is that correct?' asked Runt hopefully.

'Do you see land all around us?'

'Not really.'

'Not really, *sir*,' snapped the sailing master. He was an elderly man, used to beating rowdy young men into shape, and he wasn't going to take any nonsense.

Runt was silent, and he frowned as he heard the two midshipmen snickering. Learning navigation was hard enough without those two getting in his way, and he wished he still had his dagger. Still, there was plenty of time to find a weapon before nightfall, and come the new day it was possible the ship would be short two midshipmen.

There was a cry of 'captain on deck', and Runt glanced across the quarterdeck to see a tall, grey-haired man striding towards the wheel. The captain inspected the sailing log, eyed the rigging, then said something to the helmsman, who turned the wheel a fraction to starboard. Then, satisfied, the captain went to speak with the officer of the watch.

The captain's appearance reduced the annoying young

midshipmen to awed silence, and the lesson proceeded without interruption. Before long the sailing master nodded his approval at Runt's progress, which earned him a sour look from the two youngsters.

Then the captain went below, and Runt steeled himself for the resumption of hostilities.

'Are you a Methusian spy?' demanded Dallow, the pasty-faced midshipman.

'He's too dumb to be a spy,' said Cormley, the older one with a face like a rat. 'Berry told me he's an orphan, raised by farmers. They probably thought he was one of their sheep!'

The boys laughed, and Runt scowled at them. 'What do you know about animals, you pair of cretins? Why, I once tamed a fearsome fire-breathing dragon, and–'

At this, their laughter drowned out the rest of his words. 'Were you kidnapped by fairies, too?' said one of the midshipmen, and they both laughed even harder.

'You've never met an elf, have you?' demanded Runt. 'Or seen a knight at full charge, or fled from one of the stone people, with his bloodstained axe ready to take off your head.'

The midshipmen stopped laughing, instead looking at him with puzzled expressions. 'Elves?' said Dallow.

'Knights?' said Cormley, with a snort. 'What are you, a relic from the history books?'

'Story books, more like,' said Dallow, and they both snickered.

'They're all real where I come from,' snapped Runt. 'You two wouldn't last five seconds in my land, snappy uniforms or not.' As he saw their expressions, he realised he'd said too much. Far too much.

'You h-hail from th-the Cursed Island?' said Dallow, his pasty face now a ghostly white.

Cormley said nothing, but he was staring at Runt with his ratty little eyes as though he expected to be killed on the spot by some fantastic creature summoned from thin air.

Under normal circumstances, Runt would have enjoyed the sudden change in their manner. However, their words had carried, and in the sudden silence he realised the entire ship's crew was staring at him.

Then Tinch, the sailing master, barked an order, and two seamen ran up and grabbed Runt firmly by the arms. Another took a strip of fabric and gagged him, most likely thinking Runt would try to curse them, or cast a spell of some kind.

An officer hurried over, his hat askew, and he shouted orders at the sailors. 'Get him below. Call the bosun. I want everything out of this fellow . . . everything, you hear?'

The sailors looked at him sullenly, and then Tinch stepped forward to explain their reluctance. 'Sir, his presence is a jinx on the ship. Shouldn't we . . . you know.' He jerked his thumb towards the ocean, his meaning clear.

'He can go over the side once we've questioned him,' said the officer. 'Hurry now, for I must inform the captain.'

'I *knew* he was a spy,' hissed Dallow, but as Runt was dragged below for questioning he realised the two lads were the least of his problems now.

— 8 —

Wiltred drifted in and out of consciousness, too far gone to identify the powerful brew he'd been poisoned with, but with just enough wits about him to realise he hadn't quite died. Not yet, at least, but it sure felt like he was on death's door.

He felt himself being dragged away, and he protested weakly. First, to try and stop them, and second to try and get Tyniwon's help. Instead, he was shushed to silence, and the next thing he knew he was laid out flat on his back with a white linen sheet drawn up to his chin. No doubt the murderers were saving time, for once he expired they'd only have to cover his face before burying him.

As he lay there he experienced one hallucination after another. Strange willowy figures bent over him, speaking in foreign tongues, their long blond locks tucked behind their pointy ears. He couldn't understand the words but he recognised concern in their voices, and he felt like apologising to them, for clearly it was taking him too long to die.

Then a cup was pressed to his lips, and despite his best efforts he was forced to drink from it. Moments later he went out like a light.

When he finally woke, hours later, he was lying in bed with a towering headache. His tongue felt like a square of mouldy old carpet, and his eyeballs felt like glass cubes in their sockets. He tried to sit up, but none of his muscles responded to the rallying cry. 'Great,' he muttered. 'The poison didn't get me, so now they've paralysed me as well.'

Actually, that's what he tried to say, but all he heard was grunting and squeaking.

'Mother, I think he's returned to us,' said a female voice.

'Praise the Great Bough,' said another voice, also female but a shade deeper. 'To be honest, I feared your father's homebrew had done for him.'

Wiltred frowned at this. Homebrew? He recalled the thimbleful of dark liquid he'd knocked back at the kitchen table, and shuddered at the memory. People actually drank that stuff ... *on purpose?*

Someone gripped his hand, and Willowmere's face swam into his field of view. She was wearing a hood, and he almost laughed as he remembered his waking nightmare, where the woman had the pointed ears of an ...

'Elf!' he said. 'Elf! *Elf!*'

The grip tightened, and Wiltred stopped speaking as his wrist bones creaked.

'Mother, our secret is out. There's no point denying it.'

Wiltred stared at the duo in horror, and as his vision slowly focused, he saw them lower their hoods. Elves they were indeed, with the pointed ears and long, blonde hair of their kind. Allyance's expression was welcoming, but her mother's was neutral ... and there was a thoughtful look in her violet eyes. 'Compost. No!' managed Wiltred, before sinking back on the bed.

'You know our deepest secret,' said Willowmere. 'By the ancient rules of our kind, you must now reveal yours. Only thus can we both be assured of your silence.'

'I once stole fivepence from my mother's purse,' managed Wiltred, his voice finally under his control.

'You carry a greater secret than that. I see it in your eyes.'

Wiltred swallowed. 'I fiddled my taxes. If they find out, I'll be sent to debtor's row.'

Slowly, Willowmere shook her head. 'Reach into your soul, and tell me all.'

'Tyniwon killed King Larch by mistake. Then we killed his guards, disposed of all the bodies and now we're on the run to Elven lands.'

'I asked for your secret,' said Willowmere, shaking her head. 'In return you give me the plot outline for some ludicrous bar-room tale.'

'It's true, I swear it! We were supposed to take a mould of his face, and Tyniwon didn't stick the straws up the king's nose, and the king died, and ... and ... and...'

Willowmere stood in one fluid motion. 'That tale is *true?* The king of the Barks is no more?'

'Dead as a side of bacon, and twice as crispy,' said Wiltred morosely. 'Everything was going so well! I had a new workshop, and employees, and a health plan, and retirement benefits ... and now I'm on the run, fearing for my life.'

'What about Tyniwon?'

'Well yes, he's the one who killed the king, so of course he fears for his life also.'

'No, I mean who is he? He lives here in Bark lands, yet his accent is that of the Mollisters.'

Wiltred hesitated. He'd already given up one secret, and that was supposed to make him even. Just how many secrets did the elf want? Then he shrugged, as well as he could, for only by revealing everything could he truly ask for their help. 'Have you heard of Queen Therstie Mollister?'

'Of course I have. Why, did she perish by your hand also? A tragic clothing accident, perhaps, or a lethal encounter with a wig?'

'First, I told you already I didn't kill the king, for it was Tyniwon. Second ... to my knowledge, Queen Therstie is alive and well. It just so happens that Tyniwon is her half-brother.'

'By the Silken Green Bough,' exclaimed Willowmere. 'Mollister royalty, right here in my cottage?'

'He's not royalty, not really. Questionable parentage ... you know how it goes.'

'Nay, that is not the truth of it, for it is Queen Therstie whose parentage is suspect, my own uncle having fathered her. Indeed, it is Tyniwon who should be seated on the throne.'

'Have you seen the size of him?' said Wiltred. 'In order for that lad to become king of the Mollisters ...'

'... they're going to need a bigger seat,' finished Willowmere.

They both thought on this, and then, with an effort, Wiltred sat up. 'Wait a minute. If your uncle is Therstie's father, that means ...'

'Indeed. I am the queen's cousin. The stain on my family is the reason my husband and I were banished from elven lands these many years past.'

Allyance stared at her mother. 'I never knew that.'

'Then you will share a deep secret of your own with me later, so that we are even.'

'Never mind Therstie,' said Wiltred, with growing excitement. 'You're telling me Tyniwon is the true king of the Mollisters?' His mind, addled by the potent drink though it was, quickly conjured up visions of a large, well-equipped workshop, an even bigger wage packet and an exalted position of power within the palace.

'You haven't thought this through,' said Willowmere. 'Your

61

companion just killed King Larch, accident or not, and if word gets out that the exalted and beloved king of the Barks was murdered by a Mollister ... well, I don't have to draw you a picture.'

'It would mean all-out war,' breathed Wiltred, and his visions of a new workshop vanished with a pop.

'There may still be war in these parts, since the king left no heir. A civil war pitting brother against brother, sister against brother, brother against mother and father, mother and father against–'

'Yes, yes, I get it,' said Wiltred impatiently.

'Your first instinct was the right one. You must flee Bark lands to the east, where the Elven kingdom awaits you.'

'Why would they welcome us?'

'Why do you think? Tyniwon just killed the king of the Barks! Amongst our people, he will be a hero.'

Wiltred thought for a moment. 'Do you think they'll build me a workshop?'

Willowmere ignored him, for Allyance had caught her attention. 'Mother, one of us should accompany them, to introduce them, and translate for them, and–'

'No, daughter. Our family was banished forever, and a petty dispute amongst humankind will not undo that particular ruling.'

'You and father were banished. I was not yet born!'

'If you think we're going to send you off on an adventure with these two, you've got another thought coming,' said Willowmere sharply, sounding a lot less like a high-born elf, and a lot more like the exasperated mother of a teenage girl.

'Very well, I obey you,' said Allyance obediently, but there was a stubborn set to her features.

'Wiltred, you must rest this night and depart in the morning.

62

You will be safe here, as long as you don't drink of the fyrehose.'

'Drink of the what?'

'My husband's home brew. An ancient recipe much beloved of my kind, it seems fyrehose is far too strong for your weak and fragile body.'

'I was dehydrated!' protested Wiltred.

Willowmere patted him on the arm. 'Of course you were, my dear. Now rest here and sleep off your ... dehydration ... for you have a long journey ahead of you.'

With that, the elven women left, and Wiltred was left alone with his hangover. The strange turns of events hammered at the inside of his skull, as did the remnants of the fyrehose, until he finally drifted off into a fitful slumber.

'Make way there! Make way for the Queen's Champion!'

Addressing himself in the third person had no appreciable effect on the crowd, and Sur Loyne was forced to negotiate the narrow streets of Branche at a snail's pace. His horse didn't mind at all, for it had ridden hard that day and Sur Loyne wasn't exactly a featherweight. Then again, it had once been ridden by Sur Cumfrence, a spine-bending experience it would never forget.

The crowds were gathering for an announcement regarding their missing king, called to the capital by town criers and messengers. Since there was no heir, many radicals were calling for a democratically-elected parliament, but the vast majority of the population were expecting some noble or other to take up a temporary role. Yes, it might lead to a dictatorship, but the alternative was dozens of corrupt politicians spending ten times what the city could afford in order to shore up their vote. Quite frankly, the citizens would suffer either way, but at least with a dictatorship they only had to pay for one person's follies.

Sur Loyne didn't care about the next ruler of the Barks, for he just wanted to find Tyniwon, put him on a horse and get him back to Mollister lands. He'd been hoping to meet King Larch, man-to-man, but since that wasn't going to be possible he was forced to wait for an announcement along with everyone else. As the Queen's champion he was entitled to meet with the man in charge, not some lowly underling, but that was a problem right now because apparently nobody was in charge.

In the meantime they found a tavern with a stable, and they left their horses and belongings behind before heading off to seek an official they might question. 'Keep your wits about you,' he told Sur Kah and Sur Pryze. 'For all we know, Tyniwon is locked in their deepest dungeon, and we must be circumspect unless we want to join him.'

'Sur Cumspect? Isn't he patrolling the eastern border?'

'No,' said Sur Pryze, with a shake of his head. 'That was Sur Wendah, but they recalled him to the palace after he gave in to a bunch of rebels without so much as drawing his sword.'

'Shut up, the pair of you,' snapped Sur Loyne. 'I meant we have to be surreptitious, not some random knight of the realm.'

'Sur Reptishis *is* a knight of the realm,' protested Sur Kah. 'Mind you, he's in jail right now so I guess it's safe to impersonate him.'

'He's in jail?' said Sur Pryze, looking shocked. 'What for?'

'Some say he was fiddling the books, but others say it was circumstantial.'

'I've met Sur Cumstanceyal,' said Sur Pryze darkly. 'I wouldn't trust that rogue with my pocket change.'

By now Sur Loyne was ready to kill them both on the spot, their prattling having all but tipped him over the edge. However, he reined in his anger with an effort, and, shoving aside the odd peasant, they all made their way to the city courthouse. They'd decided this was their best option, for it was the first place to learn of any announcement about the new ruler.

'That's sublime!' said Sur Pryze, as he saw the elegant building.

'What's he doing in Branche?' said Sur Kah, looking around for their fellow knight.

'No ... the courthouse. It's beautiful!'

The others concurred, for the entire building was built from fine-grained hardwood, and the dark, smooth timbers were intricately carved. 'It looks ancient,' said Sur Pryze.

Sur Kah concurred. 'Circa 580, if I'm not mistaken. The previous one burnt down.' He hesitated. 'Actually, they all burn down, sooner or later.'

'Why?'

'Wooden candelabras.'

Sur Loyne glanced up at the buildings lining the narrow alley. Everything was made from wood, making it an absolutely terrifying deathtrap, and he resolved to leave for Mollister lands that very afternoon whether they found Tyniwon or not. The queen couldn't very well complain about her missing half-brother, since the Barks couldn't even find their own king.

The doors to the courthouse creaked open, and the three knights approached the front counter. There were half a dozen people behind the counter, and about fifty lining the big hall, each of them clutching a paper ticket.

Sur Loyne ignored the lot and strolled up to the counter, addressing the one person who seemed to be waiting for custom. 'Good afternoon, madam. I have just arrived in your fair though highly flammable city, and—'

Silently, the woman indicated a paper ticket dispenser at the far end of the counter.

'No, I just want to know who's currently in charge, so that I might petition them for information on—'

'Take a ticket and wait your turn,' said the woman curtly.

Sur Loyne gave her his most winning smile. 'Yes, look, I don't think you understand. We are three knights sent to Branche by orders of queen Therstie Mollister, and—'

'Take a ticket or leave.' The woman looked past him and raised her voice. 'Number fourteen thousand, nine hundred and eighty-six.'

An elderly man got up and approached the counter, walking with the aid of a cane. He held out a yellowed, crumpled ticket, and the woman took it and inspected it closely. 'State your business.'

'M-my sweetheart and I seek permission to marry,' said the old man, in a quavery voice.

'Leaving it a bit late, aren't you?' said Sur Loyne, with a laugh.

The man looked him up and down. 'Sonny, you won't be grinning when you've been waiting thirty-seven years. An' my woman ... she don't believe in sex before marriage.'

Sur Loyne stared at the man's ancient ticket, then hurried to the dispenser. The next number was in the hundreds of thousands, and with a sinking feeling he realised it would literally be decades before he was served. Well, he wasn't the queen's champion for nothing, and so he gathered his fellow knights to hatch a plan. 'It's simple,' he whispered. 'We take a number, then kill everyone else with an earlier ticket.'

The other two looked at him like he was mad.

'What?' protested Sur Loyne. 'It won't take long if we split up and take them on three at a time.'

Sur Kah pursed his lips. 'There is another option.'

'What?'

'We could buy someone's ticket.'

'Or we could kill them and take it!' said Sur Loyne enthusiastically.

'Tell me,' said Sur Pryze, 'did you ever consider a career as a cultural ambassador?'

'Not really, but I suppose it's an option.'

'Well, let me give you some pointers. First, visiting a foreign land and murdering the inhabitants is frowned upon, and in some quarters it can even be considered illegal.'

'But they're just peasants!'

Sur Pryze closed his eyes. 'You can get away with that sort of thing in Mollister lands, but not here.'

'Well I'm damned if I'm waiting thirty-seven years for an answer. What do you suggest?'

'How much money do we have?'

They took out their pocket change and counted it, the clink of metal coins echoing around the vast hall. Slowly, they noticed a hushed silence had fallen over the crowd, and then someone screamed '*Metal!*' and there was pandemonium. The fifty or so people waiting for an audience tried to leave the building en masse, while guards attracted by the screams tried to get in. Several people went flying, and there was a snowstorm of numbered tickets.

'Quick, give me the cash,' hissed Sur Kah.

They obeyed, and he threw the handful of coins into the departing crowd with an underarm action. The money rattled on the floor, scattering amongst the fleeing people, and in the renewed frenzy he started snatching tickets from the air.

The other knights followed suit, until they were all holding a dozen each.

'Number fourteen thousand, nine hundred and eighty-seven,' said the woman behind the counter, who'd ignored the entire fracas as though it were a common occurrence.

'Oh look, that's me,' said Sur Kah, and the three knights approached the counter while a dozen guards beat various members of the crowd senseless before charging them with possession of metal.

Ten minutes later the knights had what they were after . . . the name of the man with all the answers.

'Chief Courtier Starlow,' muttered Sur Loyne, repeating it under his breath lest he forget it. 'Let us pay this man a visit immediately, for I tire of this city and I wish to be on my way.'

9

It was nighttime, and Clunk was still cutting rolls of silk into large, rectangular panels. He was keeping a count of the various sizes and shapes as he worked, and as the piles of fabric panels grew, and the number of full rolls decreased, he decided it was time to get the others working on the construction.

First, he sent Millie and Hurm to collect the metal parts from the various blacksmiths around the city. Then, once they'd left, he collared Father M, who was boiling a kettle on the hearth. 'I need you to start the gluing process,' said Clunk, indicating the panels. 'You will notice there are four piles, arranged from the narrowest panels to the widest. I need you to take one panel from each pile, and glue the edges in a specific manner.' Clunk fetched the barrel of foul-smelling glue, took up a flat wooden blade, and demonstrated. First he laid a thin bead of glue along the widest edge of one panel, then he took a panel from the next pile, flipped it over and smoothed it out, pressing down until the glued edges formed a seam. Finally, he laid it aside and repeated the process.

Father M got the idea, and after shoving balled-up pieces of silk into his nostrils to fend off the foul fumes, he set to work.

By the time Millie and Hurm returned, Clunk had finished

the cutting. He got them involved in the glueing process as well, joining the twinned panels which Father M had been working on in order to form even longer strips, a yard wide at their thickest point, with the narrowest edges at each end. Meanwhile, he started on the crude sewing machine, and their makeshift workshop was filled with the sound of sawing and hammering ... and protests at the stench of the glue.

Twenty minutes later the sewing machine was ready, and Clunk threaded the coarse needle and gathered several fabric off-cuts. He laid them together and ran them through the machine, pressing down on the foot pedal to drive it. Afterwards, he inspected the rough stitches with a critical eye, and decided to make several adjustments to the insides of his crude device. He tested it again, and when he was happy he took up the first of the glued panels and ran it through the machine, which left a reasonably straight row of stitches across the seam.

They worked non-stop for several hours, until Clunk realised his human companions were getting so tired they risked making a mistake. He sent all three off to sleep, while he himself continued working. By the time dawn came around, the panels had been transformed into a huge, silken bag which overflowed the bench and covered the entire room with folds of fabric.

Millie was the first to appear, yawning and rubbing her eyes, and Clunk sent her to fetch breakfast for the others. When all three were awake and fed, he set them to work again, this time cutting and tying ropes, forming a mesh net which would enclose the balloon's canopy.

'What kind of fish do you intend to catch with this?' asked Millie, putting her hand through one of the giant squares in the net.

'Anyone can see that it's not for catching fish,' said Father M loftily. 'It's to keep the sea serpents at bay, in order that we might navigate the ocean in safety.'

Clunk did not correct him, for he was worried Father M and Hurm would down tools if they learned the true nature of the device. When the time came they might still refuse to board his balloon, but he was hoping that they'd go along with him if they were forced into a last-minute decision. If, on the other hand, they were given hours to brood and worry about a balloon flight over guard towers bristling with death-dealing weapons, the chance of them accompanying him was much closer to zero. He found this strange, since they seemed perfectly happy to sail the ocean depths in a boat made from the city's entire stock of dress fabric, with only a piece of home-made netting to protect themselves from humongous sea serpents. But then, nobody claimed humans were logical animals.

While the others kept working on the balloon's huge, unwieldy envelope, Clunk fetched the remains of the hand-drawn cart from the street. First he removed half the wooden boards from the base, to save weight, and then he built a railing around the rest to form a travelling basket for his passengers. With the balloon almost ready, there remained one vital ingredient.

'Hurm, I need two sacks of charcoal. Large sacks, please.'

'Is that for a large celebratory feast before we embark?' said Father M, practically licking his lips. 'That is a good idea, for we can also roast viands for our journey.'

'That too,' said Clunk. In truth, he needed the charcoal to power his balloon, and once again Father M had leapt to the wrong conclusion. There was no harm letting them roast meats as well, though, and so he sent Hurm with the wizard to fetch both charcoal and some choice cuts.

'When are you going to tell them it's not actually a boat?' Millie asked him. She gestured at the mounds of fabric filling the room. 'Father M will soon realise it's large enough for twenty people, and yet there is no keel to hold its shape.'

'Our friend Father M is so secure in his own brilliance that he scarcely pauses to question himself.' Clunk shrugged. 'Once he reaches a conclusion, it's set in stone.'

They worked in silence for some time, before Millie piped up again. 'Why do you think he's called Father, when he's clearly a wizard? Isn't that the title for a priest, or a cleric?'

'Some people pursue dual classes. Unfortunately, that usually means they master neither.' Clunk would have said more, but he heard the others returning. Hurm carried two large sacks, which had smudged his shoulders and neck with charcoal dust, while Father M bore a covered basket. They stoked up the fire, and Father M cooked several juicy steaks on a griddle, which he, Millie and Hurm ate with relish.

'A little tough, but this improves them no end,' said Father M, as he heaped more of the tangy sauce from a jar.

Clunk watched them closely, adding the weight of their food to his existing estimates of their body weight. His figures were a little rubbery in that regard, a bit like the steaks, but as long as he loaded the balloon's basket with plenty of ballast before setting off it would all work out. Hmm. Ballast. 'We're going to need a couple more items,' he said, and the others groaned. They'd run too many errands for their liking, and Clunk's mysterious project was beginning to get on their nerves. 'Nothing special, I promise you. Please, continue eating and I will prepare.'

While they chewed their steaks, with even more relish to mask the flavour, Clunk cut two dozen fabric offcuts to size and sewed them into open-necked sacks with drawstrings. He completed the job, then handed the sacks to the others as soon as they'd finished feasting. 'Fill them all with sand, and tie the necks securely.'

'Aha,' said Father M. 'You construct a sea anchor for the boat.'

Millie rolled her eyes, but she was behind the wizard and he didn't notice.

Clunk followed them outside to check the weather. It was already late afternoon, and the sun was dropping towards the rooftops. They couldn't leave until darkness, so that suited Clunk perfectly. The other issue was the wind, and he sought an open area where he could take an accurate reading. It had to be blowing from the east for their voyage to succeed, but anything more than a gentle breeze would be dangerous.

He tested the wind speed and direction, and discovered it was blowing from the north. Clunk felt a tinge of annoyance at the vagaries of the weather, the one element of his plan he had no control over, but there was nothing to be done about it. All they could do was prepare everything for departure, and then wait. For a moment or two he watched the others filling bags with sand, his busy mind automatically calculating weights and measures, and then he returned to the house to inspect every seam on his hot-air balloon.

It took a while to prepare Runt for torture. Not because the men were squeamish or hesitant, but because he was too small for their chairs, and the large iron manacles dangled from his wrists like thick metal bangles.

Eventually they lashed him to a gunner's stool, and he sat there in pensive silence as the bosun prepared a range of unpleasant-looking implements. Aside from the charcoal brazier to heat everything up, there were pokers, pincers, knives, needles, a row of six-inch nails and a very large mallet. There was a thin wire with wooden handles, too, and Runt studiously avoided thinking about the parts of his body upon which such a device might be used.

He'd been tortured before, many times, but it usually involved a safe word and cash up front. This time would be a lot more real, and lot less fun. He wasn't a big fan of pain, either, not unless he was the one applying it.

The gag had worked loose in the struggle to get him below decks, and Runt waggled his chin to get his mouth free. 'Why don't you skip the torture?' he asked. 'I'll tell you everything I know, and you won't even have to raise a sweat.'

The bosun said nothing, only interrupting his preparations to tie the gag twice as tight as before. It felt like Runt's jaw was about to come away from his skull, and tears sprang to his eyes as he pondered how unfair life was to him. There he'd been, minding his own business, stealing left, right and centre while topping the occasional victim. It was scarcely worse than everyone else in the Old Kingdom, he told himself. So what had he done to deserve this?

There was a red glow as the bosun blew on the coals. He was a thickset man, his tattooed arms corded with bunched muscles and slick with sweat. He looked like he could haul an anchor – or torture a prisoner – for hours on end, and Runt wondered whether he could request one of the weedy little midshipmen as a stand-in torturer instead.

The bosun approached him with a red-hot poker, and Runt's eyes widened at the sight. It wasn't fair ... he was gagged so tight he couldn't even shout out all his secrets! The poker came closer, and he stared at the tip in horrified fascination. Was the man going to brand his cheek, or burn his earlobe ... or was he going to put one of Runt's eyes out? He struggled with his bonds, but there was no escape, and he could feel the heat from the poker now.

'Sail ho! Sail on the larboard quarter!'

The bosun hesitated at the faint cry, and then a drum began to beat, and pipes began to twitter, and with a muttered curse the big man shoved his poker into the coals and ran for the main deck.

Runt breathed out. He'd almost wet himself with fear, but now he was relieved in a completely different fashion. His first thought was escape, and he struggled with the rough ropes as the crew's feet thundered overhead. There was an almighty roar and a succession of squeals as the cannon were run out on their wooden trucks, and then the drumming stopped and he heard shouted orders.

The bindings weren't giving in to Runt's treatment, but then he spied a dagger on the nearby table. He started rocking the stool, using the ship's rolling motion to get himself closer and closer. Finally, he was able to turn himself on the spot, and taking the knife in trembling, half-paralysed fingers, he sawed away at the ropes.

They parted in no time, and he freed his legs before ripping the gag from his face. Now he was free, and his first instinct was to tip the brazier on its side and burn the ship to the waterline. Unfortunately, that would also burn him to a crisp, since he couldn't leave the lower deck without being spotted. He was in the very tip of the bow, from what he could tell, and he was surrounded by huge coils of thick rope, one end of which fed out through the hull. He stood on tiptoes to peer through the hole, and saw the end of the rope tied to a huge anchor. Then he saw something which made him forget all about his own troubles, for there was a large ship bearing down on them, its sails filled and a huge white wave at the bow where it cut through the ocean waves.

Seconds later the other ship turned sharply, and Runt found himself staring down the barrels of about thirty large cannon. He stepped back from the hole and dropped to the deck, cowering amongst the coiled rope with his hands over his head. There was a rumble of thunder, a hair-raising howl, and a series of tremendous crashes as the enemy cannonballs struck home. Fortunately they'd hit further back, amidships, but he felt the entire vessel shake under the impact.

Before he could move there was a massive roar, a blast of thunder which lifted him bodily off the deck. Acrid grey smoke swirled into the cable locker, and his eyes smarted as it filled his lungs. The ship rolled savagely, and he realised they'd just fired back at the enemy.

There was silence for a couple of minutes, a silence broken only by the screams of a wounded crew member, and then Runt heard the rumble of their attacker's broadside. A ball smashed into the hull not five feet from his position, and when he looked up he saw a two foot wooden splinter sticking out of the opposite bulkhead like a spear. There was a lot more light spilling into his hiding place, and the reason why was immediately apparent. The enemy's shot had punched a large, ragged hole straight through the beams, even though they were twelve inches thick.

Runt swallowed at the sight. He thought he'd be safe cowering behind the hull, but the timbers offered about as much protection as a paper mache helmet. Through the hole he could see the enemy ship wreathed in smoke, and he wondered how long it would be before it fired again. Too soon, was the answer, and he decided to get the hell out of there.

10

Pentonville decided their first task was to interrogate the guards who'd been on duty when the robot disappeared. He and Islington found the men in the barracks, where the pair of them were playing cards with half a dozen others.

'Oh look, it's the beachcombers,' someone said, and the rest laughed. Many of the men around the table were grizzled veterans, and Pentonville realised their task was going to be trickier than he expected. Try and drag the two guards away for questioning, and there could be an all-in fight.

'Played with any good jellyfish lately?' called someone else, and there was another round of laughter.

'We're here under the captain's orders,' said Pentonville. 'He wants you two on the double,' he added, nodding towards the men he wanted to question.

'What for?' demanded one of them, a redhead with a bushy beard. Pentonville knew him as Nate, but whether that was the name he'd been born to, nobody could say.

'You question the captain?'

For a moment it looked like there was going to be resistance, but the men threw their cards down and gathered their coin from the table. 'Keep my seat warm,' said the second man, a blond with a scar over one eye. 'We'll be back soon enough.'

Sarminter, thought Pentonville, as he recalled the man's name. The four of them strolled to the cells, where Islington and Pentonville led them past a row of open doors. At the far end they took a set of wide, stone steps, which led to the deeper dungeons and the torture chamber. 'Captain wants to speak with you first,' said Pentonville, and he motioned Nate towards an empty bench. 'Take a seat.'

Unsuspecting, Nate sat down, and Pentonville crouched before him and snapped a pair of manacles shut, securing Nate's ankles before the man could move. Then, he and Islington secured the second man, who was now outnumbered.

'What are you doin'?' he protested, as they pushed him down on a second bench and chained his legs. 'I ain't done nuffink!'

'We'll be the judge of that,' said Pentonville. 'The captain wants answers, and if you give them freely we'll release you unharmed. Otherwise ... ' with this, he took up a pair of long-nosed pincers, rusty and bloodstained. 'Well, let's just say we're getting the answers either way.'

'The cap'n wouldn't stand for this!' shouted Sarminter. 'Let us go right now, or–'

There was a snap as Pentonville closed the pliers on thin air, and the two men stopped talking. 'First question. Who else was in the mechanical man's cell?'

'L-lord Chylde,' said Nate. 'H-he wanted to interview the prisoner.'

'We know all about his Lordship's visit,' said Islington. 'But, as I'm sure you're aware, there was another prisoner who went missing that night. A young thief called Millie, who was to be sold into labour. What happened to her?'

The two men exchanged a glance, then eyed the

bloodstained pliers Pentonville was holding. 'It weren't nothing, I swear. We just ... wanted to see if the metal man would ... do her.'

'Do what to her?'

'You know.' Sarminter made a crude gesture, and his chains rattled. 'We had a bet on it.'

'So you locked this defenceless girl in the cell with a dangerous prisoner? For *sport*?'

'That's about the size of it.'

'And what happened?'

'Nothink,' said Nate sourly. 'His Lordship showed up, demanding an audience. While he was in the cell–'

'With the girl?'

'He didn't mention her. Maybe she hid or something. Anyway, while he was in there, we got news about the Lord Chancellor's assassination, and we was ordered to attend.'

'So you left Lord Chylde alone with the mechanical creature?'

'He was just leaving, and I think I heard him lock the door.'

'You think?'

'I'm certain! When we came back, the door was all busted and the metal man had gone. H-he tore his chains apart, he did. It weren't natural, that much strength!'

'And there was no sign of Millie?'

'None. Figured she left with him, or just after.'

Pentonville hesitated. So far the information tallied with the stories he'd heard, but now they were approaching trickier ground. 'While Lord Chylde was in the cell, did you happen to hear his conversation?'

Sarminter looked shocked. 'We'd never do such a thing. Treason, that is, and a capital offence!'

'Of course, of course. But his Lordship's voice carries, and I'm sure a sentence or two must have reached your ears, even by mistake. If you recall any of his words, I'm sure we can release you immediately.' And if you can't, his expression said, you'll be down here for months.

'There was a few words, now you mention it. Impossible not to hear, since he spoke loud.'

'Go on, then.'

Nate and Sarminter exchanged a glance, before Nate continued. 'Well, he were telling the metal man to travel to Last Hope, where he was to meet a contact of his Lordship's. His Lordship ... well, he thought the queen would take the clockwork marvel to the royal palace, and he din't want that. No, he din't want that at all.'

'So what were his plans?'

Nate lowered his voice. 'I think our Lord wishes to build more of these mechanical men.'

'How?'

'His people were going to take it apart, piece by piece. Lord Chylde wanted to know what strange magic caused it to live and speak, that he might copy the technology.'

Pentonville suppressed an oath. For a moment he'd thought their quarry was heading to Last Hope, where it would be trivial to locate him. Now, it seemed, Last Hope was the last place Clunk would wish to visit, since that's where Chylde's man was waiting to take him apart. So where would he run to? He racked his brains as he thought on the problem, discarding both the elven lands and the kingdom of the stone people. Both were too far, as were the other kingdoms to the north east and north west. 'This Millie. From whence did she hail?'

'Bark lands. Her family was killed on the way to Chatter's Reach, and she fell into bad ways to survive.'

Pentonville led Islington aside, out of earshot of their captives. 'Well? What do you think?'

'I believe they're telling the truth.'

'And the robot? Do you believe this girl Millie might be leading him to Bark lands?'

'A metal creature in the wooden kingdom?' Islington snorted. 'Not a chance.'

'Well, unless we work out the way of it, we're going to be riding the length and breadth of the kingdom for the rest of our lives.' Pentonville sighed. If only they'd kept chasing Tiera instead of coming back to the city! That was the much easier task, to be sure.

'Are we going to torture these two?'

Pentonville shook his head. 'They've told us what they know, and if we harm them their mates will come after us, orders from the captain or not.'

'You speak wisely. So what, then?'

'This robot seemed an intelligent sort. What if he travelled to Last Hope anyway, but with no intention of meeting Lord Chylde's contact? It's the last place anyone would look for him. For the life of me, I cannot believe Millie would lead him into Bark lands, and he has no business with the elves or the stone people.'

Islington nodded, and they decided to ride to Last Hope.

'If the metal man isn't there, we can settle in a hostel until we come up with a new plan. Days ... or maybe weeks.'

'These things take time,' agreed Pentonville, and he set the pliers aside.

'What about these two?'

'Give the keys to someone else, and tell them to let them free in a couple of hours. I want to be clear of the city before they're loose.'

'An excellent idea,' said Islington, and the two of them left the torture chamber.

'Hey!' shouted Sarminter. '*Hey!*'

'We'll be right back!' shouted Pentonville, and then he and Islington darted up the stairs, taking them two by two.

Sur Loyne followed directions to the palace, where he approached the guards with some misgivings. It was only by pure luck – and a handful of pocket change – that they'd avoided a four-decade wait for service at the courthouse, and he was dreading the wait time at the palace.

However, as he studied the guards he realised something. One of them looked familiar. In fact, he looked very familiar indeed. 'Oxley, isn't it?'

'Not me, no sir.'

'Yes it is. You were a member of the palace guard.'

'No I wasn't.'

The second guard was staring at him now. 'You said you was a soldier.'

'I was!'

'He wasn't,' said Sur Loyne.

'I've never been to Mollister lands,' protested Oxley, the first guard.

'How did you know that's where I'm from?'

The guard lapsed into sullen silence, until he noticed the hilt of Sur Loyne's sword. Some of the mud had worn off, and there was a distinct gleam to it. 'Is that metal?'

'No,' said Sur Loyne, quickly covering the hilt with his hand.

'What about that ring? Looks like gold to me.' Oxley tutted. 'Punishable by death, that is.'

'Oh yes? You and whose army?' demanded Sur Loyne, half-drawing his extremely sharp and very metallic sword.

The guards were armed with nothing but wooden staves, and from their expressions they didn't fancy their odds of survival. 'All right, tell you what,' said Oxley. 'I'll let you through, and we'll say no more about your metal or my past. Deal?'

'Wait a minute,' said the second guard. 'You can't let them into the palace carrying deadly weapons.'

'Why not?' demanded the first guard.

'They might attack the king!'

'They'd have to find him first. Anyway, they're Mollister knights, and killing our king would start a war.'

'*My* king, you mean,' muttered the second guard.

Oxley ignored the barb. 'He was just trying to cause trouble so we'd let him through,' he said soothingly. 'He doesn't know me at all. Isn't that right, Sur Loyne?'

'Never seen you before in my life,' said the champion, and he pushed through the doors to the palace before the second guard realised Sur Loyne had never revealed his name to either of them. Sur Kah and Sur Pryze followed, and together they took a long hall to the throne room. The guards there let them pass without challenge, and the three knights paused to admire the impressive chamber. The vaulted ceilings were well-crafted, and if they noticed holes where several wooden shingles had blown away, they were too polite to point them out.

Near the large throne there was a large table, and at the table were two elderly men. One of them looked up as the knights approached, and when Sur Loyne introduced himself there was a round of bowing and shaking of hands.

'I'm sorry the city hasn't been more welcoming,' said chief courtier Starlow apologetically. 'You see, we're in the midst of a constitutional crisis, and there is no resolution in sight.' He indicated his companion, a tall man wearing what looked like a dead bush on his head. 'This is the palace genealogist, and together we are trying to identify the next in line to the throne.'

There was a pile of scrolls on the table before them, each covered in spidery lines, with rows and rows of names and dates. Sur Kah, as fond of dates as your average teenager, picked up the nearest and scanned the parchment keenly. 'Didn't you have the succession planned out beforehand?'

'There were several candidates, but it was up to King Larch to select one. He was a superstitious man, truth be told, and he kept putting the task off.'

'He may yet live,' said Sur Loyne. 'It takes a lot to kill a king.'

'Nevertheless, we need a ruler now. If King Larch should return at a later date, he will take over once more.'

Sur Kah was still buried in the scrolls, and all of a sudden he laughed and pointed at a cluster of names scrawled on a wrinkled old parchment. 'Hey, that's my grandfather! We used to call him Big Red, because he had a face like a beetroot when he drank too much. And those two are his brother and sister.' He pointed out another two names. 'Great aunt Bute, who never spoke a word, and dear old uncle Dugger, who made his living in the boxing ring.'

'These people are all your relatives?' said the Chief Courtier, with a look of astonishment.

'Of course! Mute Bute, Slugger Dugger, Big Red Kah.'

There was a deep silence as the Chief Courtier digested this new and rather catchy twist. He examined the dates, then compared them to several others. 'But that means ...' he managed at last, before his voice tailed off. He looked to the genealogist for confirmation. 'Do you agree?'

'Indeed, sir. The conclusion is inescapable. This man has Wood in his family tree.'

Sur Loyne laughed. 'There wouldn't *be* a family tree unless someone got wood.'

The other knights smiled politely, for Sur Loyne was their leader, but the officials paid the coarse joke no notice. Instead, they dropped to one knee and bowed so low their noses almost touched the wooden floorboards. 'Your Majesty!'

Sur Loyne glanced around, but the hall was empty. 'Where?'

'I think they mean me,' said Sur Kah ... or rather, King Kah.

'Yeah, very funny,' growled Sur Loyne. 'You! Treehead! What are you doing down there?'

'I await his majesty's pleasure.'

'He can't be king,' protested Sur Loyne. 'He's one of queen Therstie's knights, and he's not even a very good one.'

'His lineage is unmistakable, his ancestry impeccable.'

'This whole thing's unbelievable,' muttered Sur Loyne.

'Sire, will you lead us from these troubled times?'

'I will,' said Sur Loyne, 'but only if you give up this crazy idea. King Kah, indeed. Who'd take that name seriously?'

'I was asking his majesty,' said the chief courtier, his tone cold.

'Of course I'll lead you,' said Sur Kah, and he helped the men to their feet. Sur Loyne gave him a venomous look, for if anyone was going to be crowned king by surprise, he was surely the better man for the job. He turned to Sur Pryze for support, but the third knight still had his head bowed, and didn't notice.

Sur Kah wasn't moved by Sur Loyne's reaction though, and he gave him a look of regal disdain.

'Now, follow me,' said the chief courtier. 'There is much to do, and we must move quickly before there is any more unrest in the city.'

'Unrest? What unrest?'

'There was a protest at the courthouse, not half an hour ago,' said the courtier solemnly. 'Some miscreant threw a handful of metal coins into a crowd.'

'How terrible,' said Sur Loyne. 'You wouldn't want to have someone like that as your king, would you?'

'Indeed not.'

'You'd better get the interrogations going so they can identify the perpetrator. And did you say *metal* coins?'

'Indeed.'

'That's punishable by death, isn't it?'

King Kah frowned at the champion, but said nothing. As the ruler of the Barks he had the power of life and death in his hands, and if Sur Loyne didn't watch it he was fully prepared to make an example of him.

11

Runt peered through a crack in the door, and the sight that met his eyes made him feel like he'd been transported to some devilish level of hell. The lower deck was packed with sweating, shirtless men, who were feverishly working the guns as they strove to get the upper hand in the battle. He covered his ears as the row of guns fired in unison, the huge weapons leaping backwards on their trucks, the subsequent swirl of smoke all but filling the deck.

Even as it cleared, a man at each gun sprang forward with a dripping wet sponge attached to a long pole. They plunged the pole into the mouth of their guns, avoiding the jet of steam as the hot metal boiled most of the water away. Another gunner took a small powder charge from a wooden box, passing the fat sausage-like object to the first man, who pushed it into the gun and rammed it home with the other end of his pole. The cannonball went home next, followed by a fat wad of fabric, both of them pushed all the way down to the breech by the loader.

Finally, the gun captain rammed a metal spike down the touch-hole at the rear of the gun, piercing the powder cartridge inside, then poured in a measure of fine gunpowder. When he was ready he stepped back. 'Run 'er out!' he shouted, and all the other gun captains followed suit.

The gun crews hauled on ropes like fury, inching the massive weapons forward until the muzzles protruded from the side of the ship. When they were ready, the gun captains sighted along the barrels.

'Fire!' yelled a uniformed officer, who was watching proceedings from the far end of the deck. The gun captains pressed a glowing stick to the powder in the touch-holes, and Runt recoiled as the entire deck full of guns fired as one.

The men leapt forward to reload, and while they were busy there was a distant boom as the enemy ship fired. Runt heard the terrifying howl of incoming shot, and then the scene changed in an instant. There was a hurricane of splinters and dust as the broadside smashed into the side of the ship, and two of the guns took direct hits. The long metal guns rang like giant bells, flying backwards off their wooden trucks, crushing several of the crew. Other shots wiped away men like they'd never existed, and several others were hurled backwards like ragdolls.

The rest of the crew didn't falter, they kept working their own guns as though nothing had happened. Then Runt saw a small boy of ten or eleven years old emerging from a hatch at the far end of the deck. He was struggling with a wooden bucket packed with powder cartridges, and as he made his way along the line the sailors grabbed a couple of bags each to replenish their supplies.

The guns fired again, fewer of them this time, and the enemy fired back while the thick smoke was still swirling around. When it cleared the boy had vanished, and the bloodstained bucket was lying on its side in the middle of the deck.

Runt stared at the bucket. Without powder, the guns would fall silent in no time. And without guns, the enemy would pound their ship to matchsticks ... and him along with it. Cursing under his breath at his mad folly, Runt charged from the cable locker, scooped up the bucket and ran for the hatch. He recognised the officer as midshipman Berry, his face stained from the gunpowder and smoke, his eyes wild. Berry waited until the guns fired again, from the upper deck this time, then cupped his hands to Runt's ringing ears. 'The magazine is down the ladder,' he shouted. 'Go with speed, and you have my thanks!'

As Runt stepped towards the hatch another small boy emerged, and he watched the lad scamper up the steps to the upper deck with a bucket of charges gripped in both hands, so heavy it was almost tipping him over. Runt shook himself, and raced down the steps to the lowest deck in the ship. The magazine was nearby, illuminated by well-shielded lanterns, and inside he could see two elderly men scooping black gritty powder into the small cartridge bags. They filled them as quickly as they could, putting in a couple of stitches to seal the ends.

Meanwhile, there was a wall of prepared cartridges nearby, and Runt started packing as many as he could carry into the bucket.

'What happen' to Tom?' asked one of the men.

Runt shook his head, and the man turned away, his shoulders slumped. Despite his grief, he continued working, for there would be time to mourn after they won the battle.

If they won, thought Runt, and for the first time he realised the outcome wasn't certain. Since coming aboard, he'd been in awe of the powerful warship, with its huge guns and well-trained crew. But what if the other ship was bigger, better-served, and had even more guns?

There was no time to dwell on it, because when Runt reached

the deck above, straining under the weight of cartridges, several of the crew spotted him and beckoned wildly. He ran as fast as he could with the heavy bucket, barely pausing as the men grabbed cartridges to feed their guns.

He was two thirds of the way along the deck when the enemy broadside struck, and the violent impact threw him clear off his feet. Something grabbed at his arm, spinning him round, and he went down in a heap. Ears ringing, dazed, it was all he could do to pat himself down looking for mortal injuries. It turned out he was unscathed, but there were more dead and injured crew all around him, and he noticed the sleeve of his jerkin had been shredded by a flying splinter. A near miss, for an inch closer and it would have taken his arm off.

Struggling to his feet, Runt hauled the bucket to the remaining guns, and then he ran back to the hatch, stepping over several bodies on the way. All his instincts screamed at him to hide in the cable locker and wait for the battle to end, but he knew with stone cold certainly that every hand was needed to win this fight . . . his included.

The next half hour passed in a whirlwind of gun smoke, thunder, flying splinters and injured men. He had no idea how the tide of battle was going until there was an unexpected pause in the firing.

'She's caught!' yelled someone, and there was a ragged cheer.

Runt dropped the bucket and ran to the nearest porthole, avoiding the red-hot gun barrel to peer out through the porthole. The graceful enemy ship was now a battered hulk, with jagged holes up and down the hull, no masts, and no sign of the billowing white sails. Instead, there was billowing white smoke, and he saw sheets of flame consuming the deck as the dry timbers burned fiercely. Men were leaping into the ocean, many of them unable to swim, and then, without warning, there was a flash of intense light which consumed the enemy ship. Seconds later there was an almighty bang, rumbling across the sea in the biggest thunder blast Runt had ever heard.

When the smoke cleared the enemy ship had vanished, as had all the men in the water. There remained a few blackened planks, bobbing gently in the waves, but there was no further sign of their foe.

'Magazine went up,' muttered a seaman. 'Poor devils should have struck their colours.'

Runt's senses had been battered by the noise and pandemonium of the battle, and he staggered away from the side of the ship, barely noticing his surroundings. Vaguely, he was aware of the dead and injured being dragged away.

Then a hand clasped his shoulder, and Runt looked up to see Berry smiling down at him. 'Good job,' said the midshipman. 'We'll make a sailor of you yet.'

There was a patter of feet, and a seaman ran up and knuckled his forehead. 'Begging pardon, sir, but the quarterdeck took a direct hit. All'us officers killed, sir.'

'All of them?' demanded Berry, shocked.

'Yessir. You'm in command now. Midshipman Cormley fell too, sir, but Dallow made it.'

Berry straightened his battle-worn uniform and stood tall. 'Very well. Send a party to check the hull for leaks. Get a crew onto the guns, I want them back in working order as soon as possible. And see that the wounded are tended to, for I'll need a report on our able bodies.'

'Aye aye, sir,' said the seaman, and he saluted again before running off to obey.

'What did he mean about the quarterdeck?' asked Runt.

'Well my friend, it appears I'm now captain of this vessel, and the master of all who sail in her.' Berry stared at the damaged guns, his gaze travelling along the bloodstained deck and smashed, shattered bulkheads. 'We're going to need a friendly port for repairs, make no mistake about it. That explosion will draw more of the enemy, you can be sure of that, and we're in no condition to mount a defence.'

'What about your mission to sink transports?'

'Our mission now is to survive and fight another day. Now, you must excuse me for I have much to do. You will help by assisting the men however you can.'

Runt threw him a salute, just like the seaman had, and then Berry was gone, leaving him alone in the chaos and destruction. He'd noticed the man had called him friend, and he assumed the crew had decided not to torture him now he'd risked his life to help them. That, and there was a good chance they'd need every available pair of hands to set the ship straight.

Runt saw half a dozen men lashing ropes to a fallen gun, hoping to lift it back onto its truck, and he hurried over to lend a hand. One of the crew slapped him on the back, then showed him how to help, and before long he was hauling ropes with the best of them.

Many leagues away, in the land of the stone people, it was late evening and a coming-of-age ceremony was in full swing. All over the grassy hill, parties of dwarves sat on bearskin rugs, quaffing mead from stone jars and munching cold venison poached from the forest. Several sported black eyes and bandages, evidence of scuffles with outraged farmers less than impressed at having their stock hunted for finger food.

Near the summit, a particularly large gathering sat in a circle around a rough stone slab. Standing on the slab was the most impressive of dwarves - four feet high, five across and sporting a beard like wall-to-wall shag pile. A hole in the approximate centre of the beard was opening and closing, and when food and beer weren't entering, words were coming out.

'Sons!' shouted the dwarf. He saw an indignant pair of bloodshot eyes glaring at him from a face of matted brown hair. 'And daughter!' he added. 'We are gathered here today to witness something quite special.' He paused to drain the contents of a stone jug, then threw it over his shoulder.

'Ow,' yelled a voice. 'Watch where you're throwing those fugging things!'

'Sons *and* daughter,' shouted Rugbeard, for such was his name. 'We are *not* gathered here to drink, eat and be merry.'

There were several puzzled looks.

'Although we *will* get to that later.'

Cheers.

'We are gathered here because my son...' he paused for effect. 'My *son* ... is coming of age.'

More cheers.

'And, as is traditional at these gatherings, I would like to invite Stonesmasher to speak to you all, so that he may explain to us in twenty-five words or less exactly how he will dedicate the rest of his life to the service of our community.'

'Speech,' shouted the crowd.

'The community is our lifeblood,' continued Rugbeard. 'For century upon century we have mined and forged, forged and

94

mined until the very land has been cast in our image. Thus it falls upon our children to ensure our kind endures through the ages.'

There was a prolonged bout of cheering.

'And so, with great pride, I present... Stonesmasher!' Rugbeard threw his arms out, beaming as a hefty young dwarf with a knee-length black beard and the shoulders of a rutting bull sprang to his feet and strode confidently to the stone slab. Rugbeard hugged his son, and in time-honoured dwarven tradition, they engaged in a brief hand-crushing contest before parting with throbbing, mangled fingers.

Stonesmasher stepped into the middle of the slab and surveyed the audience with clear, grey eyes. Hearts fluttered amongst eligible and ineligible females alike.

'Speak, son!' called Rugbeard, spraying the back of someone's head with chewed meat. 'You tell 'em!'

Stonesmasher cleared his throat. 'First of all, I would like to thank my parents.'

'What's this, an awards ceremony?' muttered someone. He was quickly shushed.

'I would like to thank my brothers, who taught me arm-wrestling, sword-fighting and strip-mining.' He cleared his throat. 'I would also like to thank my sister, who taught me weapon-making and clear-felling.'

There were nods all round at the sensible choices.

'And finally I would like to thank the elves, who taught me everything I know about the environment.'

'The *who*?' yelled Rugbeard.

'The *what*?' screeched the audience.

'The environment.' In the deathly silence, Stonesmasher turned to point at the forest. 'To a dwarf, those trees are nothing but firewood.'

'As it should be!' spluttered Rugbeard. 'As it always has been.'

'And yet, they are more than a simple source of heat. Every tree harbours life, every leaf–'

'That was a fine speech,' said Rugbeard quickly, clambering onto the slab. 'And now, it's time for the coming-of-age ceremony.'

'But I haven't finished yet.'

'Oh yes you have.' Rugbeard drew his axe. 'With this weapon, you will declare your true intentions,' he said, pressing the worn grip into his son's hand.

Stonesmasher regarded the axe, then let it slip from his fingers. The steel head rang on the stone slab like a funeral bell. 'I shall cut no trees,' he said softly. 'I shall work no stone.'

There was an uproar as the crowd of dwarves leapt to their feet. Jars were shattered and cold meat was trodden underfoot as the crowd rushed the unresisting dwarf. Willing hands grabbed him and bound him with leather belts and cast-off bandages. Then the crowd parted, leaving Stonesmasher lying on his back on the slab, his face bruised and his beard awry.

Rugbeard approached. 'Son, tell me you'll work the mines?' he pleaded. 'It means a lot to me.'

Stonesmasher turned his head away. 'I shall not.'

Rugbeard bent to retrieve his axe. 'Tell me you'll forge new weapons?'

'No.'

'What can you do to serve our community?' asked the father, as he adjusted his grip on the handle.

'I can make potions,' said Stonesmasher.

'Potions?' spat Rugbeard. 'Potions?' His eyes rolled up into his head and he keeled over as if shot. At exactly the same time, every dwarf in sight did likewise, and the ground fair shook as a hundred thick heads hit the turf.

'Quite effective potions at that,' muttered Stonesmasher. He pursed his lips and blew a piercing, ululating whistle. A slender elf stepped out of the bushes, surveying the fallen dwarves as he gathered his cloak around himself. 'One of your better efforts,' said the elf, who sometimes went by the name Slimbough, but usually went by the shorter and much punchier name of Slim. 'Long may they sleep.'

'Long enough for me to escape, I hope,' muttered the dwarf. 'Unwashed louts, the lot of them.'

The elf cut his bonds with an economical use of his blade. 'Will they follow you into the wilderness?'

'No chance. They'll declare me dead by the hand of an evil wizard, and then they'll hold a massive piff-up in my honour.'

'Then let us leave this place,' said Slim, 'For I hear tree stumps crying out in anguish, and I would put some distance between myself and the harrowing sound.'

Stonesmasher nodded. Although he wasn't attuned to nature like his elven friend, he shared his pain. 'We shall proceed east, for there is a lake with fresh water, and a cave we can use as a temporary shelter.'

'We can hardly proceed west,' said Slim, 'since the only thing we'll meet in that direction is the wide ocean and a watery death.'

'East it is,' said Stonesmasher, who was determined to have the last word.

'Lead on.'

'After you.'

'I insist,' said the elf, bowing politely.

Stonesmasher sighed. Slimbough was a dear and trusted friend, but he could also be a tiny bit irritating at times. After gathering up a fallen axe and a joint of venison, Stonesmasher set off at a fast stroll, turning his back on the land of his birth and the family who'd raised him. 'Fare thee well,' he murmured under his breath, for he bore them no ill will. Then he smiled, for he'd had the last word after all.

'I'm sure they'll miss you,' said Slim, who had the sharp hearing one associates with elves.

12

While the others were putting the finishing touches to the balloon, Clunk took several spare planks and turned them into a long ladder, capable of reaching the roof. He carried it outside and set it against the eaves, then climbed it rapidly. It was dark now, but night-time didn't bother him. On the contrary, it meant he was less likely to be seen.

The roof was made from thatched straw, old and rotting in places. He tested it with his foot, then stepped onto the thatch and climbed the incline to the ridge, where the stone chimney poked out through a gap in the roofing. There was smoke aplenty, and Clunk put his hand into the chimney to measure the temperature. He also switched to infra-red vision, checking for sparks.

The smoke was hot, and he was pleased there were no burning embers. By burning the right kind of fuel, the air rising from the chimney would fill the balloon perfectly, and as a bonus it wouldn't set the envelope on fire. Next, Clunk held up his finger, measuring the wind. It had swung to the north-east, maybe a touch more, and he smiled with satisfaction. It was good enough, and the speed wasn't so high that it made their attempted flight dangerous. Well, no more dangerous than taking to the skies in a home-made balloon.

He clambered back down the ladder, and with Hurm's assistance he got the wooden basket and all their supplies onto the roof. Father M was engrossed in his work, and didn't notice. Millie realised what Clunk was up to, but said nothing.

Hurm looked fearful as he climbed the ladder, looking down constantly and taking longer and longer to move up each rung. Clunk realised the human was terrified of heights, and he decided not to tell him about the purpose of the balloon until it was far too late.

Next, Clunk took four ropes and tied the basket down, one side to each corner of the roof, lashing the rope around the poles underneath the thatch. Those would prevent the balloon flying away before they were ready, and would have to be cut when they wanted to leave.

'I need you to bring up the bags of sand and put them in here,' he told Hurm, indicating the basket. 'Put them around the edges.'

Hurm nodded, then peered over the edge of the roof with a fearful expression. Slowly, he took the ladder to the ground, where he slung four bags around his neck before climbing up again to deposit them in the basket.

Clunk left him to it and returned to the house, where he got the others to help fold the balloon into the smallest package possible. He took up a coil of rope, slung it over his shoulder, then hesitated. This was the moment of truth, for Father M was sure to raise objections once he discovered they were moving the 'boat' onto the roof. 'I'm going to need your help,' he said.

'What is it now?' protested Father M. 'I've already worked my fingers to the bone.'

'We need to move this onto the roof,' said Clunk, indicating the big parcel of silk with his foot.

'We have to do what now?' demanded Father M. Then his

face cleared. 'I get it! You've had a vision of a huge flood, and we're launching from the roof.'

'Your statement is mostly accurate,' said Clunk, without revealing which part he was referring to.

The others helped him carry the huge bundle of silk outside, and with Hurm's help they got it up the ladder and onto the roof, which creaked alarmingly under their combined weight. 'Spread out,' said Clunk quickly. 'Try not to stand together, or we'll fall right through.'

Meanwhile, Father M was surveying the horizon, scanning every point of the compass. 'I don't see any rain clouds,' he said. 'Are you sure about this vision of yours?'

Clunk ignored him, and set about securing the balloon to the wooden basket. When it was done, he ran a pair of long ropes to the small flap at the top of the balloon, and then, after a moment's hesitation, he took the neck of the balloon and dropped it over the chimney. The silk billowed and flapped as it captured the hot air, and Clunk ran a length of rope around the chimney to prevent any escape.

As the balloon filled, Father M stopped scanning the horizon and instead turned his attention to the billowing silk. He gazed at it, then at Clunk, then at the balloon again. Clunk could see the man's brain working, and he waited for the inevitable outburst.

'A ship of the sky,' said Father M slowly. 'So you see, I was right after all. Of course, I chose not to reveal your plans to the others lest they be fearful of the journey ahead.'

Clunk hid a smile. The wizard was so keen to appear right all the time, he'd been forced to take the balloon in his stride. 'You'd better get into the basket,' he told the others. 'We need to weigh it down.'

Meanwhile, the balloon was really filling out now, rising

above the house like a big fat multicoloured tick gorging itself on some victim's lifeblood. When it was vertical, and filled as much as Clunk dared, he slashed the rope holding the neck around the chimney and ran for the basket, diving in.

The balloon's envelope rose, free of the chimney, and the ropes twanged like piano strings as it reached the end of its leash, held down by the basket, which was in turn held to the roof by the four guy ropes. The basket strained upwards, hauling on the four ropes, and Clunk got to his feet and prepared to cut them.

Too late, because with a groan of tortured nails, the entire thatched roof was torn free.

The balloon shot skywards, and everyone bar Clunk ended up on the floor of the basket. There was a loud crack as the timbers which had been holding the roof together parted in the middle, and the thatched roof folded itself in half and dangled from the basket like a gigantic handkerchief.

Everyone looked down through the widely-spaced slats with horror as the ground - and their temporary and now roofless home - fell away rapidly beneath them.

Clunk realised he'd over-estimated the lift, for the balloon should have drifted across the city just above the rooftops, not rocketed into the sky with a thatched roof still attached. He couldn't cut it free, either, for without the weight of it they would rise even faster. That, and dropping the broken roof on any unsuspecting civilians below would be a less than friendly act.

Instead, he pulled a cord, letting some of the hot air out of a vent on top of the balloon. He wanted to rise, but he was also being careful not to let out too much air too soon, for there was no way to replenish it.

'You should have built a boat to travel on water instead,'

snapped Father M, as he struggled to his feet. He was none too careful with his staff, putting one end into Hurm's midriff as he regained his balance. Then he realised just how high they were, and he fell silent.

Clunk offered the other two a hand, and together the four of them watched the city sliding past below, illuminated by the occasional lantern or torch. 'Keep your voices down,' murmured Clunk. 'The sound will carry a long way.'

'What the hell could they do about it, even if they did see us?' demanded Father M.

'We're well within bowshot.' Clunk tapped his foot on the floorboards. 'These slats wouldn't stop an arrow, either.'

Father M crossed his legs, and when he next spoke it was barely a whisper. 'How high must we go?'

Clunk had been asking himself the same question. As the air cooled, they would come down again, and when that happened they'd start throwing the bags of sand overboard. Therefore, the more altitude they could gain now, the further they'd travel. On the other hand, if they went too high the air would be much colder and the balloon would cool faster. 'It's a delicate balancing act,' he said at last.

'Hurm not like,' said the fighter. He looked thoroughly unhappy in the basket, and was being careful to avoid looking down.

'It's not too bad,' said Millie, comforting him with a hand on his shoulder. 'Clunk knows what he's doing, believe me.'

'Still not like,' muttered Hurm. 'Birds fly. Hurm walk.'

There wasn't much to be said after that, especially as they were passing over the city's outer walls, with the buckled metal gates and plentiful guards. They saw two guards directly below, chatting together as the huge balloon passed directly overhead.

Fortunately the balloon was in total darkness, and there wasn't as much as a squeak as they sailed over the city limits and headed into the wasteland. Before long the city vanished behind them, and Father M cleared his throat as he realised something. 'If you can't see the ground, how will you know when we're close to it?'

'I have an inbuilt altimeter,' said Clunk.

'I used to have one myself,' said Father M. 'Alas, I misplaced it.'

'It tells me how high up I am, and as long as we stay above two hundred feet we'll be safe, for there are no hills in these parts.' He noticed they'd stopped climbing, and he decided to cut the broken roof free. It was only made of thatch and lightweight poles, and the whole thing couldn't weigh more than twenty or thirty kilos. Therefore, he didn't expect much of a change in altitude. There was one problem though, and he got the others' attention. 'There are four ropes attached to the roof below us, and if we cut them one by one, the last might tip the basket. Therefore, we must cut all four simultaneously.'

Hurm drew his huge sword and prepared for a swing. Alarmed, Clunk grabbed the blade and forced it down, for the massive weapon would have cut not only the ropes, but probably a large portion of the basket and occupants too. 'A knife is all we require,' he said quickly.

They fossicked around until each had a blade, and on Clunk's count they all began sawing frantically. His and Hurm's ropes parted first, followed by Millie's. Father M was having trouble with his, and as the roof swung below them on the last remaining rope, the basket swayed alarmingly. Clunk looked up, hoping the strain didn't pull them free of the huge, air-filled envelope, but then there was a loud twang and the roof fell away into the darkness.

He felt the balloon rise immediately, and the numbers on his internal altimeter spun crazily. When they slowed, he realised they were much higher than he expected. Then he realised something else ... although he could track their height, he had no idea how fast they were travelling. The air was completely still, for they moved with the wind, and if that wind were blowing at a hundred knots or more, they wouldn't know until they slammed into the ground and were dragged along for league after league.

Clunk decided to change his plans slightly. Instead of sailing past the watchtowers and then setting down, he intended to stay aloft as long as possible, so that they might see daybreak before landing. That way, they would also see the ground.

It was early next morning, and Wiltred was sitting at the table having breakfast. Treeborne had left before dawn to tend the crops, while Willowmere had just returned from milking the cow. There'd been no sign of Tyniwon or Allyance, and Wiltred wondered if they were off somewhere, improving elf/human relationships. The pair of them seemed keen on each other, but then again Tyniwon was keen on most young women. He just hoped the young man didn't start some kind of family riot, because he might end up in the compost heap ... with Wiltred for company.

His fears were allayed moments later, because Tyniwon came back alone, brushing bark and twigs from his leather jerkin before removing his boots just outside the front door. It seemed he'd been off collecting firewood, although when

Allyance came in through the back door with a pitcher of water, her face was suspiciously flushed. Wiltred eyed Tyniwon with suspicion, but the young man returned his gaze with a look of pure innocence.

'Did you get enough wood?' asked Willowmere.

'Oh yes. Plenty,' said Allyance, and she gave Tyniwon a quick grin.

Damn and blast it, thought Wiltred. It was Tyniwon's fault they were fleeing Bark vengeance, and now he was compounding the problem by taking an elf maiden to his bed! Didn't he realise how perilous the situation was? What next, a fist fight with Treeborne? 'Eat some breakfast,' he said shortly. 'We have to leave.'

'What, now?'

'The sooner the better,' said Wiltred, around a mouthful of egg.

Tyniwon glanced at Allyance. 'We can stay a few days, surely?'

'Not likely. Our lives are in danger.'

'But the king's guard will never find us here.'

It's not the king's guard we're in danger from, you fool, thought Wiltred, but he didn't say anything.

'Oh, mother, I still owe you a secret,' said Allyance suddenly.

Wiltred paused with a forkful of egg halfway to his mouth, and he felt a terrible clenching of the stomach. Surely she wouldn't tell them about her tumble with Tyniwon? She couldn't. She mustn't! 'Nice weather today,' he said desperately. 'And wow, wasn't it a surprise to find out Tyniwon is the true king of the Mollisters? I mean, a guy like that, you wouldn't want a stain on his character, would you?'

Allyance gave him a strange look. 'Have you been drinking fyrehose again?'

'No. Do you have any?' Wiltred decided that if he was about to check out of his troublesome life, he might as well go out blind drunk.

'I don't think that's wise,' said Allyance.

'Well, we mustn't hold you up. Tyniwon and I will be on our way, and you can have your little mother-daughter chat once we're tiny little specks in the distance.'

'Oh, yes. The secret.' Allyance turned to her mother and bowed her head. 'Mother, Tyniwon and I–'

'Ow, my leg!' shouted Wiltred, leaping up and knocking his chair flying. 'Sorry, sorry. It's an old war wound, and it plays up now and then. The only cure is to walk it off.'

Tyniwon, fed up with the older man's strange behaviour, clapped a hand on his shoulder, righted the chair and sat him down. 'You're acting like a madman. Now sit there and shut up.'

Wiltred put his mouth to Tyniwon's ear, lowering his voice to a whisper. 'If she tells her mother what you two have been up to, we're dead, the pair of us.'

'What *have* you two been up to?' asked Willowmere, who, as an elf, was blessed with supernatural elven hearing.

Tyniwon bowed. 'Your daughter and I have been discussing the idea of her accompanying us on our journey. I know you're against it, but I promise Wiltred and I would give our lives to protect her.'

Willowmere snorted. 'Your protection didn't do King Larch much good.'

'That was an accident!' protested Tyniwon.

'As for defending her, you do realise Allyance could take you both before you drew a second breath?'

Tyniwon frowned. 'How is that possible? In the woods, she was struggling to save herself from a single opponent.'

'Ah, yes,' said Allyance. 'Mother, that was the secret I wished to share.'

'Do tell.'

'I've seen Tyniwon around the city in weeks past, and I thought he looked ... cute.'

Wiltred glanced up at the seven-foot giant. The sturdy young man could be described in many ways, but he didn't feel cute was one of them.

'When I was returning from the market yesterday, I heard these two in the woods behind me. So, when the bandit attacked me I sort of let him capture me, just a little.'

'Aha!' said Willowmere. 'I wondered why you hadn't killed him outright. It was a festering sore on my mind, now soothed by your explanation.'

'Wait a minute,' said Wiltred. 'Are you saying you staged the attack so Tyniwon would save you?'

'That is indeed the case. It seemed the best way to meet him.'

'Couldn't you have, I don't know, walked up to him in the city and said hello?'

'I was going to, but when I came to your workshop I heard much swearing and angry conversation.' Allyance indicated her pointed ears. 'I heard you discussing the king's death right through the wooden walls, and so I hurried from the city in order to accost you on the way home, staying just ahead so you would catch up with me in the place of my choosing.'

At that moment Treeborne returned from the fields, where he'd been listening to every word, and he gave a great shout of laughter as his daughter finished her tale of deception and subterfuge. 'Wil, she's got to go with them. Why, without her guile they won't stand a chance on their journey.'

'I'm of a mind to ground her,' said Willowmere, but then she shrugged. 'Very well, she may go. After all, if we don't let her she'll just follow them anyway. And I suppose she ought to see the land of her birth, even if it's likely to be through the bars of a cell.'

'Mother, I thank you!' said Allyance, and she gave both her parents a big hug. 'Now finish your breakfast, and be quick about it,' she told Wiltred and Tyniwon. 'I must collect a few items for the journey, and then we leave!'

13

Aboard the balloon, everything had been running smoothly for some hours now. It was still dark, but Clunk could see a flickering light slightly ahead and far below, directly in their path. There were similar patches of light far to the left and right, much fainter, and he realised each light represented a lantern or a torch attached to a guard tower.

Now that he could see a marker on the ground, Clunk was able to judge their speed for the first time since they'd set off, and the result of his calculation was troubling. They were moving quickly, and the balloon would have to slow considerably if they were going to set down safely.

Descending was still the last thing on his mind, though. The longer the balloon stayed airborne, and the deeper they flew into the rocky wastes, the less walking they'd have to do.

'What was that?' said Father M suddenly. He jerked, and started brushing himself down. 'There's a fudding bug trying to get up my robes!'

Millie squealed as something ran up her leg, and Clunk turned his chest lamp on before they all panicked. Caught in the low-wattage beam, like an actor in a spotlight, was the biggest cockroach he'd ever seen.

Millie tried to stamp on it, but it scuttled away. Hurm raised his thick tree trunk of a leg, and brought his foot down with the force of a hydraulic ram. He got the cockroach all right, but such was the force of the blow that his foot went right through the planks which made up the bottom of the basket.

'Take hold of something!' shouted Clunk, for he'd already guessed what was about to happen. Hurm and Millie reacted quickly, grabbing the sides of the basket in time. Father M did not.

There was a loud crack as the entire floor gave way, aided by the hundred kilos or so of sandbags they'd brought along for ballast. Like a hangman's trapdoor, the floor disappeared, and so did the ballast and their sack of supplies. Father M almost went through the floor too, but Clunk shot out a hand at the last second and grabbed the elderly wizard's robes, leaving Father M dangling in mid-air with his arms and legs waving frantically.

The balloon shot upwards, the sudden movement almost tearing Father M's robes from Clunk's grip. Without ballast they were far lighter, and the occupants hung on for dear life as they gripped the sides of the basket, with nothing beneath their feet but the ground far, far below.

Without the floor, the basket lost all its integrity, and the sides began to creak alarmingly as they flexed this way and that. 'Keep still,' said Clunk urgently. 'Keep still, or the basket will tear itself apart!'

The others obeyed, even Father M, and while they were frozen Clunk released his grip, hooking his arm around one of the taut ropes holding the basket up. Then, with his fingers, he managed to tug on a nearby line, releasing hot air to slow the balloon's rapid ascent. The numbers on his altimeter were fair whizzing by, and if he didn't regain control soon they'd not only fly right over the rocky wastes, they'd be lucky to set down before they reached the lands of the stone people . . . or even the western coastline.

Slowly, he pulled Father M back up into the basket, until the wizard managed to get a firm hold on the edge. Then Clunk turned his full attention to the controls.

Eventually the balloon levelled off, but they were now so high that the illuminated watchtower had disappeared into the darkness below. Either that, or the hundred kilos of sandbags had scored a direct hit, destroying the tower in the Old Kingdom's first ever recorded bombing raid.

Unfortunately, with the loss of their ballast Clunk now had limited control of the balloon. He could take them down any time by letting air out, but there was no way of rising. Not unless someone volunteered to jump overboard, and he didn't think that was very likely.

'By Zephyr,' muttered Father M, making the wind sign with one hand. 'I thank you, Clunk, for you surely saved my life.'

'It was nothing,' said Clunk modestly.

'As for you,' snapped Father M, turning on the hapless Hurm. 'You nearly killed us all, you muscle-bound moron!'

Hurm was too busy clinging on to answer. He didn't like heights at the best of times, and the balloon ride was the scariest thing he'd ever experienced. The last time he'd been poised above a deadly drop was when a thief had tried to poison his ale, and that hadn't been terrifying at all. Well, not for him, although the thief had been pretty scared right before Hurm ran him through.

'The balloon is under control,' said Clunk, trying to inject a note of confidence into his tone. 'Also, the basket might last for several minutes yet.'

'How long before we land?' demanded Father M.

Clunk hesitated. 'Unfortunately we can't set down until

daybreak. But if the basket breaks, we can still hold onto these ropes. It will be uncomfortable, but there's no cause for alarm.'

'Great. And what happens if the ropes break?'

'If that happens we'll be landing a whole lot sooner,' admitted Clunk. 'It would also be at a rather high speed. Terminal, you might say.' He suddenly realised it would have been a good idea to run up four parachutes while he'd had the sewing machine out, but he didn't feel now was the right time to bring that up.

'I *said* this was a stupid idea!' snapped Father M. 'Why couldn't we build a sailing boat instead?'

'Because of the sea serpents,' said Millie, fed up with his carping. She didn't like the height either, but there was nothing they could do now except hold on for dear life. 'We're all in this fix now, and complaining about it won't see us through.'

'Thank you for your support,' said Clunk, grateful for her kind words.

'I'd rather have some support under my feet,' snapped Father M. 'I can't hold on like this forever.'

'Why don't you rest your staff across the basket?' suggested Millie. 'You could sit on it and take the weight off your arms.'

'What if it snaps in two?' Despite his protests, Father M decided to try. He positioned the staff across one corner, then hoisted himself up and sat on the slender wooden pole, holding onto the ropes to balance himself. 'It's not very comfortable,' was his only comment, but he looked a lot happier.

Clunk eyed the other two humans. Both had their arms outside the basket, taking their weight under their armpits, and he knew they couldn't hold on forever. So, moving very carefully, he approached Millie and Hurm and ran a loop of rope around their chests, tying it off so they couldn't fall even if they were forced to let go.

He returned to his corner and took a fresh grip on the basket, trying to brace the sides so the whole thing didn't fold itself flat like a box without a base or lid.

An hour passed in silence, until Clunk noticed the faintest tinge of light in the sky behind them. Daybreak was coming, and soon after he discovered he could see the faces of his fellow travellers. The ground was still in darkness, but as dawn broke he could finally make out trees, bushes and rocky crags. The terrain was rough, very rough, and he frowned as he saw the huge broken rocks littering the landscape in every direction. There were hills and valleys too, where the surface had buckled and cracked from unimaginable forces far below ground.

He'd been hoping for a nice flat piece of turf, where they'd set down with a feather-light touch before alighting from their flying machine. Instead, it looked like their landing was going to be the equivalent of a faceplant on an oversized cheese grater.

'So that's why they call it the rocky wastes of the west,' said Father M, eying the terrain with a sour expression.

'We're moving a bit fast, aren't we?' added Millie.

Clunk nodded. If they set down at this speed, the humans would be lucky to escape with multiple fractures, let alone their lives. They needed to go higher, to try and find flatter ground ahead, but without ballast there was simply no way to rise. Once they were low enough he could jump overboard himself, of course, but that would just send the balloon shooting into the sky with nobody aboard capable of controlling it. Anyway, there was no guarantee the terrain ahead was any better.

They'd been dropping steadily, and the ground was slowly coming up to meet them, getting closer and closer. Twisted old trees dotted the landscape, and several gnarled branches threatened to snag the remains of their basket as they flashed by. Clunk racked his brains, trying to find a way to make the balloon go up, but the laws of physics weren't going to be influenced by wishful thinking alone.

He was still considering their problem when the sun rose over the horizon, bathing them in light and warmth. Clunk noticed the increase in his skin temperature immediately, and he looked up at the balloon in new-found hope. Sunlight shone on the fabric, and as it warmed the air inside, the balloon started rising again. Sluggish at first, soon they were rising steadily, the twisted trees and rocky landscape dropping away beneath them.

'That was ably done,' murmured Millie.

'Timed to perfection,' added Father M.

Hurm was staring at the fast-moving terrain in petrified fascination, incapable of coherent speech. Actually, the latter was pretty much business as usual, but the extreme fear was certainly new.

As the balloon rose into the sky, more of the landscape ahead was revealed, and Clunk felt a rush of relief as he saw a large body of water directly in their path. It was a big circular lake, surrounded by steep cliffs on all sides like a gigantic bath tub, and he realised it would make a perfect landing spot. He ran a few calculations, then worked the controls, letting out air gradually until he judged their descent would carry them up to the nearest shore. 'Can you all swim?' he asked the others.

Father M, Millie and Hurm all shook their heads.

That made things a little trickier, and Clunk ran some more calculations. He had no idea how deep the water was, and it was going to take all his skill to set down on the very edge of the lake. Too soon and they'd hit the cliffs or drag along the shore. Too far and he'd drown everyone.

They crossed the nearest cliff, and Clunk let out a large amount of hot air, causing the balloon to fall rapidly. Everything happened in a rush from that point, but fortunately his brain was a powerful computer, and so he could slow events down and examine them carefully. As they flew over the beach he examined the shallows ahead, estimating the depth. 'Cut your ropes, then get ready to jump on my mark,' he said quickly, then resumed his scanning. The balloon was going to fly over the shallows maybe ten or twelve feet up, and he didn't want everyone jumping into knee-deep water lest they break their ankles. He plotted a couple of lines on the scene, set up a counter, then relayed the numbers to the others, who'd removed their ropes in the meantime.

'Three. Two. One. *Jump!*'

Millie closed her eyes and let go, plunging straight down even as the water came up to meet them. Father M slid off his staff, twisting it free as he fell. Hurm shot Clunk a frightened look, then held his nose and jumped.

The balloon started to rise immediately, and by the time Clunk leapt clear he was further out than the others. As he fell, he turned his head to see the humans struggling in the water, and then he splashed down and sank straight to the bottom.

Immediately, he turned towards shore, leaned forward and drove himself along the sandy lake bed with his powerful legs. He reached Hurm first, and he dragged the big human along with him, kicking and struggling. Next, he took hold of Father M's cloak, which was flapping around underwater like sheets of seaweed. Finally, he broke the surface, and he was pleased to see Millie stumbling from the lake ahead of him, water streaming from her sodden clothes.

Father M and Hurm collapsed on the gritty black sand, coughing and spluttering, and after verifying they were going to live Clunk glanced over his shoulder to seek out the balloon. It was already high up, a gleaming, multicoloured ball caught in the sunlight, and he smiled to himself as it sailed on towards the western coast. It had been a resounding success, despite a few minor issues, and he was feeling proud of himself.

'You're a bloody lunatic,' growled Father M. 'You could have killed us with that deadly contraption!'

'Hurm not like,' said the fighter, who looked pale and bedraggled.

Only Millie looked happy, her face flushed and her eyes bright. 'That was the most exciting thing I've ever done,' she declared. 'Never again will I experience such a thing.'

'Don't speak too soon,' muttered Father M. 'You have no idea what twisted plans this robot has for us. Why, I wouldn't be surprised if he suggests flying home attached to the belly of a dragon!'

Clunk had actually been planning to ride on the *back* of a suitable dragon, but he decided now wasn't the time to reveal the fact. He needed to regain their confidence first, and so he got everyone gathering dry branches and twigs before lighting a roaring fire on the shore.

As the warmth dried their clothes the others became more talkative, and even Father M admitted that the balloon flight had turned out moderately well in the end, barring suitable safety warnings and the lack of a certificate of airworthiness.

'Now we just need our supplies, and we can have a decent cooked breakfast,' he said.

'I'm afraid we don't have any supplies,' said Clunk. 'They fell out when the floor broke.'

Father M stared at him, aghast. 'You mean we're stuck in the middle of the rocky wastes, with no map, no idea where the nearest settlement is, and no food or drink?'

'If we head west we might encounter settlements,' said Clunk, trying to comfort him. 'I believe the stone people live in this area, and–'

'You want to get food from the *dwarves*?' said Father M, his voice rising. 'Are you completely insane? Why, they still eat people in these parts, and if we're really lucky they'll kill us first.'

Clunk eyed the surrounding cliffs. 'We ought to find shelter near the lake. There is fresh water here, of course, and once we have a base we can venture further afield to seek supplies and help.'

Father M grumbled more, a lot more, but even he could see they had no choice. 'Very well. Let's split up and look for a cave. Make piles of wood as you go, for we can gather them later as firewood. I will keep an eye out for game, and with any luck we might enjoy a bite of roast waterfowl or rabbit for lunch.'

Clunk studied the far side of the lake, which was half-hidden in the early morning mist, and he estimated it would take two or three hours to get there. 'Let's circle the lake in pairs and meet at the opposite side,' he suggested.

Father M agreed, and he and Hurm set off in a clockwise direction, while Clunk and Millie went the opposite way. Not long after they parted, Clunk realised he'd forgotten to warn the other two about any dragons which might be nesting in the rocks, but he decided they'd discover the presence of dragons soon enough if they stepped on one.

14

It took Allyance but a few minutes to gather her things, and then the party was ready to leave. In the elven tradition, her parents stood waiting with gifts for their journey.

'You three set off on a brave, noble quest,' said Willowmere. 'You will journey for several days, encountering all manner of difficulties, dangers –'

'– and ditches,' added Treebough. 'Deep marshy ditches full of stinking water.'

'But I'm sure you will overcome these challenges, for you are pure of spirit!' Willowmere hugged her daughter, then pressed a cooking pan brimming with stew into her hands. 'This is your favourite meal, daughter of mine. It will feed you and nourish you.'

'Don't forget to clean the pan afterwards,' added Treebough. 'That stuff's murder if you let it harden.'

Willowmere ignored him, and advanced on Tyniwon. 'For you, a twig of purest willow, to remind you of the happy times spent in this place.'

'Er ... thanks a lot,' said Tyniwon, and he pushed the twig into his pack.

Wiltred watched Willowmere advancing on him, but to be honest he wasn't getting his hopes up. She'd probably give him something truly useless like a lock of hair, or a handful of muesli bars. But instead, she pressed a small silver flask into his hands.

'Fyrehose,' she said. 'Perhaps, if you take it one drop at a time, it won't render you unconscious. For we all know you cannot hold your liquor!'

Everyone laughed politely, and Wiltred smiled and nodded as he pocketed the little vial. Privately, he vowed to empty the lethal brew into the nearest river as soon as he got the chance. At the very least, they'd be able to sup on pickled fish.

'Now you must be away, for the morning grows long,' exclaimed Willowmere. 'Farewell, my friends. Farewell, my daughter! Travel safe!'

The three of them set off across the fields in high spirits, and they were still in earshot when Treebough addressed his wife. He spoke loudly, and Wiltred didn't need supernatural elven hearing to pick up the conversation.

'Do you think they'll make it, my dear?'

'Allyance will be fine,' murmured Willowmere. 'The other two don't have a hope in hell.'

'Why, then, did you give them my hip flask?'

Wiltred missed the reply to that one, but he didn't care. His mood had soured, and as they tramped across the fields he decided he might drink of the fyrehose after all.

'Aha, I see a cave!' said Father M. 'I told you I'd find us suitable shelter.'

Hurm frowned. He wasn't that hot on interpreting dialogue, but he was pretty sure Father M's conversation over the past thirty minutes had been nothing but a string of negative statements. 'We'll never find shelter, we'll starve to death, my feet hurt, this is a stupid plan' and so on. Hurm wished he could have teamed up with Millie instead of Father M, but for some reason she'd accompanied the strange metal man instead.

'Of course, there won't be any food,' continued Father M, as they made their way up the rocks to the entrance. 'It's probably packed with killer bears, killer bees and those little biting midges that leave big red welts. I bet it's damp and dark, too.'

And we're back to the complaining, thought Hurm. He himself never complained about possible future events, because thinking about what *might* happen, rather than concentrating on the things which were *actually* happening, made his brain hurt.

However, contrary to all Father M's predictions, the cave was spacious, dry and surprisingly well lit. The two of them were carrying a few odds and ends of firewood, and Hurm took a handful of twigs and made a tiny pyramid in the centre of the cave. Then he took a few larger sticks and placed them carefully around the twigs. Finally, he sharpened a straight stick, took up a larger branch, and squatted on the ground with the branch in his lap. He placed the pointed stick between his palms and began rolling it, fast, twirling the point in a small hollow he'd dug into the bigger piece of wood.

Father M went to get some more driftwood while Hurm paused to add fragments of dry leaves and shredded bark to his branch, before twirling the stick again.

Father M returned while Hurm was still working away. He

tossed a big pile of wood on the unlit fire, which knocked Hurm's carefully constructed twigs and sticks all over the place.

By now, Hurm's branch was showing the first signs of smoke, and he knew it would only be ten or fifteen minutes before he had the first signs of fire. It was almost hypnotic, the twirling of the stick, and the rubbing noise, and the feeling of being one with nature was intense.

He wasn't going to get the chance to light his fire, though, because while he was still twirling his sharpened rod between his palms, Father M took out a small stoppered bottle and tipped a few grains of powder on the untidy pile of driftwood. Then he added a dash of some mystical liquid, and the driftwood caught with a loud woof, filling the cave with the glare from its towering flames.

Hurm paused to gaze at the roaring fire. Next, he glanced at Father M, because it occurred to him that it would have been nice to know about the wizard's magical fire-lighting potion before he sat down to rub sticks together. Then he jumped up, cursing, because the stick he'd been twirling had caught fire while he wasn't looking, and the flames had just taken all the hairs off the back of his hand.

'We don't need two fires,' said Father M. 'You should put your feeble effort out before someone gets hurt.'

Hurm stamped his stick into the dirt, then froze, his head on one side. He could hear voices, and they were both male. 'Hurm hear people,' he said.

'That'll be the others,' said Father M. 'I wonder if they found any food?'

'Not others,' said Hurm.

'Well who else could it be in these parts?' said Father M waspishly. 'Dragons don't speak, do they?'

He soon found out who it was, because at that moment a heavy-set dwarf and a slender elf entered the cave.

'So you see, Slim, it's not really a crime if they don't find out,' the dwarf was saying.

'That is a common misconception, Stonesmasher my friend,' replied the elf.

They were both armed, one with a large axe and the other with a bow, and as they became aware of Father M and Hurm, they both grabbed for their weapons. The elf nocked an arrow in the blink of an eye, and the dwarf brandished his axe as he glowered at Father M from under eyebrows the size of shaggy hamsters. 'Who the hell are you?' he demanded, in a rough voice. 'And what are you doing in my cave?'

'We seek shelter,' said Father M, or rather, he tried to. He only managed to say 'we' before Hurm drew his enormous sword and swung it at the dwarf's head.

The dwarf ducked, and the sword cut through the air with a vicious hum. The elf reacted instantly, turning on Hurm and loosing his nocked arrow, but he was too late because Hurm had already rolled to one side. The shaft shattered on the rocks, but the elf was quick too, and he loosed off two more arrows before Hurm got anywhere near him. The first hit Hurm's sword, glancing off and going straight into the fire. The second was dealt with by Father M, who'd stopped trying to say 'seek' and instead used his powers to deflect the arrow away from the fighter.

Hurm drew his sword back to cut the elf in two, but Stonesmasher the dwarf got there first, parrying the ferocious blow with his huge double-headed axe. Hurm tried again, but once more the axe foiled him.

'Wait, wait, wait!' shouted the elf. 'Stay your weapons!'

Hurm hesitated mid-stroke, and the dwarf knocked his

sword aside before lowering his axe. The two of them scowled at each other, itching to fight once more, but before they could do so the elf stepped between them.

'Hold!' The elf raised his hand. 'Do you not see? We are four very different individuals, with complementary skills. A big strong dwarf, an elegant elf, a brainless barbarian and a skinny old wizard? Why, we should form a party!'

'Form a party?' sneered Father M. 'You'll be suggesting we roll dice next!'

'You're right. It would never work. What was I thinking?' So saying, the elf stepped back and nocked an arrow, and then it was on again for young and old.

Stonesmasher swung his axe, which simply glanced off Hurm's solid skull. In return, Hurm grabbed a handful of beard and repeatedly banged the dwarf's face into the rocks. This had no effect on his face, but it certainly bruised the rocks some. Meanwhile, Father M came running to get in a cheap shot, but the dwarf lashed out like a mule with his heavy boot, back-heeling the wizard just below the belt.

'Ow, my *bells*!' groaned Father M, clutching at his groin. Then he forgot about the pain, because the elf looped his fancy bow over the wizard's head and tried to strangle him with the string.

Father M wasn't having any of that, so he reached back and plucked an arrow from the elf's quiver, jamming the point through the uppers of Slim's fancy green boot, and straight down into his fancy elvish foot. Slim cried out in pain and started hopping around the cave on his good foot, until he trod on a spent arrow. The point went through the sole of his boot, and he uttered a string of elvish curses and started hopping on the other foot. Father M saw his opportunity, and he went at his wounded opponent with a flurry of jabs and blows from his silver-tipped staff, whacking the elf around the head, shoulders, knees and especially the toes.

Hurm was still holding a handful of Stonesmasher's beard, only the dwarf was no longer attached to it. Stonesmasher threw aside his axe, which was useless in close quarters, and instead went in with bunched fists. His punches landed like steam-hammer blows, and Hurm backed away quickly, fending off the fists with the palms of his hands. Then he saw his opening, and he slapped the dwarf across the face with a lightning fast move. Stonesmasher reeled from the stinging slap, then countered with one of his own. Hurm slapped him back, and then they stood toe to toe, slapping each other repeatedly, faster and faster until their hands were a blur.

Just when it seemed the slapfight would go on forever, Hurm ducked, Stonesmasher stumbled forward, off balance, and the big fighter met him with a straight jab to the nose. He thought it was all over then, but it was as though he'd punched a rock face. The dwarf grinned at him, spat on the ground, then bunched his fists and prepared for a *real* fight.

Meanwhile, Father M was busy trying to break his staff over the elf's head, but elves had natural immunity to wood, and the blows had little effect. Slim was out of arrows, rendering his bow useless, but he was adept in the art of unarmed combat. So, he threw his weapon aside, rolled up his sleeves and took a fighting stance.

Father M smiled. He too was an adept in the art of unarmed combat, and he recognised the elf's stance as that of a lowly beginner. Confident, he side-stepped the elf's feeble attempt to grapple him, then turned sharply and drove his foot into the elf's midriff.

Or he would have, if the elf had still been there.

Slim was behind him, somehow, and Father M cried out

as the elf punched him in the kidneys with a hefty one-two, then followed it up with a cheeky kick to the posterior. The kick knocked him face-first into the dirt, and he seethed with anger as he realised the sneaky, cheating elf had fooled him by pretending to be a novice.

Now thoroughly enraged, he drew on all his unarmed combat skills, and performed a manoeuvre called the i-sting. This involved grabbing a handful of dirt and tossing it into his opponent's face, and the tactic worked perfectly. The elf stumbled around, half-blinded by the grit, and Father M gathered up a large stone and clonked him on the side of the head with it, leaving him thoroughly dazed.

Meanwhile, Hurm and Stonesmasher had moved on from prizefighting to wrestling, and Hurm was trying to get his opponent into an arm lock. Meanwhile Stonesmasher was trying to connect Hurm's left knee to his right knee ...by wrapping it the wrong way around his muscled torso. The two of them grunted and strained, but it was all in vain because they were evenly matched. Even, that is, until Father M performed his patented i-choo manoeuvre, which involved jamming a handful of dust up Stonesmasher's nose until the dwarf was sneezing his lungs out.

After that the fight ended quickly, with both dwarf and elf lying on the ground while Hurm stood over them, arms raised in victory, one foot planted on each of their chests. There was no crowd to cheer him, but Father M did give him a slow clap.

There wasn't much time to celebrate, though, because at that moment there was a deep rumble. Near the back of the cave, there was a rock which had hitherto been large and immobile. It was still large, that was for sure, but it was no longer immobile. In fact, it was rolling aside like a huge, circular door, and as it opened wider and wider Father M stared with shock as he saw the reason for this strange un-rocklike behaviour.

They were about to have more company, and the newcomers would prove to be even less welcome than the dazed foes Hurm was busy standing on.

15

'Ladies and gentlemen, we're gathered here today to pay homage to the new king.'

There was a smattering of applause from the gathered lords and ladies. Sur Pryze clapped enthusiastically, while Sur Loyne stood towards the back of the hall, wearing a sour expression.

'Of course, we're all hoping King Larch will return to us, but in the meantime we must appoint a new monarch to rule our fair land. And so, it gives me much pleasure to introduce King Kah, whose ancestors form the closest and strongest branch of the Larch family tree.'

There was a cheer as King Kah took the throne, and he smiled at his subjects as Chief Courtier Sparlow placed a crown of dried branches on the royal brow. The king's smile faltered as he noticed Sur Loyne's look of thunder, but he recovered quickly as he sipped from the royal goblet, and partook of the royal bread. Then, ceremony complete, he was swamped by nobles with claims over new land, or claims over lands which belonged to other nobles, who in turn put forth their own claims over their enemies' lands.

Sur Loyne watched the unseemly scrum, and for the first time that day a smile appeared. He thought being king involved chomping down endless feasts, accepting valuable gifts, and getting up to bedroom antics with any serving girl who caught his eye, but it seemed the king of the Barks was basically a glorified magistrate. Plus the throne room was draughty, there were gaping holes in the roof, and you couldn't get a decent set of cutlery for love nor money.

So much for the king! Sur Loyne turned his mind to the true reason for their presence in the Bark kingdom: Tyniwon Mollister. With Sur Kah's royal help, he was hoping they'd be able to round up everyone in the city who'd seen the young giant recently, before threatening to lop their heads off if they didn't reveal his location. In fact, he wouldn't mind lopping off a few heads before the questioning started, to show the others he meant business.

'Make way there,' he said loudly, and he elbowed his way through the squabbling dignitaries until he was standing before the king.

'I didn't see you clapping with the rest,' said Sur Kah.

Sur Loyne frowned. He might not be jealous any more, but he was still miffed. 'What did you say?'

The king swallowed, for Sur Loyne was a dangerous man, and he carried a large and very sharp sword. 'I, er, must have been mistaken.'

'I need to speak with you about Tyniwon.'

'Oh yes, your queen's half-brother. I will order a search party next week, after the celebrations.'

'I'm not staying in this dump for a week,' snapped Sur Loyne. 'Give me twenty men and a chopping block, and I'll leave with Tyniwon before nightfall.'

'I'm sorry, but I can't set you loose on my subjects. This isn't Mollister land, you know. We treat people well here.'

'Like making them wait forty years for service at the town hall?'

King Kah waved away a couple of nobles, then indicated Sparlow should give him some room. Once he was alone with Sur Loyne, he lowered his voice and continued. 'Our processes could use a little streamlining,' he admitted. 'But you must agree, it's a nice chance to see the locals living long enough to *wait* forty years. In Chatter's Reach, they barely survive to middle age.'

'Yes, and speaking of living a long and healthy life,' said Sur Loyne, casually dropping his hand to the hilt of his sword. 'Twenty men to help me search, we agreed, and the sooner the better. Otherwise I'll tell Sparlow you're the one who chucked a handful of metal coins into the crowd earlier today, and they'll have your head off before you can say paper-cut.'

'You're an outsider here. Why would anyone believe you?'

Exasperated, Sur Loyne took a step forward. 'Listen to me, you muddle-brained idiot. *You're* an outsider here, and as soon as the real king turns up this lot are going to have you out on your ear. And when they do, I'll be waiting for you. Got it?' With that, he turned on his heel and marched out, barging through the waiting dignitaries like a big, angry cannonball.

He paused in the hall, because he realised he'd left without extracting a promise of help, and also that the next time he tried to confront the new king there would probably be two dozen armed guards there to keep Sur Loyne at bay. Guards armed with wooden clubs and staves, to be sure, but they'd win out by weight of numbers alone.

On the spur of the moment he changed his mind once again. Instead of hunting for Tyniwon, he'd track down King Larch of the Barks. Getting the rightful king on the throne would achieve two important objectives. First, it would ensure Sur

Kah was booted from his un-earned position on the royal throne, and second, it would make Sur Loyne feel a whole lot happier.

With his scheme fully hatched and ready to cluck, he went off to inform Sur Pryze of their new mission.

It took an age to get the lower-deck guns onto their trucks, and after the work was finished there was plenty more to keep the crew occupied. They were still busy restocking cannonballs and securing the guns when Dallow, the surviving midshipmen, came down from the upper deck. 'Begging your pardon, but the captain wants to see you.'

Runt frowned. 'I thought the captain was killed?'

'He was. This request comes from midshipman Berry.'

'So who's the captain?'

'Midshipman Berry is the captain, but that's because he's the ranking officer. Since he's not been promoted, he cannot be addressed as Captain Berry, only as the captain.'

Runt shook his head, confused by the protocols. But whatever Berry's rank, the man was waiting for him and he didn't want to delay. So, he followed the midshipman to the upper deck, where if anything the scene of destruction was even greater than it had been below. In addition to shattered rails and up-ended guns, there were rows of dead sailors covered with an old sail, and the entire deck was littered with rigging blasted from the masts overhead. Runt looked up, and was surprised to see only one of the big masts still standing, with the other two hanging over the side like huge, fallen trees.

Men were busy hacking at ropes, trying to free the masts so they could bring them alongside. Others were working on the two fat stumps sticking out of the deck, getting them ready for removal so the original masts could be reshipped. They'd be shorter than the originals, but the aim was to raise sail and flee to safety, not win awards for the most graceful ship to be sunk in enemy waters.

Berry was giving orders to a group of men, who split up and ran to their tasks as Runt approached. Most were able seamen, temporarily promoted to replace the missing officers, but they knew their jobs and there was an air of calm all around the busy deck.

'The enemy will know we're in the area by now,' said Berry. 'That explosion will have carried deep into Methusian territory, and I'm sure the fleet will be dispatched to seek its cause. They will be hunting us, my friend, and we can't outrun them in this state.' He looked up at the sole remaining mast. 'There's going to be another battle, and this time the outcome will not be in our favour.'

'So what can we do?'

Berry gave him a wry smile. 'Nothing. We need a sheltered anchorage, timber, supplies . . . all the things we cannot have this far from home. If we're lucky they'll let us surrender, and we'll spend the rest of the war in captivity. If we're unlucky they'll sink us, surrender or no, as revenge for defeating one of their own.'

Runt glanced along the deck towards his little rowing boat, which had miraculously escaped the enemy gunfire. He was tempted to ask Berry to set him free, so that he might try to find his own way home. On the other hand, they were miles from anywhere, and with his luck the Methusians would pick him up. They would probably torture him, and he'd end up even worse off.

However, seeing his little boat had given him a crazy idea, and he rubbed his chin as he wondered how to present it to Berry. Unfortunately it was a tricky one, because the last time the subject of the Old Kingdom had come up, they'd dragged him below for a spot of torture. Oh well, he thought, if he wanted to get home he had no choice but to try. 'Sir, there is one place where you could repair your ship in safety.'

'Oh yes? Do tell!'

'You remember that speck on your chart, the one you called the Cursed Isle?'

'Certainly I do, for everyone knows the tales of despair, horror and woe associated with that foul place.' Berry's expression changed. 'No! Surely you're not suggesting–'

'I am,' said Runt firmly. 'As you already suspected, I'm a native of that island, and it's not cursed at all.'

Berry's mouth dropped open, and he looked at Runt as though the halfling had just sprouted horns.

'We call it the Old Kingdom,' said Runt, pressing on, 'and there are many inlets along the coast where you could repair your ship. Supplies too, if we land near a city.' Not too near, he thought, because the ruler of whichever land they chose would give his or her left arm for a ship such as this.

Berry recovered from his surprise. As the captain of a damaged ship, his mind was focussed on practical matters, and Cursed Island or no, he needed somewhere to shelter. 'I would be willing to try such a thing,' he said at last, 'but the crew . . . once they found out, they would put us both adrift in that boat of yours.'

'So don't tell them it's the Cursed Isle. Tell them it's a neutral country, or a big island you once heard of in your travels, and then act all surprised when we sail up to it.'

'These are experienced men,' objected Berry. 'Some have been sailing the oceans forty years or more, and they will not be fooled by such fanciful tales. Rumours about the Cursed Isle, once started, would be as difficult to extinguish as the flames aboard that Methusian ship we fought, and you saw what happened to those poor souls.'

'And what's going to happen when the Methusian fleet catches up with you?'

Berry was silent, for Runt made a good point. 'I have it,' he said at last. 'We will set a course for this kingdom of yours, and when the crew see land they may be too overcome with joy to consider the implications.'

Runt thought of the huge sea serpents lurking in the oceans around the Old Kingdom, and the fierce dragons living in the rocky wastes of the west, and decided not to mention such minor details to his new-found friend. After all, the ship was large and well-armed, and it could probably defend itself against the threats. Then he thought of the Old Kingdom, and the various races which called it home, and he wondered which coast was the more suitable. Not Mollister lands, for the queen would send an army to take the ship as soon as she learned of its presence. The Bark kingdom was landlocked, and the elves were right out thanks to their skill at long-range archery.

That left the two kingdoms in the northern regions, which were inhabited by savages and barbarians, and the kingdom of the stone people ... which was inhabited by savage, barbarian dwarves. He decided on the latter, because the dwarves didn't use ranged weapons, and they didn't so much swim as sink like solid chunks of rock. 'Aim for the south-western coast,' he advised Berry. 'The dw– ... I mean, the locals don't like the sea very much, and they wouldn't patrol a beach to save their lives.'

Berry nodded, and left the master in charge while he went below to plot a course on the big map. Runt stood there, enjoying the afternoon sunshine, and a feeling of joy came over him as he realised he would soon be home. Stranded in the kingdom of the stone people, sure, but at least he'd be facing all the familiar terrors the Old Kingdom had to offer, and not these new-fangled ones like sea-battles, drowning and a superstitious, cut-throat crew.

— 16 —

It was a long, hard journey on foot, but Tiera and Thonn finally made it to the city of Branche. They passed through the big wooden gates, sidestepping a beam which had worked itself loose from the splendid overhead arch, and then made their way into the depths of the city itself.

There was activity everywhere they looked, with people tying up coloured bunting, hawkers selling wares from handcarts, and unruly children running here and there, stealing food from the hawkers and pulling down the carefully-erected bunting the minute people turned their backs.

Thonn and Tiera strolled past the chaos, wondering what the bunting was for. Curious, Tiera called out to a citizen, who was leaning against a wall, panting heavily after chasing children away. 'Sir, can you tell me what you're celebrating?'

'There's to be a new king,' said the man, between ragged breaths.

'What happened to the old one? Did he die?'

'That's a question we've all been asking ourselves, lassie. One day he was here, watching over us, and the next he vanished.'

'And the new king?'

The man spat in the road. 'Some Mollister knight, they say.

Came swanning into town the day after poor old King Larch disappears, and they made him king before anyone could draw breath.'

'You don't mean the queen's champion, Sur Loyne?' demanded Tiera. She'd seen the knight on the north road, and had assumed he'd been sent to kill her. But what if he were involved in a sneaky plan to annex the Bark kingdom for the queen, Therstie Mollister? What if he wasn't looking for her at all?

'No, it was another one. Sur Kah, I think it was. Some kind of historian, they say.' The man spat again. 'Mollisters. Who needs their airs and graces?'

Tiera moved on, her mind busy with the implications. She'd come to Branche to lay low, but now it seemed the city was to become the centre of a power struggle between two major kingdoms. At this very moment, Mollister armies could be mobilising, perhaps intending to march on the city and shore up their new king. And what about the old king ... had he been quietly assassinated, the body disposed of without fuss? Tiera felt a twinge of annoyance, because if anyone wanted a king killer, they should have offered *her* the job.

'Now that we've made it to the city, what is your plan?' asked Thonn.

Leave again, Tiera almost said, but it was too soon for that. They'd travelled a long way, and the machinations of kings and queens had nothing to do with her. 'First I shall look for work, so that we might eat.'

Thonn looked doubtful. 'If you intend to sing for money, it's likely we will starve.'

'My singing isn't that bad!' protested Tiera, stung by his criticism. 'You put me on the spot last time, and I didn't have time to warm up.'

'That's as may be, but perhaps you ought to seek a different line of work.'

Tiera was silent. Her actual line of work was killing people, preferably in the dead of night, and she was well-paid for it. So well paid she had ten gold coins concealed in her boot, but they were about as useful as newly-cut rubies when it came to buying supplies, for nobody outside a wealthy lord or lady would have enough cash to exchange a single gold coin. Why, ten gold coins was enough to buy a small house, furnish it, and hire servants to fetch and carry.

That gave her an idea, and she approached a woman who was busy feeding her baby while simultaneously holding up one end of a brightly-painted paper streamer. 'Excuse me.'

'Sorry love, can't talk now. Gotta stop these damned kids ripping the decorations down again.'

'It's just a quick question.'

'Go on, then.'

'Where does one go to buy a house around here?'

'Do I look like I go around buying houses in my spare time?' said the woman acidly.

'Forgive me. It was just a question, no slight meant.'

The woman relented. 'Ask at the town hall. They'll know.'

'Thank you. And the town hall is–'

With a nod of her head, the woman indicated the direction. 'You can't miss it. It's a big wooden building with carvings.'

'Thank you.' Tiera set off with Thonn in tow, and she couldn't help noticing every building was wooden, with lots of carvings. However, when she came across a much larger building, just off the main square, she realised she'd found the place.

'I believe we've arrived at our destination,' said Thonn, in the annoying manner of a talking assistant who loved to state the obvious.

Inside, there were dozens of people sitting around holding paper tickets, and when Tiera went to the counter the woman indicated a dispenser. 'Take a ticket, wait your turn.'

Tiera obeyed, and went to sit down.

'I wouldn't bother, love,' said an old man. He displayed his ticket, which was about sixty thousand numbers lower than hers. 'The average wait time is about forty years, but if you pay them a shilling they'll come and knock on the door when it's your turn.'

'Forty years! But I just want to ask where I can buy a house!'

'Oh, you don't need a ticket for that.'

'That's a relief.'

The old man leaned forward, turning to his left. 'Mabel, you still waiting to sell that place what belonged to your grandparents?'

'That I am,' said a middle-aged woman. 'Been thirty-five years already, by my reckoning, and it's not getting any newer.'

'I might have a customer for you.' The old man indicated Tiera. 'She wants to buy a place.'

'Well, I don't know. I was only seven when I got this ticket, and I feel I should, you know, wait my turn so I can hand it in. It's been so long I want to know what it feels like.'

The old man snorted. 'Don't be daft. That ticket's just so you can offer your house for sale. They'll give you another ticket afterwards, and you'll be waiting another forty years to sign over the deeds.'

'Now you put it like that, I suppose it does make sense to avoid the queue.' The old woman eyed Tiera thoughtfully. 'How much are you offering?'

'I don't know. What kind of house is it?'

'It's got a roof and four walls. What more does anyone need?'

'Can we go and take a look?'

'Of course, dear. It's just down Splint Lane, behind the timber yard. Third on the left, it is. You can't miss it, there's a lovely red door at the front.'

'Will you wait here until I come back?'

'Are you taking the piff? All I do is wait!'

Tiera nodded her thanks, and she and Thonn set off to inspect the house. It was in the middle of a row, and the front door was open. It might have been red once, but over the years the paint had faded and peeled thanks to the lack of lead, and the door was now just plain wood. Tiera pushed it open, wincing as the wooden hinges creaked, and then leapt back, startled, as half a dozen chickens fluttered out, clucking and flapping their wings.

Inside, the floor was buried under manure, and what furniture there might once have been had either collapsed or been stolen. On the positive side, there were three rooms of a decent size, with shutters on the windows and working doors. Out back there was a small square of land, overgrown with weeds, and in the corner there was a wooden pipe with a cork in, right above a broken stone bowl. Tiera pulled the cork, and a stream of water gushed out, running over the bowl and seeping away into the dirt.

'Fresh water. That's good,' said Thonn encouragingly.

Tiera wasn't sure whether the shattered basin was meant to be a kitchen sink, a bath, a toilet, or all three in one compact unit. But yes, it was convenient. She looked over the house once more, and decided it would do. Sure, it needed a bit of renovation, but with a cheap fixer-upper like this she was sure to have plenty of money left over for paint, furniture and floor coverings. 'Let's see what she's asking for it,' she said, and they returned to the town hall.

The woman looked up as they entered, her face hopeful. 'Did you have a good look around?'

Tiera nodded, and sat down next to her. 'It needs a lot of work.'

'Superficial, that's all. The structure is sound.'

'There's chickens living in the front room.'

'So? Think of the free eggs! And there's running water, too.'

'I know. I saw it running all over the back yard.' Now that they'd fired their opening shots in the negotiation, it was the moment of truth. 'How much are you asking?' demanded Tiera.

The woman studied her shrewdly, trying to estimate her worth by sight alone. Meanwhile, Tiera could all but feel the weight of gold hidden in her boot, and she hoped the ten coins weren't singing out to the house's owner, betraying her wealth. Then a thought struck her like lightning. The coins were gold. This was the Bark kingdom, where metal was banned. So what did people use for money, if not gold?

'I can't take any less than three guineas,' said the woman at last. 'I'm sorry if that's more than you have, but times are hard and I need the money.'

'Three guineas? What kind?'

'Steelwood, of course. What other kind is there?'

Gold, thought Tiera. She lowered her voice to a whisper, and leaned closer to the woman. 'I'm new in these parts, so tell me ... if a traveller were to show up in Branche with, I don't know, solid gold coins ... what might they do with them?'

'You have ... gold?' hissed the woman.

'I'm talking hypothetically, of course.'

'Why, gold is priceless in this city. With real gold, a body

141

could leave Branche and settle anywhere in the old kingdom. One could move to Mollister lands, and have metal pots and pans, and cast iron fireplaces that don't burn your house down, and proper metal tools, and ... ' The woman's voice tailed off, and there was a wistful look in her eyes. Then she gripped Tiera's arm. 'Oh, *do* say you can pay in gold, for I would accept five gold coins without a second thought.'

'I thought you said gold was priceless? Now you're saying it's worth less than three wooden guineas!'

The woman eyed her shrewdly. 'Well, yes, but the other thing gold can get you in this city is ... dead. Takes a certain amount of nerve to carry gold, that it does. To put myself at such risk, why, it would have to be worth my while.'

'I'll pay five gold coins ... on one condition.'

'Name it.'

'I want to exchange one of those gold coins for the equivalent in your local currency. Give me half, you can keep the rest.'

'So you're offering four and a half for the house?'

Tiera nodded.

'Done,' said the woman quickly. 'I know someone who can change your money, but we'll have to meet them together. They won't deal with strangers.'

'Then we have a deal.'

'By the way, you can move in to the house whenever you like. There's no need for any paperwork.'

'Are you sure?'

'I'm certain.' The woman nodded towards the counter. 'It'll be forty years before these people realise it's been sold.'

17

There was plenty of driftwood, and Clunk and Millie gathered armfuls until they could carry no more, at which point they set it down in a neat pile before collecting more. All the while they studied the base of the sheer cliffs, looking for a cave the party might shelter in. There were plenty of fallen rocks, some as big as houses, but clamber over them as they might, they didn't find anything that could be described as shelter.

'Maybe we could build a hut out of all this driftwood,' suggested Millie. 'My family lived in a wooden hut, and it was very cosy once my father lined the outside with squares of turf.'

'You've told me little about yourself until now,' said Clunk gently. 'It must have been terrible to lose your entire family. It was a robbery on the road to Chatter's Reach, you said?'

Millie nodded. 'They surrounded our cart, intending to kill us all for our belongings. Once they learned this, my parents leapt at them, giving their dying breaths so that I might flee to safety.' She looked down at the sandy beach. 'That was six months ago, and I still feel the loss as keenly as the night it happened.'

They walked in silence for a while, before Millie spoke up again. 'How long before we travel to Bark lands?'

'Father M seemed to think that was a very bad idea.' Clunk gestured at his metal body. 'I will not be welcome, and it seems to me you would have already known this.'

'Yes, but you can wear a cape, and gloves, and ...' Millie stopped. 'Clunk, did I not tell you of the magician who lived in the woods near my village? He spoke of working metals, and when night drew close he would come to the square with marvellous tools of iron, and knives of steel, and pans of copper. These he would exchange for food and –'

'Millie,' said Clunk gently. 'I can get all of those and more in Mollister lands. There is no need for me to travel to the Bark kingdom.'

'But you need a forge, and access to metalworking tools. I swear he can help you with these things! Why, my own mother knew him as a girl, for she used to take food and supplies to his workshop. If we can but speak to him, I'm sure he will remember her!'

'Have you never met this man yourself?'

'Alas, no. But my mother told me about him when I was growing up.'

'Then how do you know this metalworker is still there?'

Millie was silent.

'Is there another reason you want me to travel to your village? Something you're not telling me?'

There was a long silence. 'Clunk, when the bandits attacked my parents, I saw them fall. But what if one or both survived? They might have returned to our village, hoping I would make my way there.'

'So why didn't you?'

'I could not travel the land alone. I wouldn't make the border without being captured, or killed ... or worse. And I had no money to hire men to guard me ... men who would probably cut my throat the moment the city was out of sight.'

'So you decided to trick me into accompanying you?'

'I'm sorry I deceived you.' Millie's head dropped. 'You are strong and kind, and I feel safe by your side, and so I used the tale of this metal-working magician for my own ends.'

'Is there any truth to the story?'

'Why yes! My mother showed me metal objects this man had made, objects which were banned in Bark. She spoke of him fondly, and with great warmth.'

Clunk walked in silence, before coming to a decision. 'Millie, everyone deserves to get home safely. Therefore, I will accompany you to your village, metal-worker or not.'

Millie looked up at him, her eyes shining. 'Really?'

'First we must help Father M and Hurm with their quest, since my needs coincide with theirs. After that, we will discuss yours.' Clunk hesitated. 'I have a new plan for travelling by air, which I hope to put into action before too long.'

'Not another balloon?'

'No, not that.' The plan would be far more dangerous than travelling by balloon, thought Clunk, but he didn't say so. 'However, if we go to the Bark kingdom and find your magician ... '

'Wiltred,' said Millie.

'If we meet this Wiltred, I hope he turns out to be as useful as you say. It would be very helpful.'

A hundred yards further on they encountered a willow tree, with branches hanging down into the water. The tree was alive with twittering birds, and Clunk eyed the little brown creatures thoughtfully. 'Do you think Father M could cook those?'

'Oh no!' said Millie, shocked. 'It's terribly bad luck to eat that breed. Our quest to catch a dragonling would surely fail, and our entire party could be thrust into mortal danger.'

Clunk looked doubtful. 'They're not very big, and they don't look particularly fierce.'

'Believe me, they are not for eating. I learned a song about them when I was a very young girl.' Moments later, Millie's voice rang out loud and clear, the sweet tones as beautiful as a dawn chorus.

My dear old pa had a saying you see
A warning to all, so listen to me
Those tiny birds, all brown and cute
You should never, ever, ever shoot.
Since you cannot be an adventurer
No! You cannot be an adventurer
Sing! You cannot an adventurer beeeeeeee
Once you stake a sparrow in the tree.

'But I wasn't going to stake them,' protested Clunk.

'I think killing them in any manner would still count. It's a song, not a legal document.'

Clunk eyed the girl thoughtfully, for sometimes, when she was distracted, she spoke with a wisdom far beyond her years. At these times Millie seemed to be less of a peasant girl who'd spent most of her life tending crops and pulling weeds, and more of a trained professional. But a professional what? That was the question.

There was a splash nearby, and Clunk turned to see a shoal of fish feeding amongst the willow leaves. 'I suppose you have a song about those too.'

'Don't be silly. Everyone eats fish.'

With that, they continued walking around the lake, pausing now and then to search the rocks for any hidden caves.

'I hope the others have found something,' remarked Millie. 'All we've got to show is more firewood.'

Clunk gazed along the shore, trying to estimate how much longer it might be before they met Father M and Hurm, but there was still a lot of mist and it was hard to tell.

'What are we going to do if we can't find shelter?' demanded Millie. 'It's going to be pretty cold near the water.'

'As you said, there's plenty of wood, and I can keep the fire going all night.'

Without warning, a shadow flew across the beach, so large it blotted out the sun and covered several hundred feet of shore.

Clunk had been around spaceships his entire life, so big things moving around in the sky weren't cause for alarm. But in the Old Kingdom, where mass transit meant people walking in a group, an enormous shadow such as this was cause for mild curiosity. So, he glanced up ... and what he saw in the sky had him grabbing Millie by the arm and dragging her towards the nearest cluster of rocks at top speed.

What he'd seen was a gigantic creature flying through the sky, much like a lizard with huge leathery wings. A lizard with a gaping mouth full of twelve-inch teeth, and claws that could have torn a mountain to shreds in two blinks of the eye.

Dragons had come up in various conversations since Clunk arrived in the Old Kingdom, but nobody had told him how mind-bendingly *huge* they were. And never mind huge, he'd scarcely believed they were real. A small part of him had been convinced that dragons were no more than a fairy tale, but that small part was now erased, formatted and ready for a whole lot of new data. He recalled the half-melted city gates at Last Hope, and he realised the people of that fair city had been very lucky, for it was obvious they'd been attacked by a baby dragon. Here, circling the lake, was a fully-grown specimen.

Did they breathe fire? Did they exhale noxious gases? Or did they land and eat all the rocks until they exposed the cowering humans desperately trying to hide? All these thoughts lanced through his electronic brain as he dragged Millie towards cover.

The shadow passed over them again, and Clunk heard the dragon's huge scales singing as they cut through the air. Aside from that, it was completely silent, with no pantomime roaring, no snapping of its huge jaws, and no jets of fiery breath.

They reached the rocks and dived into the small gap between two huge boulders, sitting down and drawing their arms and legs in to make themselves as small as possible. 'Do you think it saw us?' whispered Millie.

Before Clunk could reply, there was a huge thud, shaking the ground. Lumps of rock fell from the cliffs, striking the boulders and showering Clunk and Millie with grit and small fragments. Clunk risked a look, and he saw the dragon had landed on the beach, its huge webbed feet obliterating ten yards of their footprints. The dragon was a mottled grey colour, with patches of moss growing between some of its huge scales, and he realised they might have flown directly over a dozen such beasts in their balloon, for it blended in perfectly with the terrain. His circuits ran with ice then, because he imagined what such creatures might have done to their fragile balloon.

As he watched, the dragon lowered its massive snout to sniff at the sand. Then it raised its head, looking directly at their hiding place.

The Mollister High Council was in session, and every single member of the Council was seated at the Long Table. Queen Therstie sat at the head, as was her right, and Lord Varnish had the second-most important seat at the far end, where he was surrounded by scrolls containing reports on the kingdom.

In between there were forty empty chairs, twenty on each side of the table, for Therstie was not one for bureaucracy. Extra council members cost money, and some of them might even try to make suggestions, neither of which appealed to the queen.

'The High Council is in session,' said Therstie. 'Can we have the minutes of the previous meeting?'

'Eh?' called Lord Varnish, for the Long Table was very long indeed, and he was so far away her voice hadn't carried.

'Minutes!' shouted Therstie.

Lord Varnish took up a scroll and began to mumble his way through the contents. 'Guards struck down ... incurable disease ... with an unwilling goat ... woodcutter's daughter with huge ... lack of messenger squirrels.'

'What?' called Therstie.

Varnish passed the scroll to a servant, who started the lengthy trek along the table to the queen's position. Meanwhile, the spymaster took up another scroll and peered at it, shaking his head.

'What?' shouted Therstie.

'No money!' shouted Varnish. 'We're broke!'

'Why don't you tell everyone?' muttered the queen. She eyed the Long Table with disfavour, for although it had been used for generations, she felt a small round table in a nice cosy room would be far more suitable for discussing private matters of state. With their current setup, spies from the other kingdoms didn't even have to infiltrate the palace to pick up

149

juicy bits of news. No, they could stand two hundred yards away, outside the palace walls, and still hear the queen and Varnish yelling state secrets at each other.

The servant finally arrived with the scroll, and Therstie's eyes widened as she read a disturbing tale of woe, danger and illicit love. It was engrossing stuff, unlike just about any of Varnish's reports, ever, and she checked the title to see which of her settlements it referred to. That's when she realised he'd sent a draft of a short story up the table, instead of the report.

She waved the scroll and nodded, and Varnish made a note in the minutes. For all Therstie knew, she'd just ordered the burning of some village or other, or perhaps everyone in the land would now be forced to wear green on Wednesdays, but she wasn't about to go through the whole palaver of sending the story back and waiting for the real report. 'You. Tell him to sit here beside me. And hurry!' she told the servant, and she waited impatiently while the message was relayed to the far end of the table.

The servant gamely jogged back to the spymaster, moving quickly despite his advanced age. Varnish frowned as he received her order, and he was still frowning as he gathered his scrolls. Finally, with much huffing and puffing, he took a seat near the queen. 'This is most irregular,' he began. 'Protocol dictates that I sit at the far end of the table.'

'Stow it. I'm fed up with running meetings like this. In fact, you can get the royal carpenters in, because I want the Long Table shortened for the next session.'

Varnish glanced along the impressive table. 'It would be a shame to destroy such a valued piece of furniture.'

'It's not valued by me. Chop it down to size and burn the rest.'

'How long would you like it?'

This was a question the queen often asked herself, but in this case the answer was simple. 'I want to fit two people at once.'

'As you wish, Your Majesty.'

'Now, what else do you have to report?'

'My spies tell me King Larch has gone missing.'

'Really?' Therstie eyed him keenly. 'Any news of the succession?'

'There is none. I suspect there'll be disarray for years while all the minor nobles stake their claim to the throne.'

'Interesting.'

'As their neighbour and ally, might we offer to send a small force to help keep the peace?'

'No.'

'Your Majesty, it would be our chance to drive a thin wedge into their capital.'

'I don't want a thin wedge, I want a huge mallet.' Therstie smiled, and it was not a pleasant sight. 'Call in the troops, for I intend to send our entire army. We are going to take over the whole of the Bark kingdom.'

Varnish stared at her. 'Annex the Barks while they're weak? That is a bold plan indeed, and a mighty expensive one.'

'Raise taxes. Everyone will pay up when they're promised rich new lands.'

'But–'

'Right, you want to vote on it?' Therstie raised her hand. 'I vote yes. Anyone against?' She looked along the huge, empty table. 'Didn't think so. Now put the plan into action.'

'Your Majesty, what of Tyniwon? If you don't get your half-brother back first, they'll use him as a hostage.'

Therstie frowned. 'You raise a good point, for my dear

brother means everything to me. Have you no word on his whereabouts?'

Varnish hunted through the scrolls littering the table, even checking the tiny messages which still sported traces of squirrel droppings. 'No, Your Majesty.'

'Hmm. Raise the army, but put the invasion on hold until Tyniwon is safe. They must not have an excuse to harm a single hair on his head.'

'Yes, Your Majesty. Now, if we might turn to other business?' Varnish unrolled an official-looking document. 'There are rumours the elves are mobilising. It's only a matter of time before the dwarves respond, and I'm afraid we're looking at another ... situation.'

'They're going to war with each other?'

'Perhaps.' Varnish unrolled a map and pointed out their respective countries. 'As you know, their lands are situated on either side of the Bark Kingdom, and to get at each other they must first enter that country.'

Therstie's eyes widened. 'They've heard about King Larch too! They intend to take the Bark lands for themselves! Varnish, the invasion plan is back on. Ready my armies. Forge mighty weapons and armour. Recall my knights, and have them lead our brave men to victory.'

'But what about your brother?'

'Forget Tyniwon. After all, he's only my half brother, and it's his own stupid fault if they're holding him prisoner. What did he want to go to Bark lands for anyway?' Then she remembered something. 'Wait, we have a Bark prince staying in our household at this very minute.' More like staying in her bedchamber, but Therstie didn't need Varnish to know that.

'You refer to Feine Greyne?'

'Yes. Lock him up in our deepest dungeon, and we'll swap him for Tyniwon once this is all over.'

Lord Varnish hesitated. 'Actually, Your Majesty, he's already in our deepest dungeon.'

'That was fast, even for you.'

'I grew suspicious of the man, for he used the wrong cutlery at the dinner table, and no prince would commit such a social faux pas. Therefore, I had him spirited away in the night for a spot of questioning.'

'Oh, so that's where he went. I thought he'd gone for a piff and forgotten the way back.'

'Under torture, Grayne admitted to being nothing more than a common messenger, putting on airs and graces to impress you.'

'I'm shocked.' Therstie shrugged. 'Oh well, it happens. But don't put him to death just yet, Varnish. I may have use for him.'

'Your Majesty, he's an imposter. He claimed royal blood!'

'He's a good messenger though, and boy, can he lick a stamp.'

'We must make an example of him.'

'Nonsense. My word on this matter is final.' Therstie got up. 'Meeting over. Finish your minutes, add some heroic flourishes and get the orders written. We go to war this very week!'

18

Father M gazed upon the wide passage at the rear of his cave in horror, for a dozen green creatures were standing just inside gazing straight back at him.

'What the 'ell are they?' demanded one of the creatures, a portly green specimen around five feet tall. It had pointy ears, a pointy snout and pointed teeth, and it was clutching a wooden club in its pointed claws.

'Beats me, Pointy,' said another of the creatures, studying Father M with a look of open surprise. 'I ain't seen nuffink like this before, so 'elp me.' He thought for a moment. 'Could it be a yewman?'

'Dunno Snick, but it sure looks tasty.'

'Get a move orn, you two,' called another of the creatures. 'I ain't had my supper yet, and I'm famished!'

''old up, sunshine,' said Pointy. 'We got some intruders nosing around our gaff.'

'Well get yer skates on and kill the beggers.'

By now, Father M had recovered from his initial shock, and with a feeling of dismay he recognised the species. 'Oh no!' he exclaimed. 'Gorblins!'

Hurm leapt off his previous foes, who were still lying on the dirt floor, and he readied his sword to kill the new ones. Father

M stood shoulder to shoulder with his valued companion, ready to sell his life dearly. Then he thought better of it, and stood directly *behind* his valued companion instead. After all, big strong barbarians were ten a penny, whereas his own life held immeasurable value.

There was a groan as Stonesmasher sat up, rubbing his head, but when he saw the gorblins he grabbed his axe and staggered to his feet, taking his place with the humans. That left Slim as the last to recover, but after collecting his bow and taking a heroic stance beside his new allies, he proclaimed himself ready. Then he realised he'd run out of arrows.

'Now, now,' said Pointy, placatingly. 'There's nah need for a dust up. Just turn around and walk away, and nobody gets hurt.'

'You are the ones who will be hurt, evil creatures,' snapped Stonesmasher, for dwarves hated gorblins as much as they hated everyone else who wasn't dwarvish ... which was quite a lot. 'Flee to your stinking sewers, or I will end the lot of you.'

Pointy grinned, exposing his sharpened teeth. 'You don't count too good, rugface. There's four of you and ... ' here, he turned and counted his companions, doing it twice because someone moved the first time. 'At least ten of us,' he finished somewhat less confidently.

'Looks more like twelve to me,' said Father M, who was a bit of a stickler for accuracy, truth be told.

Pointy counted again, the task made difficult because there was a small gorblin at the back who was jumping on the spot to try and see what all the fuss was about. 'You behind Mike and Fred. Stand *still* laddie!'

The small gorblin stopped jumping, and their leader finally got an accurate headcount. 'I make it eleven and change,' said

Pointy triumphantly. 'In a fair fight, you'd have no chance, and let me tell you something sunshine ... we ain't fair fighters.'

'Correct, since you're lousy fighters,' quipped Slim, and he stuck his elvish hand up for a high five.

The others left him hanging.

'Last warning,' said Pointy, hefting his club. 'I'm going to count to three, and when we open our eyes you'd better be gone. Right lads? Eyes shut!' All the gorblins closed their eyes, and when they were ready, Pointy held up a finger. 'One!'

Hurm and Stonesmasher set to work with their mighty weapons, and sixty seconds later the entire gorblin patrol was lying around in various stages of decapitation, their eyes now permanently closed. Only the smallest, youngest gorblin remained standing, for the two burly fighters had been saving him until last, like a sweet dessert after a hearty meal.

Splodge had been brought up on tales of victorious gorblin battles, but this clearly wasn't one of them, and so he dropped to his knees and put his hands up. 'I surrender!' he said quickly. 'I ain't gonna fight you, on me mother's life.'

Stonesmasher drew back his axe, but Hurm grabbed the dwarf's shaft, preventing him from dealing the finishing blow. 'Not kill,' said Hurm, for even barbarians have a code of honour.

Stonesmasher struggled to free his axe, because dwarves didn't, but in the end he shrugged and lowered his mighty weapon. If nothing else, they could force the prisoner to dig a big hole and bury all the bodies.

'You gents are too kind,' said the gorblin. 'I'm Splodge, by the way. Pleasure to meet you.'

'Hurm.'

Stonesmasher merely grunted, for to his kind the gorblins ranked only slightly higher than those evil, blighted people who came banging on his front door and tried to sell him things.

Meanwhile, Slim had gone to investigate the gorblin tunnel, placing his feet so as not to get any green blood on his fancy footwear. It was pitch dark inside, but his curiosity got the better of him and he took one step too many.

'Argh!' went the elf, as he pitched head-first into a deep, dark hole.

Father M hurried over to look, but the hole was deep indeed, and he couldn't see the bottom. In fact, it was so deep he couldn't even see any of the careless elf's body parts. 'Hurm, pass me a torch!'

Hurm passed him a torch all right. It was about four feet long and six inches thick, and it blazed with heat and flames. Father M staggered to the hole and heaved it in with both hands, then put his head to one side, listening for the sound of its landing.

'Ow! What the fugging hell?' shouted Slim, his voice echoing up the shaft.

'This is bad news indeed,' said Father M, and he didn't just mean Slim's new injuries. 'I judge the bottom of the hole to be at least seven levels down.'

'Eight,' said Splodge, who was now standing beside him, peering into the hole as well.

'What would you know?' snapped Father M. 'We've already established your kind can't count.'

'I know it's level eight,' said Splodge doggedly ... or rather, gorblinly. 'I know, 'cause I live down there.'

Father M pursed his lips and considered the situation. The elf had taken their side in the fight, for sure, but on the other hand it would be a right royal pain to rescue him. They'd have to fight their way through seven, or maybe even eight, levels of gorblin tunnels, and there was no guarantee of success. He wondered whether it would be better to mark their new comrade as missing in action, before moving on without him. After all, a party of three was much more manageable than four, and they had a prisoner to worry about.

'Hurm rescue!' shouted the fighter, and he grabbed another burning brand from the fire and charged into the gorblin cave system, leaving long streamers of flame behind him.

Father M considered the merits of a two member party, but then Stonesmasher grabbed a burning branch and ran after Hurm, leaping right over the deep pit in the middle of the tunnel before vanishing into the distance like a dwarf running down a tunnel with a torch.

Now Father M was alone with the prisoner, and he was most emphatically opposed to the idea of a party with just one member. After all, who was going to do all the heroic dying while he fled from danger? So, he took up a handful of burning sticks and prodded the diminutive gorblin with his staff, forcing Splodge along the passageway ahead of him. 'Try any tricks and I'll do for you,' snapped the wizard.

'I only know one trick, and I ain't very good at it,' said Splodge sadly. 'I keep losing all me money.'

'Silence, gorblin!'

They reached a crossroads, where Hurm and Stonesmasher were arguing over which route to take. 'You want to go right,' said Splodge, without hesitation. Then he looked at Father M fearfully, lest the wizard punish him for opening his mouth. But Father M was not a cruel man, and he said nothing. He *was* a cunning and vain man though, and he wondered whether he could get the gorblin to whisper directions in his ear, so that he might impress the others with his path-finding skill. There were only two problems with this. First, if they ran into a gorblin patrol the others would immediately blame Father M for leading them into trouble. And second, their gorblin captive was so short, and the wizard so tall, that he'd have to perch Splodge on his shoulders to hear his whispers, and he didn't think the little gorblin had bathed for months. If ever.

So, instead of relaying whispers, he contented himself with repeating the gorblin's directions seconds after he heard them.

'Next right,' said Splodge, as they went deeper and deeper under the mountain.

'Take a right here, lads,' called Father M, as they reached an L in the passage.

They continued until they came to a rough set of steps cut into the rock. Here, Father M called a halt. 'So far we haven't met any gorblin patrols,' he said, and Hurm nodded at this sage observation. 'The lower levels may be infested though, and we should douse our torches lest we give away our presence.'

Hurm nodded again, even though he had no idea what all the long words meant. Stonesmasher, though, disagreed. 'We already lost Slim down one hole. How will we avoid others in darkness?'

Father M clapped the gorblin on the shoulder, then surreptitiously wiped his hand on his cloak. 'Splodge here will guide us.'

'Splodge here is a *member* of said patrols,' said Stonesmasher. 'The only place he's going to guide us is somewhere we don't want to go. I ought to chop his head off right now ... with my axe!'

'I promised to help, squire,' protested Splodge, for the axe was mighty and the neck was weak. 'You ain't seen any patrols because there's just the one, and you wiped that out. It were more of a hunting party, anyway.'

Father M studied the gorblin, trying to work out whether he was telling the truth. Then he shrugged. 'Very well, the torches stay alight. Now let us proceed, for one of our number lies injured and we must rescue him.'

'He's only injured because you dropped half a tree on him,' muttered Stonesmasher.

'What was that?' demanded Father M.

'Nothing.'

They took the steps, going down three flights before ending up in a store room with dusty shelves. There were a few evil-smelling haunches of some animal or other, too far gone to identify, and several jugs of what looked like fermented blood.

'What do you call this foul brew?' demanded Stonesmasher, after taking a generous swig from the nearest vessel.

'Floor cleaner,' said Splodge.

Stonesmasher smacked his lips, then shrugged and took another swig. He was used to weird-tasting liquor, because dwarves usually drank everything in sight before it had finished fermenting, and this stuff was better than anything he'd been served before. Had he been more of a businessdwarf, he'd have set up an export business with the gorblins and made a tidy fortune, but sadly the closest he got to commerce was the business end of his axe.

They passed through the store room and took another passage, and when they reached the far end they encountered even more steps. So far, Father M had been singularly unimpressed with the gorblin lair, because if he was in charge he'd have packed tenants into every nook and cranny, before charging them every penny they owned for rent. 'Where is everyone?' he demanded.

Splodge looked up at him. 'What d'you mean?'

'Where are the rest of your kind?'

'You ain't gonna see anyone up here, squire. Level eight is the roof of the world, far as we're concerned, and most gorblins won't get any closer to the surface than level twenty.'

'But you live on level eight. You said so!'

'I ain't exactly royalty, know what I mean? All us outcasts live on level eight.' He sniffed. 'If you can call it living.'

'So why don't you move to a lower level?'

Splodge pulled up the sleeve of his rough shirt, revealing a dark X tattooed into his green skin. 'Reject, see? Any gorblin with that mark goes below level eight, an' they're going in the pot.'

'You *eat* each other?'

'Sure. Easier'n hunting, innit?'

On this bombshell the party continued downstairs, and in time they reached the eighth level. Splodge led them to a side room, where they found Slim lying on his side next to the huge branch, now burnt out. 'About fudding time you got here,' he snarled. 'Which monumental idiot decided to throw this tree trunk at me?'

'It was Hurm,' said Father M.

The elf looked up at the huge fighter, with his corded muscles, thick legs and gigantic cleaving sword. 'Well don't do it again,' he said lamely, and then he allowed the others to help him up.

'Where does it hurt?' asked Stonesmasher.

'Everywhere.'

'Did you break anything?'

'Only my fall,' said the elf drily, and this time Stonesmasher gave him a high five. Mollified, the elf turned to Father M. 'You know there's an evil little gorblin standing behind you, right?'

161

'Indeed, for he is our guide. We'd never have reached you without his aid.'

'Without his kind, and their intrusion, I wouldn't have fallen down the hole in the first place,' remarked Slim.

'I thought elves could see in the dark?'

'Sure, but have you ever walked from the sunny outdoors directly into a darkened room?'

'Indeed, but I've never been daft enough to walk directly into a big hole in the floor.'

'Gents, could you leave the squabbles until later?' Splodge asked them. 'This is a living area, and someone might hear you.'

'You're right, of course. Come, everyone, let us depart this foul place!'

'It's not that bad,' murmured Splodge. Then he looked around. 'Actually, you're right. It's a spit-hole.'

So saying, they returned to the stairs and began the long climb to the surface, with Splodge leading the way.

— 19 —

Pentonville and Islington were feeling extremely nervous as they went to see their sergeant. Last time they'd encountered Showt, he'd given them a severe talking to, making their ears ring before they'd managed to tell him about their important mission. After that, he'd relented and handed over a clutch of valuable weapons for their use.

Now, having sold those weapons for a tidy profit, the two of them were forced to ask the sergeant for more.

'You can do the talking,' muttered Islington, as they entered the barracks. 'He likes you better.'

'Don't give me that spit. You know the sergeant doesn't have favourites. He hates everyone equally.'

'Maybe we could pay someone else to ask him?'

'And maybe the captain will change his mind, and we don't have to go looking for this metal man after all.'

Their footsteps slowed as they reached the sergeant's cubbyhole, where they found Showt polishing his spare pair of boots. He was rubbing so hard he was sweating, and the torchlight gleamed off his shiny forehead. 'Ah, I was wondering when I'd see you two,' he said calmly. 'Brought me weapons back, 'ave you?'

Islington swallowed. 'Not quite, sarge. See, we got in a bit

163

of a fight, and it didn't go so well.'

The sergeant looked him over, from head to toe. 'Don't look like you got any injuries.'

'We managed to escape, but the weapons ... well, we don't have anything left.'

'I see.' The sergeant spat on his boot, and rubbed it vigorously with a cloth. 'Well, no 'arm done. Those weapons was useless to me anyhow. Load o' fancy junk.'

Islington breathed a sigh of relief, but he didn't relax. They'd only got past the first hurdle. 'So, er, the captain. He's sending us on another mission.'

Showt stopped polishing, the cloth poised above his boot. Then, without a word, he continued. Now the strokes were slower, more deliberate, and as the two men waited nervously for his response they couldn't help noticing the sergeant's face was getting redder and redder.

'So you want more o' me weapons, do you?' he said at last.

'Y-yes sir.'

'Well, you're going to have to earn them.' The sergeant looked up from his polishing. 'Lefty McGraw owes me fifteen shilling' and ninepence from last week's game, and he's been duckin' me ever since. I've heard he's drinking at the Severed Goat tavern this fine day, so if you two lads nip over there and get me cash, I'll sort you out with some weapons. Deal?'

'Deal,' said Islington quickly. He'd never heard of Lefty McGraw, nor the Severed Goat, but anything was better than another roasting from the sergeant.

'See you shortly, then,' said the sergeant, and he went back to polishing his boots.

Outside, Pentonville grabbed Islington's sleeve. 'What did you agree for? You know this is a suicide mission, don't you?'

'This Lefty character can't be that bad.'

'He's worse, and so are the twenty members of his gang. And why did it have to be the Severed Goat! Do you know what they *serve* there?'

'Goat?'

'Not likely. One of my mates ordered a pork roast there once, and he found a prison tattoo on the crackling. He wouldn't have complained, but he once knew the prisoner.'

'Well, we've agreed to get his money now. We can't back out.'

Pentonville thought for a moment. 'You know, we could just ...desert.'

'Run away, you mean? Never come back?'

'Sure. The men of the city guard have a proud tradition of laying down arms and deserting at the drop of a hat. We could chuck all this and start again somewhere else.'

'Forget it. I've already got enough trouble on my plate, and I don't need to spend the rest of my life looking over my shoulder. Anyway, we've only got a handful of shillings between us.'

Pentonville's face cleared. 'That's it! We don't have to stick our necks out confronting Lefty and his people. We can use our own money to pay Showt! You know, the money we got from the arms dealer!'

'You're right! That was fifteen shillings ...'

'And ninepence,' finished Pentonville. Realisation dawned, and the two of them cursed the sergeant under their breath. Somehow, via his contacts, Showt had found out exactly how much they'd sold the weapons for, right down to the last penny.

'I suppose we were lucky, in a way,' said Islington. 'He could have asked for double.'

Half an hour later they were fifteen shillings and ninepence lighter, and the sergeant graciously let them have a rusty old sword each to protect themselves with. The swords had been sharpened so many times over the years that the blades were barely a foot long, and they kept falling out of their scabbards. The sergeant laughed to himself as they clutched their useless weapons, but there was nothing they could do about it.

But the sergeant wasn't done yet, for he'd had another nasty shock for them. They would not be travelling alone, for a minor knight was to accompany them on their quest. The man was the fifth son of some unimportant noble or other, and he'd earned a knighthood by reading the queen a particularly moving poem. In the royal chambers. After midnight.

Now, while Islington and Pentonville rode their sway-backed nags towards the city gates, Sur Rhyff accompanied them on a white charger, the harness made from polished leather with silver detailing, his gleaming black boots supported by a pair of ornate stirrups.

'I wish we could go without Sur Rhyff,' muttered Islington, but he wasn't the type to disobey a direct order, so he put a bold face on the situation.

'It could have been worse,' whispered Pentonville. 'It might have been Sur Leigh.'

Islington winced, for the crotchety old knight was a fabled grouch.

'Where to?' asked Pentonville, as they rode out of the city. 'Bark lands, or Last Hope?'

'Last Hope,' said Islington firmly. 'No metal man would travel to Bark lands.'

'No sane man would willingly travel to Last Hope,' sniffed Sur Rhyff.

You took me there, for I was a fool,

166

to this horrible cesspit, known by all.
An uncultured wasteland, the likes of which
I owe you for, you son-of-a ...

'Hey, wait for me!'

Pentonville and Islington were already crossing the river, and upon reaching the far side they set off through the woods without waiting for the wordy knight. 'You know,' said Islington. 'A group of bandits has been attacking travellers in the woods. If we encounter them, we should ask whether they've seen the metal man.'

'Are you crazy?' Pentonville brandished his blunt little sword. 'There are but two of us, and we're armed with nothing but rusty bread knives.'

'They don't know we're alone. We might be part of a larger force.'

They both looked round at Sur Rhyff.

'We might be well-armed and rich also ... but we're not,' said Pentonville. However, with no other leads he was forced to agree to Islington's plan, and they rode on, waiting for a hail of bandit arrows to cut them down.

'Ah-choo!'

It was thirty minutes later, and the explosive sneeze came from just ahead, startling them. They reined in their horses, and the two guards dismounted, leaving Sur Rhyff to mind their mounts. Of course, he couldn't let the opportunity pass, and they were regaled with one of his finer efforts.

I await thy return with bated breath,
And I trust thee go not to thy deaths.

The two men trod carefully as they made their way through the undergrowth, but they needn't have bothered because the frequent sneezes masked any sounds they were making.

'Ah-choo!'

'Ah-choo! Ow, by dose.'

Islington parted the bushes, and saw three men and a woman sitting around a campfire. They were huddled in blankets, and while two of them had their backs to him, he could see the others had red eyes and runny noses.

'How'b de stew?' asked one of the men.

'Id dill cookin,' said another.

'Ah-choo!'

Islington and Pentonville exchanged a glance. These four looked like bandits, but they were stricken with colds and didn't look strong enough to rob a newborn babe. So, they stepped out of the bushes, hands on hilts. 'City guard. Don't move!'

'Ad if,' said the woman. 'I god so maddy aches and pains I can't ged up.'

The others concurred.

'Arrest us,' said the woman, holding out her arms. 'Lock us up. Just make it subwhere warm.'

'We don't want to arrest you. We just want information.'

The woman shrugged. 'I dobe care any more. Ask away.'

'Have you seen a man of metal in these parts?'

'Seed him? He's the one what chugged us all in the river! Freezing code, it were.'

'Really? Do you know where he was going?'

'Anywhere he wants,' said the woman morosely. 'No power in the land can stop that thig, not the mightiest dragon nor the biggest hill giant.'

'We have information he might have been travelling to Last Hope,' said Islington.

'Or the Bark kingdom,' added Pentonville.

The woman blew her nose lustily. 'Sorry. No idea.'

'Please think. This is an important quest.'

'Think? I can barely breathe!' protested the woman.

'I have sixpence for information,' said Pentonville.

'Oh, in that case they were going to Last Hope.'

'Really?'

All the bandits nodded.

'Definitely.'

'Uh-huh.'

Pentonville eyed them doubtfully, then tossed a coin to the woman. 'Thank you for your help. And when we ride back this way, you'd better be gone or we'll take you in.'

'When you come back this way, we'll be fighting fit again,' muttered the woman.

On that cheery note, Islington and Pentonville returned to their horses, where they found Sur Rhyff crouching behind a bush. 'You can come out now,' said Islington. 'It's safe.'

'I had a stone in my boot, else I would have rushed to your aid.'

They all mounted up, and the party set off for the western road. 'Did you believe those brigands?' asked Islington.

Pentonville shrugged. 'They helped make our choice for us. Anyway, it will be easier to search Last Hope than the entire Bark kingdom.'

Islington concurred, and the three men rode on through the woods.

Runt leaned over the rail at the ship's prow, eager for his first sight of home. Over the last few hours the crew had repaired the battle damage as best they could, and the ship was sailing almost as well as it had done before the attack. Every stitch of sail was rigged and drawing, and Runt could hear the water foaming under the bows as they cut through the waves. The happy burble seemed to be whispering of the Old Kingdom, and the adventures which lay ahead.

There had been one sad note, which was when Berry had overseen the burials. Three dozen crew members had been committed to the deep while he slowly read their names aloud, the remaining crew standing bare-headed in the sun as they remembered their fallen comrades. Each body went into the sea with a splash, and Runt couldn't help wondering if a huge sea serpent would snap them up like a trail of tasty breadcrumbs.

But that was an hour ago now, and thoughts had soon turned to the future.

Their first task after reaching dry land would be to replace the temporary patches in the hull, for several enemy balls had struck near the waterline and it was impossible to plug the holes properly at sea. Next, Runt decided he'd lead a raiding party to the nearest settlement, to secure victuals for the crew. That would put him in good standing, for once they'd had their fill of fresh food and beer, they were sure to cheer on his next plan. This involved sailing right around the Old Kingdom, raiding towns and villages on the way, gathering gold and valuables as their reward.

Some might see this as a betrayal of his fellow countrymen, but Runt put the thought out of his mind. After all, he asked himself, what had his country ever done for him?

Once they'd completed the journey, Runt would be set ashore in a safe harbour, near a town they hadn't raided, attacked and razed to the ground. He'd be fabulously wealthy, set up for life, while his new-found friends would sail back to wherever they'd come from.

He hadn't actually cleared this ambitious plan with Berry yet, nor the rest of the crew, but that was only a minor detail. Runt was practically a hero now, and he was convinced they'd hang off his every word.

'Land ho!' came a shout from the very top of the tallest mast, and Runt turned his gaze to the horizon, even though he knew it would be a while yet before the Old Kingdom was visible from the deck. He heard footsteps, and when he looked round Berry was at his elbow.

'So, my friend,' said the captain. 'There is your land, as expected.' He hesitated. 'Are you certain they have no ships? No navy at all?'

'That rowing boat of mine is the biggest vessel in the land.'

Everyone on board was staring at a point off the port bow, which was just as well, because when Runt looked over the starboard bow he saw the unmistakable shape of a giant sea serpent swimming alongside, maybe forty yards away. It seemed to be shadowing them, and for a split second he wondered whether to raise the alarm. Instead, he held his tongue, because if the ship turned and ran now, he would never get the chance to go home again.

The serpent was twice as long as the ship, and could probably have snapped it in two, had it felt the need. Instead, it swam alongside, keeping it company. Runt tried to keep an eye on it whilst pretending to look the other way, because if it looked like attacking he'd be forced to raise the alarm, whatever the consequences.

Moments later, land came into view off the port bow, and Runt felt a lump in his throat as he gazed upon his home. Soon he would step upon the shore, the first resident of the

Old Kingdom to return from a sea voyage in many a long year. Then he'd set about raiding the place, in order to make off with as much treasure as he could carry in his short little arms.

As he daydreamed about fabulous gems, and rivers of gold and silver, he felt a solid bump on the ship's hull. He glanced to his right, but the sea serpent had vanished.

'Leadsman, take a sounding!' shouted Berry, from the quarterdeck.

Several of the crew were peering over the railings into the water. They were still a long way from shore, and it was clear they were puzzled about the bump, for the sea was deep and there were no obvious obstructions. Runt kept quiet about the serpent, hoping the ship had given it a bump on the head, and driven it off. His plans for getting home would come to naught if the ship turned around and fled.

He watched a sailor coming towards him with a big coil of fine rope slung over his shoulder. The man was holding a weight in one hand, and as he got closer he pulled a yard of rope free and swung the weight underarm until it was a blur. Then, judging the moment, he released the rope, and the weight sailed ahead of the ship to land in the ocean with a splash.

Instantly, the sailor took in the slack, and as the ship sailed over the weight he pinched the rope between two fingers, just as it pointed straight down. 'By the mark, twelve!' he shouted, then hauled the rope in hand-over-hand.

He continued to take measurements as they sailed along the coast, while the captain, the master, and both midshipmen studied the shore through spyglasses.

'What do you think?' asked Berry. 'That cove yonder?'

The sailing master nodded, and Berry called out the new heading. The ship heeled over, and seconds later they were

172

heading directly for solid land. As they got closer, sailors furled most of the sails, until the ship was barely moving. The leadsman called out the depths, and the land grew closer until Runt could make out individual trees and bushes. The cove was circular, with a narrow entrance between towering rocky outcrops, and the ship passed between the cliffs with barely twenty yards on each side. A dozen sailors were at the rails, keeping a wary eye out for rocks beneath the surface, but the channel was deep and they sailed through without incident.

Runt had no idea where they were landing, in relation to the rest of the Old Kingdom. His intention had been to go ashore in the dwarven kingdom, but with the big sea serpent trailing them he felt it better to set down anywhere, as long as it happened quickly.

As they approached the sandy shore, Berry called for the anchor. There was a big splash, and as the last remaining sails were taken in, they came to a slow, gentle halt. The water was as flat as a millpond, and the big ship just sat there, stable and immobile for the first time since Runt came aboard.

'Break out provisions,' shouted Berry. 'Give the crew a meal, for they've deserved it!'

There was a loud cheer from the men lashing sails to the yards, the men lining the rails, and the men tending to the rigging and especially those standing at the wheel. Runt wondered whether they'd be cheering quite so loud if they realised the welcoming cove was part of the Cursed Isle they feared so much.

20

Queen Therstie had just finished breakfast, and after her maid took away the tray, Therstie requested Lord Varnish's presence. He arrived soon after like a vial of poison ... silent, odorless, and fatal to anyone who tasted him. 'Varnish,' she said imperiously. 'I wish to inspect my army.'

'Your Majesty ...'

'You have one hour. Assemble the troops on the eastern field, that I may view them from the tallest tower.'

Varnish hesitated. 'My Queen, if I might –'

'That is all. You are dismissed.'

'But Your Majesty ...'

'Uh-uh,' said Therstie, wagging her finger. 'I gave you an order. No speaking, just leaving.'

Varnish bowed low and departed without further objections, although his expression was troubled.

Therstie breathed a sigh of relief, for she was certain that Varnish would one day refuse to take orders from her, and she had no idea what she'd do next. Call the guard? But they were scared of him too! Call for her champion? No, Sur Loyne was in Branche, doing her bidding. Therstie sighed as she thought of the brave knight, for while he could be annoying in close quarters, he at least had a big sword with which to run Lord Varnish through.

The queen thought of Hurm, whom she'd dubbed Sur Rogate. He had the most impressive weapon of all, but the barbarian was even now engaged in some meaningless quest dreamt up by Lord Varnish, a quest from which he might never return. Why, if she didn't know better, she could almost believe the spymaster's primary function was to keep all these men from her bed! And yet he was the one who insisted she produce an heir to the throne, to ensure succession.

An hour later, dressed in her ceremonial uniform and carrying her ceremonial sword, Queen Therstie left her chambers flanked by two guards. Her metal-shod boots rang on the flagstones, and the armour pinched her in all the wrong places, but she bore the noise and discomfort with grace. After all, her army would soon depart on their campaign, and then she could slip into something more comfortable and call for afternoon tea.

When she reached the eastern tower, the guards paused to form a chair with their arms, and Therstie sat down so they might carry her to the top floor. It wasn't her idea, for she would have walked the steps and more herself. No, the problem was that rousing speeches tended to have little impact if the speaker was panting for breath, their brow running with sweat.

Near the top she was met by Lord Varnish, and for a moment she considered standing on her own two feet. One push from the spymaster, and she and both guards would tumble down the stairs, most likely ending in her death. She'd tumbled with a pair of guards before, but never down ten flights of stone steps.

But before she could dismount, Lord Varnish turned with a

twirl of his black coattails, and led the way up the final flight of stairs.

The top of the tower was windswept and bare, apart from the two guards, Lord Varnish and Therstie herself. As she stepped down onto the stone floor, she noticed tension in the air. She'd felt it before, usually when some member of her family lost a power play, and was about to go to the executioner's block. She glanced around the circular room, just to be sure, but there was no axeman and no block. Anyway, who'd perform an execution ten floors up? They'd have to carry the body all the way down again! Then she noticed the arrow slits in the walls, and swallowed. They wouldn't need to carry anyone, when they could push a headless body straight out the window.

She paused at that thought. What if she ordered the guards to throw Varnish off the tower? But no, he was a portly fellow, and while they were puffing and straining, trying to get him through the slit, he'd be offering them gold to throw her off instead.

These thoughts took but an instant, and were not betrayed by her expression. Stepping forward confidently, the queen addressed Lord Varnish. 'Are my troops assembled?'

After a sidelong glance out of the nearest arrow slit, Varnish nodded. 'But Your Majesty, if I might just have a word? You see, tomorrow would be a much better time to—'

Therstie raised her hand, silencing him. 'Do not tell me I laboured up ten flights of stairs for nothing.'

'No, Your Majesty. Come, come to the window and speak.'

Therstie approached the arrow slit, which was a deep, narrow hole in the stonework. The stones were close-fitting, and smooth where generations of archers had rested their elbows as they took aim at enemy troops ... or tried to shoot down wild birds for their supper. She got within three or four feet, and then Varnish raised his hand. 'That is close enough, Your Highness. Your voice will carry from here.'

Therstie stood on tiptoes, but all she could see was the stone windowsill and a narrow strip of green field maybe four leagues away. 'I can't see the troops, and they cannot see me.'

'They will know your voice, Your Majesty. And look, the shape of the window will amplify your speech.'

Therstie shook her head. 'I must look into the eyes of my men as I order them to war. It is only right. Now step away please, for you leave me no room.' Guards or no guards, she did not want to stand at an open window with Varnish right behind her.

Varnish nodded, and reluctantly withdrew. Once he was out the way, Therstie covered the rest of the distance and looked out of the arrow slit. Stretching out from the base of the tower, all the way to the distant hills, was an impressive expanse of . . . empty fields. Frowning, Therstie craned her neck to look straight down, and she saw a dozen men standing to attention far below her. Only two had armour of any kind, and the three who were armed had swords so old and rusty they looked like rejects from a junk shop. Therstie studied the men for several long seconds, then pulled her head in and gave Varnish a look of pure anger. 'This? *This* is my army?'

'Your Majesty, the rest are coming,' protested Lord Varnish, beads of sweat standing out on his polished pate. 'It takes time to draw men from the fields, and the workshops. There are crops to tend, and animals to feed, and –'

'And enemies to kill, and countries to conquer!' shouted the queen, now thoroughly incensed. She clanged a mailed fist on her steel breastplate. 'You dragged me up here in this sorry excuse for an outfit, without warning me I was about to give a rousing speech to three farmhands and a bunch of dung collectors?'

'In truth, Your Majesty, farmhands and dung collectors form the backbone of our army at the best of times. All the best men are enrolled in the palace guard, to protect you from harm.'

'Lord Chylde has a city guard. Why are they not here at my command?'

'They're busy protecting him, Your Highness. And keeping the peace, and–'

'Enough!' Therstie eyed the miserable bunch lined up below, in particular their armour. 'How goes your enquiry into Sur Roybot, the missing man of metal?'

'Proceeding, Your Majesty. My best people are on the case.'

'Well, if you remember, Sur Roybot promised to modernise our army with new, stronger materials. He is vital to the war effort, and if he's not found soon, you can put these best people of yours into the army instead.'

'Yes, my queen.'

'Tomorrow, at this hour, I will make the long, hard trip to the top of this tower once more, and if the field below is not packed from one side to the other with heavily-armed troops I will ensure that you ... ' here, she hesitated, for she was on the point of threatening Varnish's very existence. However, even consumed by anger as she was, she knew that her demand for a huge army in such a short time was unreasonable, and if she cornered this dangerous man he would fight back. '... I will ensure you receive funds from the treasury to encourage more volunteers,' she finished lamely. 'Now let us end this charade for today, and meet again on the morrow.'

Lord Varnish bowed deeply, then snapped his fingers at the guards. Immediately, they formed a seat for Therstie, and together they began the long, slow trek to the bottom of the tower.

'I don't understand,' protested Sur Pryze, as he was bustled out of the palace. 'Why do *we* have to look for the missing king?'

'Because they've crowned Sur Kah their new king, and I'm not having a Mollister knight sitting on a throne with everyone bowing and scraping to him. Not unless it's me. Now, we can't kill him, but we can do the next best thing, which is to find the real king and have him boot Sur Kah the pretender off his throne.'

'And what about the mission the queen actually sent us on? You know, to find Tyniwon Mollister?'

'We'll enquire about him at the same time.' Sur Loyne thought for a moment. 'We'll tell everyone we're a missing VIP taskforce. We can have fake badges made and everything, in case we need to question nobles.'

'Only if they're wooden badges,' grumbled Sur Pryze. 'Anyway, we can't set up a task force without the king's permission.'

'If you think I'm going to to beg a favour from Sur Kah, you're crazy,' snapped Sur Loyne. 'First, he'd humiliate me, and second, he's hardly going to agree to a taskforce whose sole purpose is to get the old king back. In fact,' he mused, 'I wonder if he had anything to do with King Larch's disappearance?'

'How, when he travelled with us?' protested Sur Pryze.

'Also, he had no idea he was next in line for the throne until he spotted his grandfather's name on those old documents.'

'He could have used a third party to sneak that document into the palace. You know he's fascinated by history, and dates, and dead people. He probably knew the old king's family tree by heart, and he saw a way to heave himself aboard the gravy cart for life.' Sur Loyne thumped his fist into his palm. 'That cunning little spit must have been planning this for months, but he's not smart enough to outwit me. Oh no, I will find out what happened to King Larch, and then there's going to be another royal death. A public execution of the usurper, no less!'

'You're really taking this to heart, aren't you?'

'Of course I am! Knights can't go around slaying kings and taking their places. Why, our entire civilisation would crumble. Peasants would demand an eighty-hour week. Children would be educated, and they'd probably invent a cure for those funny little warts that make your toes fall off. It would be utter chaos!'

'So how are we going to start this unauthorised investigation of yours? Grab people off the street and torture them, or bribe people for information?'

'We're flat broke, so bribing is out. No, what we need is a base. Somewhere close to a ready food supply, so we can steal what we need.'

There was a sound of sawing as they passed a lumber yard, where all manner of logs were stacked in neat piles. A man was cutting a log into planks with long strokes of a broad-bladed saw, pausing now and then to wipe sweat from his brow.

'You there,' called Sur Loyne. 'Worker person! Where can

two knights of the realm find lodgings in these parts?'

The man put his hands on his hips. 'There's a nice inn two streets over.'

'You misunderstood. I don't wish to pay, I'm seeking somewhere to sleep.'

'Oh, well in that case there's a derelict halfway down the street. You can't miss it, it used to have a red door.'

'So what colour is the door now?'

The man thought for a second. 'Not red, I guess. Anyway, it's the only one without a dozen kids inside. Might be some chickens, too, if the kids ain't taken 'em.'

'Thank you, good sir. Enjoy the rest of your day.'

The man looked down at the huge log, the heavy saw, and considered the hours of back-breaking labour ahead of him. 'Sure. Thanks.'

With the sound of sawing receding behind them, the two knights entered Splint Lane and located the house in question. The front door was bare wood, and there were indeed several chickens inside.

'What if the owners come back?' asked Sur Pryze, looking around nervously. He was a big strong knight, sure, but he could still have his throat cut while sleeping, just like anyone else.

'You heard the man. It's a derelict.' Sur Loyne up-ended a ruined table, laying the top against the wall. Then he dug in his belongings until he found a roll of parchment. 'I want a board with all our suspects, and a timeline for the king's disappearance. Go and find me some pins.'

'Metal pins, you mean?'

'Of course.'

'In this city? Where metal is forbidden?'

Sur Loyne cursed. 'All right, get me whatever the locals use.'

After his companion left, Sur Loyne inspected the rest of the house. It didn't take long, and as he strode across the floor, with its layer of chicken manure, he decided he'd send Sur Pryze for a wooden spade next. If this place was going to be their official headquarters, he wasn't going to be strolling around on chicken spit all day.

Sur Pryze returned a few minutes later, carrying a small wooden box with a quantity of wooden thumbtacks. Sur Loyne gave him the new errand, then tore his parchment into neat squares and started pinning them to the erect tabletop.

At least, he tried to. Unfortunately, the tabletop was seasoned teak, and the little wooden pins snapped, blunted and sheered off, as they were completely unsuited to the task. So, in the end he removed his dagger from its sheath and rammed the point into the table, pinning the squares of parchment in a fan. Then he took out a quill, and wrote Victim: King Larch on one of the squares. On the next, he wrote Suspect: Sur Kah, and on two others he wrote Clues and Time-line, leaving the rest blank.

Sur Pryze came back with a shovel, and Sur Loyne decided to take a break outside while his fellow knight cleaned up years of muck. When Sur Pryze was finally done, heaving and panting, he'd exposed an old stone floor, worn with age.

'Right,' said Sur Loyne, reappearing now the hard work was almost done. 'Get a few buckets of water and sluice this clean, and then we'll go and find some firewood and something to roast for dinner.'

'But we don't have any money!'

'I know, but the lumberyard will have offcuts, and you can hunt down a couple of those chickens. Now come on, get the floor clean. This place is supposed to be the headquarters of the VIP task force, not a sheep pen.'

21

Tiera and Thonn accompanied the house vendor down a series of ever-narrowing streets, and on the way they learned the middle-aged woman was called Annie, and she had two grown sons in the city guard. They also discovered Branche had a shady underbelly, with thieves, pickpockets, confidence tricksters, and moneylenders with eye-watering rates of interest.

By the time they reached a nondescript wooden door in a back alley, Tiera had thwarted two pickpockets and a determined mugger, and she was beginning to wonder whether the city was the right choice. Then again, given her line of business, she wouldn't be short of well-paid work.

Annie knocked on the wooden door, thrice then twice, with a pause in between. The door opened a crack, and then they were admitted to a small, gloomy tavern. There was a bar across the rear, and four or five tables with various drinkers at each, all of them in deep shadow. Muted conversations were cut off as the newcomers were studied, evaluated, and finally ignored.

'Over here,' said Annie, leading them to a table where a portly, bald man in a sheepskin waistcoat was flanked by two huge bruisers. As they got there, the previous client was just finishing his business. He was a small, thin man with a very nervous expression, and he was twisting the brim of his hat into a mangled mess.

'I'll have the money day after tomorrow, I swear.'

'I know you will,' rumbled the money lender. 'Otherwise I will have the rest of your fingers.'

The nervous man got up, bowing and knuckling his forehead. Literally knuckling it, for the fingers of his right hand were stumps.

'Got some business for you,' said Annie.

'Annie, my child. How is your family?'

'Very well, thanks.'

'Your boys, they do a good job. No more arresting the wrong people.'

'Thank you. The youngest ... well, his leg is healing, and they both promised to check with your people before raiding any more gambling dens.'

'As it should be.' The bald man glanced at Thonn, then transferred his gaze to Tiera. He looked her up and down, and she saw a hunger in his expression. 'The boy I pay you five shillings. The woman ... two crowns.'

'Oh, they're not for sale, Mr Marnay.'

'Please, Annie. Call me Ashtag.'

'Yes, Mr Ashtag.'

'And if not for sale, why are they here? Do they need a loan?'

'We're here to exchange money,' said Tiera. She knew the rate would be horrendous with a crook like this, but time was pressing and she had no choice. On the way to the establishment she'd managed to separate one gold coin from the rest, and now she placed it in the middle of the table, where it shone like a miniature sun in the candlelight.

The coin vanished into Ashtag's meaty paw, and he bit down

on it, hard, with huge tombstone teeth. 'Is good,' he said. 'I give you half a guinea in local currency.'

'Mr Ashtag,' said Annie. 'I know it's not my place, but this lady is buying my house, and ...'

'You have more gold?' demanded Ashtag, without taking his eyes off Tiera.

'She's paying me four gold coins for ...' began Annie.

Before anyone could move, Ashtag gestured at his thugs, who sprang from their places and came around the sides of the table like two charging bulls. Tiera backpedalled, giving herself room, but the men were fast too. One of them swung a heavy wooden club directly at her head, but she ducked the blow and drew her dagger in one swift move. The steel blade gleamed in the light, and as the thug's momentum carried him past her, she twisted and stabbed him in the side of the neck. He stumbled, clutching at his throat, then fell across a table which collapsed under his weight. The table came crashing to the floor, scattering tankards of ale and playing cards and customers.

'Tiera, look out!' shouted Thonn.

Tiera spun round just as the second thug prepared to take her head off with his club. She mule-kicked him in the midriff, and as he bent double, the air knocked out of his lungs, she stabbed him in the back.

There was a thud as the man went down, then silence.

Annie had her hand to her mouth, and she was staring at the bleeding corpses in wild-eyed shock. Meanwhile, Tiera leant across the moneylender's table, her dagger dripping warm blood. She didn't have to say a word, because Ashtag started counting wooden coin with fumbling fingers, until there were several tidy piles. Tiera said nothing until he added another pile, and then she nodded. After he bagged it all up, she wiped her dagger on his collar and turned to leave.

'I could find work for one such as you,' called Ashtag. 'I have many enemies.'

Tiera hesitated in the doorway. 'I'm not surprised,' she said, then continued outside.

'W-who are you people?' demanded Annie, once they were back in the alley. 'How could you kill those men so easily?'

'I'm a singer,' explained Tiera, sticking to her cover story.

'Well, you must work some pretty rough venues,' remarked the woman, and she fell silent as they made their way back to the main road. Here, Tiera gave Annie the rest of the payment, and after bidding the woman farewell, Tiera and Thonn made for their new house.

When they arrived, the front door was ajar. 'I thought I closed that?' said Tiera, with a frown. Half-drawing her dagger, she eased the door fully open and looked in. There was an even bigger surprise awaiting them inside, for someone had cleaned and scrubbed the floor. 'It's still damp. They must have only just left.'

'Do you think Annie organised a cleaner?' asked Thonn.

'Doubt it.' Tiera crossed the room to a drier patch of floor, where she stopped and stared. There was a trail of wet prints across the floor. 'Knights!' she muttered. 'Worse . . . Mollister knights!'

'How'd you know that?'

'Recognising tracks . . . it's part of my training.'

'Why do you think this is here?' Thonn asked her. He was standing next to the upended table, inspecting a sheaf of parchment squares pinned to the wood with a steel dagger. 'It's got King Larch's name, and–'

Tiera went to look, and she frowned as she saw the notes

with their headings: Suspect, Timeline, Victim and Clues. 'This is the work of Sur Loyne!' she muttered.

'You recognise his writing?'

'No, but it's plain to see. He and the other knights are not here to find me, they're here to investigate King Larch's disappearance.'

'But he's listed Sur Kah as the only suspect, and Sur Kah is the Mollister knight who is now king of the Barks.'

'You do pay attention, don't you?' said Tiera, giving him a look of approval.

'The first man we spoke to in Branche told us about it. But I ask you, why is Sur Kah a suspect?'

'Never mind that. These knights wish to use my new house as a base for their investigation, and I'm not leaving.'

'You think Annie sold it to them as well?'

Tiera shook her head. 'Someone must have pointed the place out as a derelict.'

'So what are we going to do?' Thonn looked worried. 'Sur Loyne tried to kill me in Chatter's Reach. He also saw you locked up in the cells, when you were speaking with Captain Spadell. He's going to recognise both of us!'

'So what? He was present when Queen Therstie knighted me. Would he raise his hand against one of his own?'

'Tiera, Sur Loyne is a base animal. I do not think this will end well.'

'It won't end well for him.' Tiera remembered the way Sur Loyne had manhandled her in the cells at Chatter's Reach, inspecting her teeth as though she were a breeding mare. Her blood boiled as she remembered his swagger, but she couldn't afford to finish him here, in her new house. Instead, she must encourage him to leave. 'When they return, I'll tell them we've just bought the house and moved in. I'm sure he'll go and find somewhere else, especially if I threaten to call the city guard.'

'They would side with him.'

'Take a look around, Thonn. Does it look like they're conducting official business to you? No, Sur Loyne may be running an investigation into the missing king, but he does not have permission, nor the authority.' She saw Thonn's doubtful expression, and continued. 'Trust me. He will not want to make a scene, for it will go worse for him than for us.' Failing that, she thought, there's always my trusty stiletto, new house or not.

The crew had eaten their fill, and Runt was listening in as Berry and the sailing master organised repairs to the ship's hull.

'We'll have to beach 'er,' Tinch informed Berry. 'We'll get the cutter out, and they can take a rope to shore. T'other end will be fixed to the stern, and they can pull us closer as we pay t'anchor out for'ard. Once she's beached, we'll roll her on her beam ends wi' ropes, an' shift the stores if need be.'

'Very good, Mr Tinch. Carry on.' Berry adjusted his hat. 'I will take Runt and Dallow off in the rowing boat. We'll circle the ship first, so I can take in the hull, and then we'll make for shore.'

'Aye aye, sir,' said Tinch, and he paused to salute before hurrying away to order the crew into action.

Meanwhile, Berry sent a seaman to fetch a spare pair of oars for Runt's wooden boat, and another to find Midshipman

Dallow. When the lad appeared, he was sporting a blood-stained bandage across his forehead, and there was another tied around his left calf. 'You've been in the wars, Mr Dallow,' said Berry.

'Just a scratch, sir.' But under the bandage, his face was paler than usual.

'Are you up for a spot of rowing?'

'Aye, sir. I-I'll do my best.'

The first sailor returned with the oars, and a few minutes later Berry, Runt and Dallow were sitting in the boat as it was lowered towards the water, with Dallow using an oar to fend off from the side of the ship.

'Watch my paintwork,' murmured Berry.

Runt saw a ragged hole where an enemy ball had punched clean through the thick hull, and he winced at the damage. Then they were past, and once the boat settled on the calm sea Berry and Dallow released the ropes. After he'd settled again, Dallow shipped the oars, and soon they were pulling clear.

'Around the ship, Mr Dallow,' said Berry. 'Circle her once, then pull for shore.'

As they rowed around the warship, Berry examined her closely. Partly to get an idea of the repairs needed, but mostly, Runt guessed, to inspect his new command. On the way, Runt couldn't help noticing the two men were wearing weapons at the hip. The weapons had stocks and triggers like crossbows, only with a short barrel instead of the bow part. He assumed they were miniature versions of the guns aboard the ship, and he wondered how they worked.

Berry noticed his interest. 'It's a pistol,' he said. 'Only one shot, but it'll go through just about anything.'

'What do you do when you've fired the shot?' asked Runt.

'Use it as a club,' said Berry drily.

Then, with their lap of the ship completed, they set off for shore.

By now Runt was beginning to feel a bit queasy, and he wasn't sure why. He'd been aboard the ship a while now, and he'd got used to the gentle rise and fall of the deck. He'd gained his sea legs pretty quickly, but ironically, he was feeling sick now that the motion had stopped.

'It's the change in motion,' said Berry, smiling at him. 'Lie in the bottom of the boat for a while, and it will surely pass.'

Runt obeyed, and as he was lying there he heard Berry exclaim in surprise. 'There's a river beyond those trees,' he said. 'What luck, if there's fresh water to refill our casks!'

Runt hadn't seen any rivers from the ship, but he assumed the mouth was hidden.

Dallow kept rowing the boat towards the beach, and Runt heard the gentle lapping of water on the shore. Then, as the man kept rowing, the noise faded. 'Where are we going?' he asked Berry.

'We enter the river. It's shallow, but navigable in a boat such as this.' Berry put his hand over the side, scooped up a handful of water and tasted it. 'Pah!' he said, spluttering. 'Salty.'

'It's the sea,' remarked Runt. 'Of course it's salty.'

'It will be fresh further up.'

Runt sat up. His head was spinning, but even he could see they'd left the cove behind, and were rowing up a narrow, slow-moving river. The banks were lined with overhanging trees, and as they rowed along in the shade he began to feel better. When he looked back at the cove, he could see the warship approaching the beach, and even as he lost sight of it he thought it had just shuddered to a halt.

They rounded a bend and kept going, until they took a

second bend and stopped. Berry tasted the water once more, and declared it good, and then he eyed the much wider river of which theirs was an off-shoot. Runt looked around, thinking the place looked familiar, but then one tree-lined river was much like the next.

By now Dallow was panting, with sweat running down his brow and soaking his shirt. He'd removed his fancy hat and uniform coat, and he looked all-in.

'We'll return to the ship presently,' Berry told him. 'First, I want to make sure there's nobody around to surprise us.'

There was a loud braying noise, and Runt stared towards the bank in shock. There, standing on a patch of grass, was a mule. It wasn't just any beast either, it was Happy, the mule which had swam to safety just before Runt had drifted out to sea. Runt stared at it, then broke into a smile. 'Nice to see you, old fellow!'

Berry glanced at him. 'If you tell me the animals talk in this place, I can guarantee ... '

'No, no,' said Runt quickly. 'That's my mule, Happy.'

'So you know this place?'

Runt realised the implications. If this was the river that had carried him out to sea, then the settlement of Breen was nearby, and the city of Chatter's Reach would be further along the coast. He thought they'd set down a lot closer to dwarven territory. 'There's a big city nearby,' said Runt. 'They have armed guards, big stone walls ... '

'Then let us take a look at this city,' said Berry, and the sunlight glittered off the buttons on his uniform as he sat back in the stern. 'It may be that we can negotiate with the local ruler, so that our ships can use this land to launch attacks on Methusia.'

'If you do that, won't Methusia launch attacks on *us*?' Runt pictured the Old Kingdom involved in someone else's war ... two someone elses with big ships and huge guns. 'They will ravage the place!'

'Relax, my friend. The Methusians won't know where our ships are coming from.'

There was no arguing, not with the midshipman turned captain, and so Runt settled back in the boat, lost in thought.

22

In the coastal city of Chatter's Reach, Lord Chylde was unhappy. First, the mechanical man which he'd presented to the queen, and then stolen back, had broken out of its cell and departed for who knew where.

Next, the queen's recent visit had drained his coffers and foodstuffs, including all his best wines.

And finally, after years of peace, there were now rumours of uprisings, and gathering armies, and the possibility of wars between the various kingdoms. The one thing Lord Chylde knew about wars was that they were expensive. They ruined trade, bankrupted great families, and after one considered all the fresh blood which would soak into the weary land ... what exactly did wars achieve?

So, he was not in a fantastic mood when a messenger intruded with news of some fantastic vessel which had appeared out of nowhere.

'It's moored at Shadow Cove,' said the messenger breathlessly. 'Huge it is, with masts as tall as a bell tower.'

Certainly taller than the High Priest's bell tower, thought Chylde, gazing across the city. An act of Nature had torn the top story asunder, killing the High Priest in the process, and even now several dozen workers were dangling from the structure as they tried to repair the damage. And, if they didn't finish quickly, he'd make sure they dangled there for good.

The messenger cast a meaningful look at the wine jug. 'Rode for hours I did, non-stop, just to report the news.'

'Then be sure to water your horse,' said Lord Chylde. 'This ship ... do they come to trade?'

'It has the appearance of a warship,' said the messenger. 'I did not recognise their weapons, but the men are repairing damage, as though it were involved in a battle.'

'Very well. You are dismissed.'

After a lingering glance at the wine, the messenger left, and Chylde ran through his options vis-a-vis the warship. First off, he needed a proper report, for the fool had clearly been exaggerating to gain favour. 'Masts as tall as a bell tower indeed,' he muttered. Most likely it was a small fishing vessel from the Darant kingdom in the far north-west, for their people were ever trying to conquer the seas. A storm had caught the vessel, no doubt, and the tiny thing had been carried all the way to Mollister lands before beaching. Chylde took up a quill and wrote out an order for Spadell, despatching the captain and a couple of armed men to the location. Let them take these fishermen into custody, and capture the 'war ship' while they were at it. Darant natives were wise to the ways of the ocean, and if they shared their knowledge of fishing with the Mollisters, willingly or not ... well, Lord Chylde wouldn't mind the occasional fillet of cod for his tea.

'Fudd me!' breathed Captain Spadell. '*Fudd* me!'

He was lying on a grassy knoll, peeping over the top at the 'tiny fishing boat' Lord Chylde had sent him to capture. Behind him, some way back, were Smith and Dawson, two of his most trusted men. Beyond them were the three horses the group had ridden from the city.

Smith and Dawson exchanged a glance as they heard the shock and awe in their captain's tone. He'd told them to stay put while he investigated, but now they crept up the bank to see what had surprised him so.

'Fudd *me!*' breathed Smith, as he looked over the top.

Dawson said nothing, for words had failed him, and he wasn't much into cursing anyway.

Spadell rubbed his eyes and looked again, but the scene didn't change. If anything, the scene became clearer, which made it a whole lot worse. With an expression of disbelief he unrolled his orders, read the line about capturing a 'tiny fishing boat' once more, then peeped over the top of the knoll at their target. 'Fishing boat, my big hairy bells,' he muttered.

Below them, anchored in the cove, was the biggest ship Spadell had ever seen. To be fair, he'd only encountered rowing boats, so that was hardly a fair comparison. No, this ship was bigger than most of the *buildings* he'd encountered in his life. And instead of holding a couple of fishermen, it appeared to be crewed with a hundred or more well-drilled men, who obeyed orders without question, and worked silently and efficiently as they carried out repairs on the huge vessel. In fact, Spadell was so awestruck by the precision and efficiency, he had half a mind to go and ask whether he could join the crew.

As for capturing the thing ... well, he laughed at that idea. Very quiet laughter it was, and he kept his head low in case he was spotted by lookouts.

195

'Fudd me,' murmured Smith. 'Is that a ship, or a wooden fort with sails?'

Eyeing the vessel once more, Spadell noticed a series of small doors along the side of the hull, two entire rows of them, and he could only imagine what kind of weapons they concealed. Even more worrying, the ship's crew looked to be twice as numerous as the entire city guard of Chatter's Reach, which meant that rather than Lord Chylde getting his hands on the vessel, it was more likely the vessel's crew would soon get their hands on Lord Chylde ... if they had a mind to.

'What are they doin'?' asked Dawson.

'They're repairing the hull,' said Spadell, using up his entire stock of nautical know-how. 'It is likely they were damaged in battle, and must repair their vessel before sailing away.'

Dawson glanced at the ocean. 'Do you think there are more of these ships out there?'

'It would appear so.'

'Well I don't want to meet the ship that beat *this* one,' said Dawson, with feeling.

Silently, Spadell agreed with him. There were always rumours about other lands beyond the wide oceans surrounding the Old Kingdom, but nobody had volunteered to take a rowing boat out for a quick look. Not when they were likely to be eaten by a sea serpent while they were still in sight of land.

Smith altered his position to get a better look at the terrain. 'Cap'n, should we charge them front-on, or split up and get them with a pincer movement?'

Spadell eyed the man with disfavour, for he felt the jest to be in poor taste. However, Smith seemed to be serious. 'Are you insane, man? They outnumber us thirty to one! They have weapons of immeasurable power, they are moored a hundred yards from shore, and will see us coming a mile away.'

'Yes, but *we* have orders.'

Slowly, Spadell took the parchment scrawled with Lord Chylde's risible request, and tore it in two. 'We came to investigate, but by the time we arrived the ship had already left. Is that clear, both of you?'

'I still think we should, you know, challenge them,' said Smith stubbornly.

'Have you been drinking particularly strong coffee?' demanded Spadell. 'That ship is a death-dealing instrument of unlimited power.' He shook the two halves of their orders in Smith's face. 'If you go near it, they'll cut you in two . . . like this!'

Smith was silent.

'Now listen. This ship is not attacking our fair land. It's just using the bay as shelter while it completes its repairs, and when they're done they'll lower those sail things and go away.' He could see Smith wasn't convinced, so he tried an example. 'Think of it as a very large dragon, sunning itself in your back garden. Do you poke it with a stick and try to scare it away, or do you hide until the sun goes down, when it may very well leave of its own accord?'

'I'd probably call my mates for a barbecue,' said Smith. 'However, I get your point. We hide for a while, then we go back and tell Lord Chylde we saw nothing.'

'Good man,' said Spadell, and he settled down to keep watch.

'What are we going to do?' whispered Millie, her eyes wide as she stared at the huge dragon through a gap in the rocks.

'Stay hidden,' replied Clunk. 'Maybe it'll go away.'

The dragon did no such thing. Instead, it came closer, lowering its massive head as it sniffed the rocks loudly. Clunk and Millie sat frozen in their hiding place, neither of them knowing what the huge creature was going to do next.

As the dragon got closer, Clunk could see the overlapping armoured scales around its flared nostrils, and the long, sharp teeth filling its mouth. At that moment he decided the only way to save Millie was to make a run for it, and he hoped the dragon would chase him down the beach while Millie fled to a new, and hopefully safer, hidey-hole.

Unfortunately, Millie was hanging onto his arm with both hands, and he couldn't ask her to let go for fear the dragon's hearing was as impressive as its size. He didn't want to pry her loose, either, in case she objected, or fought back. So, he sat still and bided his time.

The dragon reached out with a three-fingered claw, scraping at the top of the huge rock which concealed them. There was a horrible sound as the dragon's nails grated across the rough surface, and fragments of stone cascaded from above. Then the dragon put its head on one side, sniffing and trying to see into the gap behind the rocks. It seemed to be getting more excited, like a dog who'd followed a rabbit to its burrow, and could now sense it was just inside the hole. It used both claws on the rocks, and despite the massive size of the boulders forming their shelter, they actually began to move. There was a sharp report as a big piece snapped off, and Millie dragged her legs in just as half a ton of broken stone crashed down, covering both her and Clunk in dust and grit.

Things were getting dangerous, but Clunk still couldn't see a way out. He came up with several crazy ideas, but was forced to discard them all. Digging into the cliff face with his bare hands. Hurling rocks at the dragon, trying to hit it in the eye. Shouting and waving his arms. Pointing across the lake and shouting 'Look, more humans!' None of these ideas passed muster, and so he found himself rooted to the spot, trying to get out of a situation from which there was no escape.

A memory floated into his consciousness, that of listening to a human in a flight suit spouting crazy ideas while he, Clunk, acted as the voice of reason. Clunk frowned, for the voice was as familiar as his own, and the face was one he knew he should recognise, but the memory faded again before he could get a proper grasp on it.

Meanwhile, the dragon had tired of the gentle approach, and it reared up before coming down on its forelegs with a hefty thud, shaking the entire cliff face. Clunk heard a rumble of thunder, and, looking up, he saw something that froze him to the core. The entire cliff was falling on them!

Grabbing Millie's hand, he dragged her from under the rock, moving on hands and knees like a wind-up toy with a turbocharger. They scurried into the open, taking cover under another jumble of rocks just as the cliff face smashed down on their previous hiding spot. The noise was immense, with huge slabs of stone tumbling and sliding across the beach, and thick clouds of dust which turned Millie's hair and eyebrows white.

Rocks were still falling when the dragon decided it had had enough. It took off with a flap of its mighty wings and flew away across the lake, the draft blasting away the dust in an instant. As Clunk watched it go, he pinched his nose and blew, clearing fine white powder from his vents in a big puff of dust. Millie brushed herself down, then glanced towards their earlier hiding place, now buried under tons of rubble.

'Thank you, Clunk. I honestly didn't think we'd make it,' she said, her face grim.

'It was the least I could do,' said the robot. 'Now, we must find the others and warn them, for they will be lost if that beast catches them unawares.'

Millie hesitated, about to say something else, but then she nodded and set off beside him.

23

Father M and the rest of his party finally made it back to the surface, where Hurm single-handedly closed the big stone door, blocking off access from the gorblin tunnels. Then, as Hurm began to clear away the gorblin corpses from their earlier battle, Father M realised there was an extra pair of hands at his disposal. Splodge, their undersized guide to the gorblin lair, was trapped on this side of the barrier.

'Why are you wasting all that food?' asked Splodge, as he watched Hurm carting gorblin warriors outside.

'We do not each such foul meats,' said Father M, with a shudder.

'Have you ever tasted gorblin?'

'No, and if you tell me it tastes like chicken I will cast a spell that makes you crow like a rooster whenever you open your mouth.' Father M shooed the gorblin away and turned to more important matters. Now that they'd all stopped trying to kill each other, he felt introductions were in order. 'Slimbough. Stonesmasher. I am Father M, and my companion is Hurm.'

'Well met,' said the elf, and everyone shook hands. Then everyone wiped gorblin blood off their hands, for Hurm was still busy ferrying corpses outside.

'Sorry about the earlier ... misunderstanding,' said

Stonesmasher. 'I have just left the lands of my family, and it was not a happy parting.'

'Do tell,' said Father M.

'There's not much to it. Dwarves love breaking rocks, cutting down trees, and building things, and yet I find myself drawn to nature. Slim here was on a business trip, buying up raw materials, and when he spoke of the elven ways I decided to see for myself.'

Slim looked uncomfortable. 'Well yes, but bear in mind a lot of what you've heard is myth and legend. We've been trying to modernise, and we don't all live in trees nowadays.'

'Still, I want to see the elven lands for myself.' Stonesmasher glanced at Hurm, who had almost finished clearing gorblin bodies, and then he turned to Father M. 'And you two? What brings you to the rocky wastes?'

'We seek a baby dragon. We must capture one, and take it to Queen Therstie Mollister before Hurm can become her champion.'

Stonesmasher and Slim laughed long and hard, and then the dwarf clapped Father M on the shoulder. 'Many a tall tale have I heard, but yours towers above them all. Well done, old man! Very well done indeed.'

Father M decided not to spoil the moment by revealing that his merry jape was actually the truth.

'I have a story too,' said Splodge, from the back of the cave. The others all looked at him.

'What? I don't get to join your party?'

'This is scarcely a party,' said Father M.

'Yeah, yeah. You say that now, but I bet you team up the minute you've left me behind.'

'But you are a gorblin, and this is your home.'

'Well I wish it wasn't.' Splodge hung his head, cutting a

pitiful figure. 'I've always wanted to travel and see the world, but nobody would go with me.'

Father M felt the gorblin would be hacked to pieces the moment they reached a settlement, but if Splodge really wanted to tag along . . . well, it was a free world, wasn't it? 'If you want to, I suppose you could carry a pack or something,' he said at last.

'You won't regret it,' said Splodge, beaming all over his green, snoutish face. 'I have a great sense of smell and you'll never want for fish. Real good at catching them, I am.'

Speaking of food, thought Father M. 'Hurm, when you've done with that, can you go and trap a few juicy rabbits?'

Hurm nodded, then grabbed the last corpse and hauled it outside. There was a thud as he deposited it with the rest, and then he disappeared from view, moving quickly and silently.

'Why didn't you warn him about the dragon?' asked Splodge, once Hurm was out of earshot.

'What dragon?'

'The dragon that eats everything within twenty leagues of this lake. The dragon that forces we gorblins to cower underground in our tunnels, afraid to visit the surface lest we catch his eye. The huge, ravenous dragon that is probably snacking on your friend at this very moment.' Splodge looked around at his audience, who were hanging off every word. 'The only thing scarier than this dragon is . . . '

Everyone leaned in.

'His mate!' finished Splodge. 'She's twice as big.'

Father M glanced at the cave entrance. He knew he should go out and call Hurm back, but. . . dragon.

'It's no use hiding in here,' said Splodge, reading the wizard's mind. 'One puff of breath a hundred yards away, and you'll be reduced to a small pile of ash.'

The ground shook, causing several small stones to fall from the roof. 'Sounds like one of them just landed,' remarked Splodge.

While Father M peered out through the entrance, trying to get a sight of this new and unexpected threat, Slimbough hurried around the cave picking up spent arrows. Once he had a dozen or so, he faced the others. 'Hurm came to our aid when the gorblins attacked. Now it falls on us to save Hurm. Who's with me?'

Father M pretended he hadn't heard, and Stonesmasher busied himself putting more wood on the fire.

'I'd help,' said Splodge, 'but I don't have a weapon.'

Stonesmasher stopped poking the fire and offered his mighty weapon. 'You can have my axe.'

'Thanks, but I couldn't even lift it.'

'Shh!' went Father M, for he'd just spotted the dragon. It was on the far side of the lake, wreathed in mist ... or maybe the smouldering corpses of its victims. Even at this distance he could see the thing was enormous, but luckily it had its back to them.

At that moment Hurm strolled into the cave with half a dozen limp rabbits. He proceeded to skin and gut them, then pierced them with sticks and jammed the makeshift skewers into the ground. The meat began to sizzle immediately, and the sound and smell of roasting meat gave Father M an unpleasant reminder of the fate that was likely to befall him. 'Hurm! Dragon!'

'Where dragon, where?' said the barbarian, drawing his sword with a *riiiissk*.

Give him his due, he's certainly keen, thought Father M. He raised his finger and pointed across the lake, and when Hurm saw the mountainous leathery bulk of the beast, with its hundred-yard wingspan and fifty yard tail studded with foot-long spikes, he silently put his sword away. Hurm's actions forced Father M to revise his opinion of the barbarian, for clearly he wasn't quite as dumb as he looked.

'What's it doing?' asked Slim, peering around Father M.

'Chewing on the cliffs, I think.' Then Father M remembered something. Making their way around the far side of the lake were his travelling companions, Clunk and Millie. Judging from the time of day, their estimated walking pace, and allowing for wind speed, he reckoned they'd probably made it to the exact same rocks that the dragon was clawing at. He debated whether to mention Clunk and Millie to the others, but decided to keep quiet. The more people who ran off to mount a rescue mission, the fewer would remain to protect him from more dragons or another gorblin patrol. 'Splodge, come here a minute.'

'Why?' said the gorblin, who was nowhere near as dumb as Hurm.

'I want you to identify the dragon. Is that the big one or the small one?'

'It doesn't matter. They're all fudding dangerous.' Even so, Splodge came closer, edging his way across the dirt floor with his little green feet before taking a quick look outside. 'Oh, that's the male.'

The dragon appeared to be clawing at the rocks, and Father M could only imagine what it was like for Clunk and Millie if their hideout was slowly being scraped away. 'Slim, can you hit the dragon with one of your arrows?'

'Yes, but I'm not going to.'

'I believe it's trapped our companions. We really ought to distract it.'

'But then it will come over here and trap us instead.' Slim paused. 'Wait. What companions are these?'

'One is a rare creature with a keen mind and an exquisite body. The other is a man made from metal.'

They heard a rumble as the distant cliff face collapsed, and the dragon was momentarily hidden behind a cloud of dust.

'Well, I guess the metal one might still make it,' remarked Slim.

Then, flapping its powerful wings, the dragon rose from the shore and flew across the lake, directly towards the cave.

'It's after us!' hissed Father M, and there was a frantic scramble as they all tried to take cover at once. However, the dragon soared into the sky at the last second, before landing on the beach outside. At first Father M thought it had spotted them, but instead it had seen something far more interesting: a free meal.

They heard a crunch of bones, and when Father M peered cautiously out of the cave, he saw the dragon tucking in to the gorblin bodies Hurm had laboriously piled up outside. Even as he watched, the dragon took a gorblin by the legs, tossed it high in the air, then snapped its jaws shut after the body disappeared into its cavernous mouth. Crunch, crunch, swallow, gone.

Father M winced and turned away, and they were forced to cower in silence as the dragon finished its noisy snack, one morsel at a time. Then, with much flapping of its mighty wings, the huge beast took to the skies and vanished from sight.

24

When Sur Loyne and Sur Pryze returned to their temporary headquarters, bearing an armful of firewood and two plump chickens between them, they were surprised to find the front door shut and bolted. Sur Loyne raised his gloved fist and hammered on the woodwork, making the door shake from the blows. Moments later it opened, and a dark-haired young woman looked out. She wore a simple peasant's dress, and there was a tough, uncompromising look on her lean face. 'Yes?' she demanded. 'What do you want?'

Sur Loyne was taken aback. Peasants usually prostrated themselves before his magnificence, and he wasn't used to having one of them look him directly in the eye. The woman seemed supremely confident, and just for a moment he wondered whether he'd come to the wrong house. Then he saw his tabletop over her shoulder, with the dagger and the torn squares of parchment. 'What are you doing in this house?' he demanded.

'I live here.'

The woman spoke with a thick country accent, but even so Sur Loyne felt a twinge of recognition. Something about those hard, flinty eyes was familiar, and also the shape of her lips and her even white teeth. He'd spoken to this woman before, he knew it, but he simply couldn't place her. 'It's not your house. It's the site of an important operation!'

'To be honest, I think it's a bit late to save them,' said the woman, eying the dead chickens Sur Pryze was holding by the legs.

'Not that kind of operation!' snapped Sur Loyne. 'I meant an important–'

He got no further, because the woman had just closed the door in his face.

'Maybe we could find another place for our headquarters,' suggested Sur Pryze.

Sur Loyne wanted to kick the door in and run the woman through with his sword, but he knew it would bring guards to investigate, and that was the last thing he needed. Instead, he throttled his anger and knocked politely on the door.

It opened once more, and the woman waited for him to speak.

'I'm sorry, ma'am,' said Sur Loyne, mustering all of his charm. 'We were told this house was abandoned, and we've left it too late to find another. What say we use the front room for a day or two?' He gestured with the timber offcuts bundled under his left arm. 'We have firewood, and chickens to roast and share.'

The woman eyed the chickens.

'Come now,' said Sur Loyne. 'We toiled for hours to clean your floors, and you have to agree it was a mess. And think, with two knights such as us in your household, you will be safe from thieves, and murderers, and those annoying people who knock on the door at odd hours of the day, trying to sell you overpriced wares.'

'All right,' said the woman at last. 'You can have the front room, but be warned. The first hint of trouble, I'll call the watch on you both, and then you'll have to explain that metal knife.'

Sur Loyne felt a rush of gratitude, for the hour was getting late and he didn't fancy sleeping rough. 'There will be no trouble, I promise. We will stay out of your way.'

After she let the knights in, Tiera hurried to the rear of the house to find Thonn. He was in the tiny back yard, pressed against the wall with his eyes closed.

'Have they left?' he whispered.

'Not quite.' Tiera hesitated. 'Thonn, I have to speak with you.'

He opened one eye. 'What is it?'

'The knights. I said they could stay.'

'What?' hissed Thonn. 'Have you taken leave of your senses?'

'They're just going to use the front room for a day or two, that's all.'

'But ... I can't hide from them for two days!'

'You won't have to. Sur Loyne didn't recognise me, and he won't recognise you. Not in that cape, at least. Sur Loyne beat a skinny young prisoner in a loincloth, not a peasant living peacefully in Branche. Anyway, you were due to be executed, and he won't know you were freed.'

'But why, Tiera? Why did you let them stay?'

'If I hadn't, they would have broken in after dark and killed us both, I'm sure of it. This was the only choice.'

'Talk about keeping your enemies close,' muttered Thonn.

'They're going to share their roast chicken with us,' said Tiera encouragingly.

But Thonn was thinking along more practical lines. 'What names should we give?'

'I will be ... Tara. You can be–'

'Tom.'

'Then it is settled. I will tell them you're my younger brother, and then we'll stay out of their way. Believe me, Thonn–'

'Tom.'

'Believe me, I want revenge on Sur Loyne as much as you do, but there is no profit in killing them here. They will soon finish this investigation of theirs and then they'll be gone, and you and I can begin to build our lives in this place.'

Thonn nodded.

'Excellent. Then let us offer to prepare those chickens of theirs, for I wish to hear their plans.'

They went indoors, where Sur Pryze was busy lighting a fire in the grate, while Sur Loyne was studying his makeshift incident board. They looked up as Tiera entered, and when she introduced Thonn there was no flicker of recognition. Relieved, she passed the still-warm chickens to Thonn, who took them away to be prepared, while Tiera eyed the notes Sur Loyne was working with. 'This investigation of yours,' she began. 'Is it very secret?'

'Completely. You must not speak a word of it.'

'I won't.'

She turned to leave, but Sur Loyne hadn't finished. Now that he had an audience, he wanted to make full use of it, secrets or not. 'You will learn this anyway, so I will tell you now. We seek your regent, King Larch.'

'Yes, I see his name on your board.'

'You can read?' said Sur Loyne in surprise.

'Just a few words here and there,' said Tiera quickly. She cursed inwardly, for her innocent peasant girl ruse wouldn't hold up if she kept making mistakes like that.

'It must have been devastating when he disappeared. Your beloved king missing, and this foul imposter seated on the Bark throne.'

'Er, yes. Indeed.'

'Well, my friend and I will soon rectify matters. We intend to find King Larch and restore him to his rightful position.'

'That's nice,' said Tiera, and she turned to leave once more.

'Unfortunately, we lack resources and manpower. And I can hardly question members of the Bark city guard, not as a famous Mollister knight.'

'Have you thought about wearing a cape?' suggested Tiera. 'You'd be amazed how that throws the eye off.'

'Disguising yourself as a common peasant is harder than you think,' said Sur Loyne casually. 'People slip up. They make small mistakes. They tell innocent lies which form layers of deceit, until there are gaping big holes in their stories. And then, when they are found out ... ' Sur Loyne plucked his dagger from the table, scattering the notes pinned to the woodwork. Tiera's hand went to her sleeve, ready to fight for her life, but instead of attacking her, the knight put his knife into the sheath on his belt. 'Well, let's just say they regret every little lie,' he finished.

Tiera wasn't sure whether he was speaking generally, or whether he was letting her know he was onto her. She didn't think Sur Loyne was that subtle, but perhaps he'd been watching for her reactions, and she realised she'd gone for the knife concealed in her sleeve without thinking. Maybe, just maybe, Sur Loyne was a lot smarter than he looked.

Sur Loyne picked up the parchment squares and arranged them on the floor. 'As you see, we don't have much to go on.'

'Why is the timeline empty?' asked Tiera. She knew she should leave, but her natural curiosity kicked in. 'Can't you find out where the king was before he disappeared?'

'Perhaps you can help me there. Where were you when you heard about the king?'

I was just arriving in the city, after fleeing the cells in Chatter's Reach, thought Tiera, but she decided not to say it out loud. 'Someone shared the news. I was in the city, near the main square.'

'Did you help with the search effort? I believe a reward was offered, and everyone turned out to look.'

'Yes, but it didn't help,' said Tiera, without specifying which question she was answering.

Sur Loyne looked her up and down. 'What do you say to a special mission?'

'How much are you paying?'

'The reward is knowing that you helped your king.'

Great, thought Tiera. *He's not even my king*! 'What is it you need?'

'There is a tavern where the guards drink. I want you to go there and ask questions.'

'I'm not sure I–'

Sur Loyne ignored her. 'Who saw the king last? Was one of their number spending a lot of money in the days and weeks before the disappearance? Are there any unexplained absences?'

Despite herself, Tiera had to ask. 'You think a guard was bribed to help with the king's disappearance?'

'It's the most likely answer. Every man has his price, and the price for a king is high indeed.'

'So King Larch might still be alive? Then why aren't the local authorities doing more to find him?'

'What else can they do? The city has been turned upside-down, the countryside searched, and all to no effect. Most of them believe the king to be dead, and the rest think he's hiding on purpose. Either way, there's no enthusiasm for an ongoing investigation.'

At that moment Thonn came in carrying two freshly-plucked chickens. Sur Pryze took the fowl and placed them carefully in the grate, close enough to cook them, but not so close that they were burnt to cinders. The flesh began to hiss and spit, and a pleasant smell filled the small room.

'Tom, I was just telling your sister that King Larch may yet live,' said Sur Loyne. 'Isn't that wonderful news?'

Thonn nodded but said nothing, keeping his face averted from the knights.

'Well, these birds will be a while yet,' said Sur Loyne. 'Tara, why don't you carry out your mission now, and you can share in this feast upon your return.'

'As you wish,' said Tiera, and she led Thonn into the back room.

'Mission?' hissed Thonn. 'First you let them in, then you *work* for them?'

'The sooner they finish this investigation of theirs, the sooner they leave.'

'But–'

'Thonn, you and I must live in this city, and if we help to find the king ... well, it would improve our standing no end. Now take them some wooden platters, and listen to everything they say.'

'I don't like it,' muttered Thonn.

'Look, Sur Loyne almost killed you, and you want revenge.

213

I get it, I really do, but you'll just have to believe me when I say he'll get his punishment in the next life, if not this one.'

'Do you really believe that? Is there an afterlife where he might suffer for all eternity?'

I hope not, thought Tiera, as she recalled the hundreds of people she'd been paid to stab, drown and choke during her short but lucrative career as an assassin. Coming face to face with all her victims was the last thing she wanted. But Thonn didn't know about that part of her life, and she wasn't about to tell him. 'Of course there's an afterlife. All the religious texts say so, and who would doubt the holy word of Zephyr?'

'What about you? What will you do while I serve these monsters?'

'I must visit a tavern.' And, after putting up her hood and drawing her cape around herself, she left.

25

After a long journey, during which Sur Rhyff composed poetry out loud without seeming to pause for breath – or, indeed, to seek proper rhyme – Pentonville and Islington finally spied the gates of Last Hope in the distance. As Sur Rhyff launched into his latest effort, the two of them hunched their shoulders and doggedly rode on.

Dear, thine eyes gleam like fresh red wine,
Come, dear, come, lay down with me.
For on this night thy thighs art mine,
And I will part them with my knees.
'I wish he'd shut the fudd up,' muttered Islington. 'If I hear one more thou, thy or thee, I swear I'll piffed-off be.'
Pentonville snorted. 'Thy words tickle my ears like a brush.'
'That doesn't even rhyme, you unlettered oaf,' growled Islington.
Meanwhile, Sur Rhyff appeared to have noticed the city in the distance.

Oh my, oh me! Art those gates I see?
Are the delights of heaven awaiting me?
It wasn't entirely clear whether he was finishing the previous

poem or starting a new one, but by now Islington had had enough. 'Heaven? You've not been to Last Hope before, have you?' he remarked, and he spurred his horse on before the wordy knight could reply with any more sentences tortured to fit the iambic pentameter. Pentonville followed, and after pausing to find a suitable rhyme for 'uncouth barbarians' and 'ill-educated ruffians', Sur Rhyff set off after them.

'I wonder what happened to the gates?' asked Islington. He heard Sur Rhyff riding up and raised a gloved hand, forestalling the inevitable poem. 'I wasn't asking you.'

'They're all melted,' said Pentonville.

'Yes, well if you're just going to state the obvious I *will* ask him.' They rode into the city, and Islington spotted someone nailing wooden boards to a blackened timber frame. 'You there! What happened to this place?'

'Fire, sir. Not three days ago, these adventurers forgot to blow out a candle. Burnt down the tavern it did, and the house next to it too. Also, the house next to that, and the one on the end isn't looking that special either, if you get my drift.'

'I do indeed. Tell me, have you seen a man of metal in these parts?'

'Oh yes. He put the fire out. Regular hero, that one.'

Islington's spirits leapt, for the end of their quest was surely close. 'Where is he?'

The man shrugged. 'Gorn.'

'Gone?'

'Left us, he did. One night he were right there in the house we leant him, the next morning ... poof!'

A metal man with little hair
doth vanish gently int' thin air.

216

Islington closed his eyes. If Sur Rhyff piped up one more time, he'd cut his fudding tongue out and shove it up his–

'My good man,' said Pentonville quickly. 'Which house was the man of metal staying in?'

'Just down there. You can't miss it, since they tore the roof off when they left.'

'They?'

'It weren't just him. There was this girl, Millie her name was. And an old man with a sparkly cape and a tall pointy hat. Oh, and a barbarian with the biggest sword you ever did see.'

'What a curious party,' remarked Pentonville.

'Oh, I don't know that they were having a party.' The man frowned. 'Although, now you mention it, the old guy did look like a children's entertainer, or maybe a circus act, so it could happen they were planning a celebration after all.'

'Thank you for your help, sir.'

'Don't mention it,' said the man, and he went back to nailing up wooden boards.

The three of them rode down the main street until the indicated side-turning, and they immediately spotted the damaged house. There was loose thatching all over the dirt road, and when they dismounted and went inside they found a table covered in dried glue, an evil-smelling barrel, dozens of short lengths of rope and hundreds of silk offcuts. On the table there was a curious machine, the likes of which they'd never seen before, and when Islington pressed the foot pedal they all leapt back, for the thing whirred and chattered most disconcertingly.

'What devilry is this?' whispered Pentonville.

Islington had a mechanical bent, and after inspecting the device he tried it with a small piece of fabric, keeping his

217

fingers clear of the needle. 'Oh, I know what it is!' he said, as the thing left a row of stitches across the silk.

So did Sur Rhyff, and he wasn't going to let the opportunity slip.

Surely sir, thou dost join me in knowing,
for it seems this machine is built for sewing.
'Please help me,' groaned Pentonville.

Islington wasn't listening. He was trying to work out what the odd group had been doing here ... and more importantly, where they'd gone afterwards. He glanced at the grate, which was half buried under the ashes of a burnt-out fire, then at the two empty sacks which must have contained charcoal, and then at the chimney, and the missing roof. He felt the offcuts of silk, and as he ran his fingers over the smooth material he wondered just how much they must have used, if the large quantity that remained was nothing more than waste.

'What are you thinking?' Pentonville asked him.

'They built something large, but what? And why the big fire? It must have been damn near hot enough to burn the whole place down.' But try as he might, he was unable to make the leap from scraps of fabric, rope and charcoal to whatever device these people had made. 'It's a proper mystery.' Out the corner of his eye he saw Sur Rhyff open his mouth, and he quickly raised a finger to silence him. The last thing he needed was yet another distraction.

Still frowning, Islington went outside, where he found a wooden ladder propped against the side of the house. This only served to deepen the mystery, because it seemed the four of them must have climbed onto the roof, which had then vanished ... taking them with it. As he weighed the evidence he came to an inescapable conclusion, and he hurried inside to tell the others. 'You're not going to believe this, but I've got it,' he said. 'They were building a huge harness.'

'To what end?' asked Sur Rhyff, so eager to hear the answer he forgot to spout more poetry.

'In order to ride beneath a dragon.'

Islington expected surprise or disbelief, but instead the pair of them stared at him for a second or two before bursting into wild, uncontrolled laughter. Annoyed, he could only stand there while they doubled over and struggled for breath, tears running down their faces. Finally Sur Rhyff straightened, and he put a hand on Islington's shoulder. 'My friend, I thank you. It is months since I laughed so hard.'

'I wasn't joking,' said Islington sharply. 'They built a device which carried them away, and a dragon is the only creature big enough for such a feat.'

'But how did they attract it?' demanded Pentonville, wiping tears from his eyes. 'It's all very well throwing crazy ideas around, but there has to be some logic to it.'

'There's the reason for all the charcoal. They must have roasted huge joints of meat, trying to attract it with the scent.'

'But ... surely the inhabitants would have noticed a huge dragon?'

'In the middle of the night?'

'And even if it set down on the roof ... how exactly would you fit a harness to such a beast?'

'I said it's what they must have done. I didn't say I knew how they did it.' Suddenly Islington snapped his fingers, for another piece of the puzzle had just fallen into place. 'That man said one of the party was dressed in fancy robes. If he was a wizard, they could have used magic!'

'Magic is banned,' said Pentonville automatically.

'Oh, don't be wet. All the authorities have done is drive it underground, and not very successfully. Why, we passed a magic shop on the way here, openly selling spells and potions!' Warming to his theory, Islington continued. 'Don't you see? The metal man builds the sewing machine and crafts the harness. Another of their number stokes the fire to roast the joints as bait, the magician charms the dragon when it arrives, and the final member of the party fits the harness so they can leave. Then they all climb aboard, and as the dragon takes off it snags the roof, destroying it.'

'It would be a whole lot easier to walk out the city gates,' remarked Pentonville.

'But think! With a dragon they can cross the whole kingdom in hours, instead of days. They can land on the highest mountains, and–'

'Yes, but why?'

Islington thought for a moment. 'The only reason they'd take to the sky ... '

'Yes?'

'Is to reach a place they cannot access on foot.' Islington spun on his heel and marched towards the main road.

'Where are you going?'

'To find a map,' called Islington over his shoulder.

The others caught up, and they made their way to the mayor's office, where a middle-aged man in worn robes was sitting behind a desk on a large, ornate chair. He looked up as they entered, and frowned. 'You're not thinking of adventuring, are you? It's strictly forbidden in these parts.'

'No, we're city guards from Chatter's Reach, and this is Sur Rhyff, a Mollister knight. Together, we are looking for the metal man who recently stayed in your fair city.'

'I know the man you mean. And this city isn't fair, it's falling down.' The man got up and extended his hand. 'I'm the mayor, by the way.'

'A pleasure to meet you, sir.'

A fine old fellow is the Last Hope mayor,
ruling the city from his big wooden chair.

'Ignore him,' said Pentonville, as he noticed the mayor's raised eyebrows. 'He's always doing that, but you sort of get used to it.'

Sur Rhyff noted something on a piece of parchment, then tucked it away.

'So why do you seek this metal man?' asked the mayor.

'We're under orders from Captain Spadell, and he's under orders from Lord Chylde himself. The metal man escaped captivity, and we're here to bring him back.'

'Well, good luck. The last we saw, he was cooped up in a house round the corner, his people buying all manner of goods. Why, there isn't a bolt of fine cloth or a coil of rope left in the city! My wife and her friends came by this morning, complaining they wouldn't get a decent length for months. And then, after buying up all our goods ... these people just disappeared!'

'Yes, we inspected the house.' Islington decided not to reveal his findings, instead returning to one of the mayor's earlier statements. 'You said adventuring is forbidden. Why is that?'

'People are always coming here to mess with the dragons. They go traipsing off to the rocky wastes, stir up some angry beast, and after it's finished devouring them it comes here and burns half the city to the ground. So, I put a stop to it.' The Mayor indicated a map on the wall, which showed the city of Last Hope just inland from the coast, and a red line just

221

beyond which crossed the entire map, cutting off the rocky wastes and the dwarven lands from the rest of the continent. 'We built a wall, see? Nothing comes in, nothing goes out.'

'Except dragons, because they could fly right over it.'

'Yes, except dragons.'

'What's the wall made of?'

'Well it's not a wall, per se, because that would be a monumental waste of taxpayer's money, and sneaky adventurers would just cut holes in it. No, it's more like a network of watchtowers, fifteen of them in all, every one equipped with a pair of archers and a wrangler for the messenger squirrels.'

As Islington studied the map, he realised exactly where Clunk and the others had gone. They'd used their tame dragon to cross into the rocky wastes, avoiding the watchtowers completely. By flying at night, nobody would have seen them. Then he noticed a pin next to one of the towers, and he pointed it out. 'What's that?'

'Oh, that was the strangest thing. Last night, someone tried to knock it over. It was like they fired bags of sand at it using a catapult. Nobody hurt, apart from a few squirrels, but the roof's off and I've had to send a repair crew.'

Islington traced his finger across the hand-drawn map, drawing a straight line from the city to the damaged tower, and then further into the rocky wastes until he encountered a lake. He paused with his finger over the lake, and then he noticed something. 'Are there no rivers?'

'Underground streams.'

Islington tapped his finger on the lake. 'This place. What is it?'

The mayor shuddered. 'That's the drinking hole for two of the biggest dragons you've ever seen. Worse, there's a gorblin nest on the far shore.' The mayor made a wind sign with his left hand. 'Terrible place, terrible.'

Nevertheless, Islington knew in his bones that their quarry had gone there, for where else would they obtain drinking water? 'I need you to authorise passage through the defences for myself and my companions.'

'Impossible.'

'We're not adventurers. We're here on the queen's business.'

'I don't care if Zephyr himself sent you, I'm not losing my city to a pair of angry dragons.'

Sur Rhyff cleared his throat, and Islington braced himself for another poem. However, this time he was spared.

'Sir, as a knight of the crown I am authorised to take over your city in wartime conditions. Therefore, I would ask you to follow my man's orders.'

'Wartime?' protested the mayor. 'But we're not at war!'

Sur Rhyff casually placed a hand on the hilt of his sword. 'Do you want to bet on that, my good man?'

'Fine! So be it!' The mayor grabbed a square of parchment and a quill, and after scribbling furiously he thrust it at Islington. 'You people are cleared through the watchtowers, but when the dragons come to burn the city down, I assure you every penny we spend in repairs will be deducted from the crippling taxes Queen Therstie levies on us every year.'

Islington didn't care who paid, or when, as long as he could finish his mission and go home. 'Thank you, mayor. And I promise you, we will take care not to disturb the dragons.'

The mayor snorted, and the last they saw of him he was studying the map, no doubt wondering where the dragons would attack from when they came.

As they retrieved their horses and rode through the main gates, Sur Rhyff relived his victory over the mayor.

A verbal battle was fought and won
Now let us tackle the other one!
For the gorblins small and the dragons large
Will have our skins if we lack cour . . . age.

26

Tiera heard drunken singing long before she reached the tavern, and she was still fifty feet away when the smell of sweat and stale beer assaulted her nostrils. Still, she had a job to do, so she pressed on.

Inside, there were dozens of men and women seated at long wooden tables, drinking heavily and singing at the top of their voices. Nobody paid Tiera the slightest attention, and so she bought a mug of ale and took a seat in the corner to watch. The patrons were a mix of off-duty guards and field workers, mostly sitting with their own kind. There were a few good-natured insults floating around, but nothing that might start an all-in brawl.

Tiera knew exactly what she was looking for, and it wasn't long before she identified two or three hopefuls amongst the peasants and off-duty guards. The ones who laughed extra loud at other people's jokes, hoping someone would notice them. The guard who was sitting alone, after his two comrades went to join a bigger crowd. The woman who was popular when she got a round of drinks in, but was ignored afterwards.

In other words, the loners and misfits.

Tiera took her ale to the far end of the table, where a guard was sitting alone. He'd drunk his fill already, and was struggling to sit up straight, but in her experience that just made it easier to extract information. Better, the next day he wouldn't even remember the conversation.

'Buy you a drink?' Tiera asked him, raising her voice over the crowd's noisy rendition of a heroic dragon-slaying song.

The guard stared at her owlishly, and she realised he was even more far gone than she thought. So, she sat next to him and leaned closer. 'Shame about King Larch, wasn't it?'

The man nodded, and slowly began to tip off his chair. Tiera caught him just in time, propping him up against the table. 'What's your name?' she shouted.

'Vic.'

'I'm Tina.' She wasn't sure if he even heard her, but at that moment the singers got in a tray of fresh drinks, and as the rousing song ended she could finally hear herself think. 'Were you on duty when the king vanished?'

Vic frowned. 'Don' remember,' he said, slurring his words. 'Think so, maybe. They asked m' a lot of questions about it.'

'I'm sure,' said Tiera.

'They din't ask Ralph though. Him 'n Bent Tommy, they din't ask them anything.'

'Oh? Why not?'

Vic shrugged. 'Ain't seen 'em to ask.'

Tiera felt a quickening of her senses. 'Where are they?'

'They says the two of 'em deserted, but who does that just b'fore payday?'

Vic started to lean over again, and Tiera pushed her arm through his, holding him upright.

'I liked Ralph,' said Vic sadly. 'He said bye just b'fore he went to the kitchens. Thought he meant see you later, not ... goodbye.'

'The kitchens?'

'Yeah. Escorting some noble he was. An in-in-inspection. All hush hush.' Vic looked around furtively. 'I heard it was something about casting *metal*,' he hissed, breathing beer fumes in Tiera's face.

She barely noticed. 'Why didn't you tell anyone about this?'

'Din' want to get him in trouble. Metal is a hanging offence roun' these parts.' Vic drank deeply from Tiera's mug of beer, then studied her closely. 'You're pretty.'

'Yes, yes. But you mentioned the kitchens. Why would a noble tour those?'

Vic shrugged. 'It weren't even the proper ones. Just the old palace kitchens what burned down.'

Tiera got up, leaving Vic with her drink. She had a lead, however odd it seemed, and she decided to leave the tavern and ask around, to see whether she could find out more about these ruined kitchens. She pictured an old, blackened building, perhaps with a cellar, and she wondered if King Larch was being held captive, right here in the city. She certainly hoped so, for that would get Sur Loyne off her case.

Tiera turned for the exit, but had only taken three steps when she was surrounded by drunken guards. 'It's a new face, lads!' shouted one of them.

'Sing for us, miss!'

Tiera tried to push through, but someone had taken her elbow. There would be no escape unless she got her knife out, and that was out of the question. So, with as much good grace as she could muster, she clambered up on the table.

The crowd fell silent, and as Tiera gazed around their upturned, expectant faces she wondered if they had any idea what they'd let themselves in for. Oh well, she thought, at least most of them are blind drunk. And so, after clearing her throat and taking a few deep breaths, she began.

Life in the kitchen is desperate and cruel,
fighting to survive with ladle and spoon.
No chicken for supper, but plenty of gruel,
And don't touch the soup, for it tastes like spittoon.

The crowd eyed her dubiously, for they'd been expecting a rousing sing-song. A few pushed away the half-empty bowls of soup sitting in front of them.

And then the flames came, the kitchen's on fire!
Burning the dishes, the roof and the cook.
Some food tastes better, some is still dire.
But the roasted old cook now, he's done like a chook.

'Sing it!' shouted Tiera.

But the roasted old cook now, he's done like a chook!

Everyone sang the final line with her, and after the song was finished there was a rousing cheer and a thunderous stamping of feet. Tiera took her chance, jumping off the far end of the table and slipping away before anyone could ask for an encore.

Outside, the night air was chill, and once she was clear of the tavern she drew several deep breaths, clearing the smoke and fug from her lungs. She ought to go back to Sur Loyne, to let him know what she'd found out, but the lead was flimsy and she felt like investigating further in case it turned out to be a red herring. But first she had to find out where the old palace kitchens were.

There was a burst of laughter, and a couple of guards emerged from the tavern. They were walking unsteadily, and as Tiera approached them they studied her with their heads on one side. At first she thought they were thinking deeply, but then she realised they couldn't hold their heads up. 'Can I ask you something?' she said.

'Anything for you,' said one of the guards.

'The kitchens ... the ones that burnt down. Where are they?'

'Nowhere, they burned down,' said the second guard, and they both dissolved into fits of laughter.

'Where did they used to be?' asked Tiera, holding her irritation in check.

'Down there.' One of the guards pointed. 'They put up a new building a few days ago. Very secret, it is.'

'Shh!' went the second guard. 'It's ... secret!'

They both spluttered with laughter, and Tiera turned on her heel and left.

'Nice singing!' one of them shouted after her, but she ignored him.

Tiera found the building immediately, for not only was it new, but the houses on either side still showed signs of fire damage. There was a door, and she sidled up and tried the handle. Locked.

Pursing her lips, she looked up and down the street. It was dark, and there was nobody around, so she took out her dagger and worked the tip inside the crude wooden lock. Seconds later there was a loud clunk, and she opened the door and slipped inside the building.

Moonlight shone through windows set high in the walls, illuminating a large area with a big, circular oven in the middle. There was a musty smell, as though it hadn't been used for days, and as she walked across the floor her feet scrunched on the gritty surface.

Near the big oven were three large sacks, each filled with ashes, and Tiera dug her hand in and let the fine dust run through her fingers. Then she left the main area to explore a smaller side room, where she found a workbench, a couple of chairs and a metal bowl filled with a hard, white substance. It looked like bread dough, but had set like stone. There was a small bag, too, half-filled with white powder, and also a small wooden bowl containing grease. She felt the white powder between her fingers, then sniffed it. Plaster.

Frowning, Tiera set the bowl aside and picked up a white, oval shape. It was smooth on the outside, apart from a few bumps, but when she felt the inside it was detailed, like a cast. She took the thing to the window, letting the moonlight play on the inner surface, and as the shadows filled in she almost dropped the thing in shock. The cast was of a human face, the eyes closed, the lips slightly parted. It was an eerie, lifelike rendering, and she could only wonder at its purpose.

Further along the bench were two more face masks, each with different features. Frowning, Tiera wrapped them in a small sack and set it aside to take with her when she left.

There wasn't much more to see. She found a couple of rough sketches lying on the workbench, the parchment of good quality and fairly old. Tiera looked closer, and could tell it had been scraped and reused several times.

Finally, before she left, she walked every inch of the floor, stamping her foot to see if there were any hollow sounds. However, the floor was solid everywhere, and she realised the king could not be hidden in that place.

So, she gathered the face masks, the bag of powder, the jar of grease and the loose pages, and let herself out of the workshop, pulling the door to behind herself.

On the way to her new house, and the waiting knights, she wondered whether the items she'd found would solve the mystery of King Larch's disappearance. She truly hoped so, because she needed to get Sur Loyne off her back before Thonn grew impatient and did something stupid.

The watchtower was an impressive feat of engineering, rising from the landscape as it did on four thick legs, with angled braces all the way up to the platform. There was a roof over the platform, and walls to protect the occupants. A ladder started halfway up, and Islington realised the archers in the tower had pulled the lower half up to prevent anyone taking them by surprise. Near the top, coils of wire and metal spikes prevented anyone climbing the legs.

Next to the watchtower stood a small cottage, with smoke rising lazily from the chimney. There was a vegetable patch nearby, and a knee-high dam blocked a stream to create a pond for fresh water.

It all looked very homely and peaceful, but Islington wasn't fooled. He knew the tower held archers, for the mayor had told him so, and if the party rode any closer without announcing themselves they were likely to get shot. So, he called a halt and dug out the parchment the mayor had given him. 'Hello there!'

Twang!

Islington felt the parchment jump in his hand, and when he looked at it he saw a neat hole right through the middle. Next, he saw a messenger squirrel scampering down one of the big legs supporting the watchtower, its little tail bobbing like fury as it raced for the ground. Even at this distance Islington could see the scroll tied to its back, and he realised the archers in the tower were sending for reinforcements.

'Hey!' he shouted, waving the orders again. 'We have orders from the mayor!'

'Why didn't you say so?' demanded an angry voice.

'You didn't give me a fudding chance!'

An archer popped into view above the watchtower's wooden wall, aiming off to the right, and there was a twang as he loosed his arrow. Seconds later there was a squeak as the message requesting reinforcements was cancelled. Sur Ryhff, moved by the waste of life, chimed in with an epitaph.

See the squirrel with its tail so pretty
They shot it dead, and more's the pity.

Meanwhile, there was a clatter from the watchtower as the ladder was lowered to the ground, and seconds later an archer in forest green tights descended. It was a woman, her bow slung over one shoulder, and as she reached the ground Islington noticed the second archer remained in the tower, covering her.

The woman advanced on Islington, and he dismounted to hand her the parchment. She examined it, then turned to give a thumbs-up to her fellow archer, who lowered his bow. He still held it at the ready, in case of treachery, but at least there was no chance of getting shot by mistake. 'You could have killed me,' said Islington, his heart still pounding from the near miss.

'I could have, but I decided to shoot your piece of paper instead.' The archer looked up from her orders. 'Passing into the rocky wastes, are you?'

'That's the plan.'

She shook her head. 'Wouldn't be in your shoes, not for all the gold in the Old Kingdom.'

This was hardly encouraging, but Islington had his orders

and he meant to carry them out. 'Did you see a dragon last night?'

'No, it was dark.'

'Hear one, maybe?'

She snorted. 'You never hear a dragon, not until it's too late. It's not like you can outrun them.'

Unfortunately, Sur Rhyff heard her.

Lo the mighty dragon, silent and deadly,
'tis certain death if thou movest bipedally.

Islington wasn't really surprised the archers hadn't seen the dragon, because this wasn't the watchtower he'd been looking for. He'd taken a southward path to avoid the biggest hills, for he knew it would prove quicker in the long run, and they must have veered a little too far south. 'Do you get many dragons around here?'

'No, but there are certainly enough to snap up any damn fools heading into their territory.' The woman looked him up and down. She was in her thirties, hard-bitten and capable, and she seemed reluctant to let him pass despite his orders. 'What business do you have in the wastes, anyway?'

'We're looking for a group of fugitives. Lord Chylde himself orders their capture.'

'You know they're probably dragon dung by now, right?'

Islington thought of the metal man, which had apparently survived a plunge from the heavens as well as who knew how long soaking in seawater. 'Not all of them.'

'Well, I can't stop you, but I can tell you you're wasting your time.' She handed the orders back. 'Good luck. I doubt we'll meet again.'

Islington nodded, then went to mount up.

'You might want to leave the horses,' suggested the woman.

'But we have a long journey ahead of us. It will take twice as long to reach our destination on foot.'

'Yes, but at least you'll have a chance of getting there.' The woman turned and walked away, heading for the ladder, while Islington just stood there with the reins in one hand.

'Is the way ahead difficult?' he called after her.

'It is for your horses,' she replied over her shoulder. 'Dragons love their flesh, and if you're riding when a dragon decides to feed . . . it's goodnight one and all.'

Islington looked at the others. Slowly, Pentonville dismounted, but Sur Rhyff was still thinking.

Much loved by the dragon, is thy humble old horse,
And the rider on top makes a great second course.

By now the archer had reached the top of the watchtower, and they heard the ladder squealing as it was withdrawn. The woman leant over the wall and raised her voice. 'Leave 'em tied up in the shade of the house. We'll feed and water them until you return.' She finally gave them a smile, and it wasn't a warm, encouraging one. It was more of a wry grin. '*If* you return, that is.'

Sur Rhyff finally dismounted, and Islington and Pentonville exchanged a glance. Both were thinking the same thing . . . could they leave him behind as well? But no, they had their orders.

With the horses secured, they donned their packs laden with provisions. The sun was high, the air clear and bright, but there was a gloomy pall over the party as they took their first steps past the big, solid watchtower and set off for the rocky wastes of the west.

27

Dallow was fading fast at the oars, and none was more relieved as the little boat made its way round the final bend in the river. Runt craned his neck for a better look, and he saw the crossing point where Father M and Hurm had abandoned him and the mule several days earlier. And there was the wooden jetty, from which his ill-fated voyage had begun. Beyond, in the distance, he could see the top of the city walls at Chatter's Reach, as well as the shattered bell tower.

There was an old man sitting on the end of the jetty, a fishing rod in his hands, his bare feet dangling over the water. He was stooped and wrinkled, with a bushy white beard and a floppy hat which was so old there were more holes than fabric.

Berry murmured an order to Dallow, who altered course for the shore. The fisherman watched their approach, and as they prepared to land he got up and hurried along the bank.

'Take off your uniform coat,' Runt whispered to Berry. 'Quick! The locals may think you're an enemy soldier of some kind.'

Berry did so, stowing the neat blue jacket under the seat before laying his tricorne hat on top. Then he cupped his hands to his mouth. 'You there!' he called to the fisherman. 'A hand to the line, if you please!'

The man obeyed, catching the rope and hauling it in until the boat's keel scraped on the gritty soil, his corded forearms making short work of the job. Then, without a word, he tied the rope off around a post with short, sharp gestures.

Runt wasn't the best judge of character, but he could tell the man was angry about something. Oh well, he thought. Perhaps we scared the fish away.

'Thank you, my good sir,' said Berry. 'Would you mind looking after our boat while we–'

This was too much for the elderly fisherman, who rounded on them, his face livid. '*Your* boat?' he shouted. 'So it's *your* fudding boat now, is it? First you piff off with it, and then you want me to *mind* it?'

'I'm sorry, my good man. I was not aware–'

'Don't you good man me, you pilfering little whippersnapper.' The fisherman turned and raised his voice . . . even more. 'Guards! *Guards!*'

'Shh!' said Runt urgently. 'Believe me, you old loon, nobody stole your boat. It floated away by mistake!'

The fisherman looked like he was going to take a swing at him, but Berry intervened quickly. 'Let us settle this amicably. Runt here will pay you a fair rate for the hire of your vessel.'

'What?' said Runt, who rarely paid for anything he could steal. 'Are you kidding?'

'We've been starving!' growled the fisherman. 'No food for me family, and seven mouths to feed. Had to use all me savings to get by.'

'Which was it?' demanded Runt. 'You starved, or you got by on your savings?'

Berry laid a hand on his arm. 'Pay the man, Runt. Fair recompense.'

Muttering under his breath, Runt dug out a copper coin.

Then, seeing the fisherman's look of anger, he added another. 'There you are.'

'Two pennies? Is that all?'

'It would have been more if you'd left the damned oars in it,' snapped Runt. 'I could have drowned at sea, and then where would your precious boat be?'

The fisherman took the coins grudgingly, tucking them into the pocket of his shabby waistcoat. Berry held a hand out, and they shook to indicate there were no hard feelings. Meanwhile, Runt retrieved his coins from the old man's waistcoat with a slick piece of pick-pocketing.

They were about to go their separate ways when a man on horseback appeared over the crest of the bank. He was wearing well-used armour, and had an impressive sword, and there was a no-nonsense look on his face.

Runt frowned, for he was sure he'd seen the man before. He was still trying to place the face when he heard a cry.

'Make way there. Make way for Sur Cumfrence!'

'Oh, *spit*,' muttered Runt, and sure enough the generously proportioned knight appeared, his big, round body encased in gleaming armour. His horse was panting hard as it struggled to carry the weight, and it looked like it might snap in two at any minute. Runt would have pointed and laughed, but the last time he encountered the big knight he'd pushed his luck to the limit, and had almost ended up with his neck on the executioner's block. Now, he just hoped he wasn't recognised.

Sur Cumfrence was flanked by a dozen hard-bitten men and women on horseback, and together the group rode down the shallow bank towards the river. 'What was all the shouting?' demanded Sur Cumfrence, in a thin, reedy voice. 'Who is this rabble, and why do they stare at one so?'

'Shall I kill them all, my lord?'

'No, don't bothah. You always get blood on my armour.'

'Yes, sir.'

'I don't like that impish fellah, though. If he gets in my way, drag him away an' strangle him.'

Berry and Dallow were staring at the procession with open-mouthed astonishment, and Runt realised that, to them, knights on horseback were straight out of fairy tales and legends. Either that, or they were dumbfounded by the sight of the big metal-plated egg with arms and legs.

As the group rode up, the fisherman yanked his cap off and bowed his head. Runt didn't have a cap, but he bent his head too, more to hide his face than to show deference.

'What was all the racket?' demanded Sur Cumfrence. 'Was that your yellin' disturbing one's ride?'

'No sir. I mean, yes sir,' mumbled the fisherman. 'Just a misunderstanding, sir.'

Sur Cumfrence eyed Berry and Dallow, who eyed him right back. The knight didn't like it, for these men weren't behaving like obedient peasants. Angrily, he reined in his horse. 'You there. Do you not bow to your betters?'

'I do indeed,' said Berry, gazing up at him.

Sur Cumfrence reddened at the slight, for Berry hadn't so much as nodded. 'That head of yours would look better on a spike,' he spat.

'First you would have to take it,' said Berry, so quietly that only Runt and Sur Cumfrence heard him.

The knight swore and spurred his mount onward, and moments later his horse was knee-deep in the river. The rest of the men followed, fanning out to protect their leader, and Berry and Runt exchanged a glance. 'You could have just nodded,' growled Runt.

Berry glanced at Sur Cumfrence's ample back, the polished

armour gleaming in the sunlight. 'I could have drilled him with a single shot.'

'And then what?' demanded Runt. 'Club the other twelve to death single-handedly?'

Meanwhile, the fisherman was untying his boat, and as he prepared to cast off he spotted the navy jackets under the seat. 'Hey, you forgot your uniforms,' he said, holding them up and shaking them.

The departing group heard him, and Sur Cumfrence raised a plump hand, calling a halt. Then, with much to-ing and fro-ing from his horse, he managed to turn and face them. He spotted the jackets before Runt could snatch them away, eying the unfamiliar epaulettes and shiny gold buttons with a stony look. Then he gestured to his men. 'Enemy soldiers. Grasp them! Grasp them immediately!'

Berry's hand dropped to his weapon, while Dallow was frozen to the spot and didn't move a muscle. There were too many to fight, though, and Berry ended up pushing his pistol deep into the top of his boot before raising his hands in surrender.

'Six of you will take them to the city, where you will have them arrested as spies and locked in the deepest dungeon. Tell his Lord Chylde that Sur Cumfrence captured these enemy troops single-handed, and that he presents the rascals for torture with his compliments.' He gestured. 'The rest of you will accompany me on the hunt. Onwards!'

Runt, Dallow and Berry were quickly searched, and Runt's dagger was taken away. The men were in a hurry and didn't think to look in the officers' boots, which was just as well because Dallow had followed Berry's lead and concealed his pistol there as well.

Next, the prisoners were secured, with rough ropes tight

around their wrists, and a loose hobble at their ankles to prevent them from running. Then they were led towards the city walls, stumbling along behind the men's horses.

Berry looked up as they approached the city gates, eying the walls with interest. He muttered something to Dallow, who snorted with laughter, but Runt missed it.

'Shut up!' shouted the nearest guard, a man with a face like worn leather. He carried an axe at his belt, the head well-used and frequently sharpened. 'Any more talking and I'll cut yer heads off meself.'

There was no more talking.

The horses' hooves clattered as the party rode under the archway, and then they came to a halt. One of Sur Cumfrence's men spoke briefly to a city guard, and then Runt, Dallow and Berry were transferred to their new captors. Done with their mission, the lord's men spurred their horses and set off for the river, intending to rejoin the hunt.

'Enemy soldiers, eh?' said the guard. He looked Berry up and down, then turned his attention to Runt. 'You're not in uniform.'

'Of course I'm not in uniform,' snapped Runt. 'I'm not a soldier.' He was grateful to Berry for his rescue, and the kindness the Stalyans had shown him aboard their ship, and for a whole lot of other things too, but he wasn't grateful enough to share in whatever punishment the guards had in store for the naval officers.

'You would say that, wouldn't you?' The guard frowned. 'Wait a minute, you came through here the day after the High Priest copped it. You and that big fighter and the children's entertainer.'

'That's right!' said Runt enthusiastically. 'You remember me,

240

I was just a harmless tourist.' He held up his bound wrists. 'Let me go, and I'll say no more of this misunderstanding.'

'You ain't an enemy soldier,' said the guard. 'You're worse than that. You're a spy!'

'What? Wait, no, I–'

Runt said no more, because the guard took a piece of rag, none too clean at that, and gagged him with it. Then he turned to Berry and Dallow. 'And you two. Thinking of invading us, were you?'

'Of course not,' said Berry calmly. 'Our ship lies in a nearby cove, where we're engaged in repairs after a sea battle. Once we're done, we'll leave your people in peace.'

'Ship? Sea battle? Leave us in peace?' the guard looked them up and down, taking in the navy blue uniforms and the elaborate tricorne hats. 'Where did you come from again?'

'From the republic of Stalya.' Berry couldn't doff his hat, not with his wrists tied, so he bowed instead. 'The Methusians are our mortal enemies, but we have no quarrel with you. Release us, and we will be on our way. Harm us, and the might of Stalya will crush your nation under its mighty iron boot.'

The guard scratched his head. 'Well, you do tell a good tale, but it's not up to me. Sur Cumfrence ordered you locked up, and there's gonna be questions.' He glanced at Runt. 'Oh yes, there will be questions indeed.' So saying, he gagged the other two then put his fingers to his lips and blew a piercing whistle. Moments later three of his comrades emerged from a nearby tavern, wiping foam from their mouths with the backs of their hands. 'Here, lads. Take 'em to the cells and secure them good and proper. It seems Sur Cumfrence captured them single-handedly.'

The guards stared at him, then burst out laughing.

'All right, all right,' said the first guard. 'The how of it doesn't matter. Just get them off the street.'

Runt, Berry and Dallow were handed to the newcomers, who led them down a side-street to the barracks, and from there to the cells. There were several flights of stairs, and the air grew colder and staler the further they went. There were groans from other prisoners, and they passed several cells with hapless inmates lying naked in drifts of filthy straw. Runt saw his companions exchanging worried looks, and Berry's earlier confidence had evaporated.

Finally, they were led to an open cell, where the guards shoved them in before cutting their bonds. There was a single wooden pallet for sleeping, a pile of old straw, and a wooden bucket ... already full. Runt was still examining his comfortable new quarters when the door slammed shut, the bolt driven home with an air of finality.

'Why didn't you shoot them?' hissed Runt.

'Two shots, three guards,' said Berry calmly. He indicated the door. 'And who knows how many more between us and freedom?'

'They're going to torture us. You know that, right?'

'Then we had better hope for rescue, or plot an escape ourselves.'

Runt went to try the door, but it was solid and didn't budge. Angrily, he gave it a swift kick, then hopped on one foot clasping his throbbing toes.

So much for capturing the Old Kingdom with the help of Berry's powerful warship. Instead, the Old Kingdom had captured them.

28

Spadell stood before Lord Chylde's magnificent desk, hands clasped behind his back. Chylde had already kept him waiting ten minutes, and Spadell's anger grew as the older man continued to scribble on a sheet of parchment. However, he knew better than to cough, or fidget, because such a thing would only ensure he waited ten minutes longer.

Chylde finally finished writing, and after shaking fine powder onto the wet ink from an ornate pot, he took the parchment and blew it clean. Then, at last, he glanced at Spadell. 'You return from your expedition. What kind of vessel was it? Was it a fishing boat after all?'

Spadell hesitated. To him, obeying orders was as instinctive as breathing, but if he told Lord Chylde the truth about the huge ship in the cove he'd be sending a lot of good men and women to their deaths. It was certain his lordship would try to capture the ship, and the city guard would fall in swathes against the might of that vessel. 'Sir, we did not see any fishing boats,' he said, skirting the truth.

'A pity. I tire of steak and chicken.' Chylde toyed with a piece of parchment. 'What news of my metal man?'

'None as yet, sir. The men have not been gone long.'

Chylde folded a corner of parchment, then unfolded it again

and smoothed it flat. He was dangerously calm, and Spadell awaited the outburst. Sure enough, Lord Chylde swore and slammed his fist on the desk, making his pens and inkpots rattle. 'It's not good enough!' he barked. 'Tell me why I shouldn't fire you? Why, I ought to put a better man in charge, for there are plenty to choose from.'

'I offer my resignation, sir.'

Spadell spoke quietly, but the words seemed to hit home. Chylde suppressed his anger with an effort, and he twisted his lips into a forced smile. 'Now don't be hasty, my good man. You've served me a good many years, and I value you greatly.'

But now that Spadell had voiced the idea, his mind was racing. *Why not?* he thought. *I've had my fill of guard duty, and of leading the men. I want to settle down, find a wife, raise a couple of kids and spend my days fishing and relaxing. All this death and bloodshed is tearing me apart.*

'You're not really thinking of quitting, are you?' demanded Lord Chylde. 'Tell you what. Why don't you take a furlough? Wander the land for a couple of weeks ... or a month, even. Grow a beard, bed as many women as you can, and come back to me when you've got this itch out of your system. How does that sound?'

Unbidden, a memory came to Spadell, as vivid as the midday sun. It was the moment when he'd rescued Tiera from the damaged tower, and he could suddenly feel her lithe, naked body cradled in his arms. Later, in the cells, when he'd put his cape around her for warmth, she'd tucked a lock of hair behind one ear and smiled at him, and that smile still shone in his memories. They'd only spoken two or three times, but there was something about her, something mysterious and dangerous, and he realised he wanted to see her again. *You fool*, he thought to himself. *No wonder you can't keep your mind on the job!*

'What say you?' Lord Chylde asked him.

Slowly, Spadell nodded. 'I will do as you say.'

'All right, you're dismissed,' said Chylde. 'Send me a list of names before you leave the city, and I'll pick one of them to lead the guard in your absence.'

Spadell bowed, then left Chylde's chambers with a spring in his step. For the first time in weeks, it felt like his life had purpose. So what if it was a fool's errand, chasing after a young woman who barely knew him?

Better a hopeless quest than living with no purpose at all.

When Tiera opened the front door to her house she was greeted by laughter and the welcome smell of roast chicken. To her surprise she found all three men in the front room, where Sur Pryze was putting on a mime act while Sur Loyne and Thonn cheered him on. Sur Pryze was good, surprisingly so, and as he finished Tiera clapped with the others.

Sur Loyne fetched her a plate of hot roast chicken, and in the meantime, Tiera set down the items she'd brought from the workshop.

'What do you have here?' asked Sur Loyne, taking up one of the oval moulds. Then he set it down again hurriedly. 'A death mask? You know how to sour a cheery gathering.'

'Death mask?' said Tiera. 'Couldn't they be casts taken from a living face?'

Sur Loyne shook his head. 'There are no breathing holes, neither at the mouth nor the nose.'

Thonn picked up one of the masks and inspected it. 'Who were they?'

Tiera swallowed a mouthful of chicken. 'No idea. I found them in a workshop, which was recently built over a burnt-out palace kitchen. According to one of the guards, a noble was taking a tour of the premises the day the king vanished.' She took another bite of chicken. 'Apparently, the two guards who accompanied the noble also vanished.'

All of them looked at the plaster casts. 'Three missing people, three death masks?' said Sur Loyne. 'That cannot be a coincidence, but this noble ... what concern is he of ours?'

'It may have been the king,' said Sur Pryze. 'Royalty often adopt a lesser persona so that they might travel amongst ordinary folk. Nobody recognises them without their crown.'

'I would,' said Sur Loyne. 'There is a portrait of King Larch at Queen Therstie's palace. I have seen it many a time.'

Sur Pryze stacked the three masks and handed them to him. 'Then you are best placed to inspect these properly, to determine whether any belong to the missing monarch.'

Reluctantly, Sur Loyne took the masks, and while Tiera demolished the rest of the chicken he checked them one by one, turning them this way and that, to see whether a trick of the light might enable him to recognise the features. 'They are all different people,' he said at last, 'but it's not easy to recognise a face when it's reversed like this.'

Tiera set her plate aside and took up the bowl of grease. 'Spread this on the inside of each mask,' she said, handing it to Sur Loyne.

The knight took one look at the sticky grease and passed the bowl to Sur Pryze. 'You may wish to use a rag,' he said.

Sur Pryze passed it to Thonn. 'You have the nimblest fingers of us all, lad. Why, I can barely polish my own sword without cutting three fingers off.'

Thonn looked at Tiera, but she got up and left for the rear of the house, taking the small sack of plaster with her. On the way she collected a bowl, and when she reached the back yard she emptied dry plaster into it, before removing the stopper from the water pipe. When she judged the mix was wet enough, she stoppered the pipe and stirred the plaster with a stick, blending it to a smooth consistency.

Back in the front room, Thonn had finished greasing the moulds, and it took Tiera only a moment to pour plaster into each one. Then she sent Thonn to clean the bowl out while she waited for the plaster to dry.

As soon as it was set, she borrowed a knife from Sur Loyne and levered the solid lump of plaster out of the mould. It came free with a sucking sound, and then she was holding a positive image of the dead man's face. It sent a shiver up her spine, and she passed it to Sur Loyne while she extracted the second face. Finally she got the third one out, and that's when Sur Loyne muttered a curse.

'King Larch!' he muttered. 'That is him, or I'm a penniless begger.'

'Well,' said Sur Pryze. 'Now we know for certain the king's dead. The question is, what do we do about it?'

Sur Loyne was silent. His plan involved finding the king alive, so that the pretender Sur Kah might be kicked off the throne . . . and perhaps executed for treason. Now, it seemed, his ideas had come to naught.

Meanwhile, Tiera was inspecting the sheets of parchment she'd rescued from the workshop. Both were covered in intricate diagrams, and each had the same writing in the corner: This document is the property of Wiltred of Tharn. 'Does anyone know of this man?' she asked.

Everyone shook their heads.

'Well, either that was his workshop, or someone stole these plans from him.'

'It won't take long to find him,' said Sur Loyne with conviction. 'After that we'll torture him until he confesses to the killing.'

Tiera turned one of the sheets over, and she saw it was covered in dense scrawl. It appeared to be notes or instructions concerning the diagrams, and in several places she saw the phrase 'as suggested by Tyniwon.' 'What about Tyniwon?' she asked the knights. 'Have you heard of him?'

Sur Loyne jumped as though he'd been shot, and he snatched the parchment from her fingers, inspecting the writing by torchlight. 'Tyniwon? Tyniwon! But ... this is a blessing indeed.'

'Who is he?' asked Tiera.

Sur Loyne and Sur Pryze exchanged a glance, but the name was hardly a state secret. 'Queen Therstie has a half-brother, one Tyniwon Mollister. He has been living in the Bark Kingdom these past few months, and she sent us to get him back.'

Tiera eyed the death masks. 'He's not one of those, is he?'

'No.' Sur Loyne realised something, and his expression changed. 'You know what this means?' he said quietly.

The others looked at him.

'Queen Therstie ... she must have sent this Wiltred to assassinate King Larch. And her brother Tyniwon, he was to assist in the clean-up afterwards.' There was admiration in his voice, for he appreciated the queen's cunning. 'You can see her plan, can you not? All along she planned to put one of her knights on the throne in King Larch's place, to ensure the Bark kingdom becomes a Mollister province. It's genius!' Then his face fell. 'Alas, this makes our task harder, for should his involvement become apparent, the Bark kingdom will have no choice but to declare war.'

'Even with Sur Kah as their monarch?' asked Sur Pryze.

'If he refuses to fight us over the death of King Larch, the Barks will execute him first and *then* go to war,' said Sur Loyne.

'Then what should we do?' asked Sur Pryze.

'We must find Tyniwon and smuggle him swiftly from the kingdom,' said Sur Loyne firmly. 'His involvement must never become public knowledge.' He gave Tiera a grateful look. 'You have done well by us. Finding that manuscript with Tyniwon's name has probably saved countless lives. If it fell into Bark hands ... '

At this, Tiera took both parchments, scrunched them up and threw them onto the fire. She added the bowl of grease, which began to spit and crackle before flaring up. 'What of the masks?' she asked.

Sur Loyne handed them to Thonn. 'Take these outside, and hammer them until every piece is smaller than your fingernail. Every piece, mind!'

Thonn left, and soon they heard hefty thuds as he obeyed.

Meanwhile, Sur Loyne was staring at Tiera. 'Chatter's Reach!' he exclaimed. 'That's where I saw you! You were in the cells with the captain! And the boy ... he–'

'You beat him near to death while he was chained to the wall,' said Tiera quietly.

'Did the beating addle his brain? For he acts as though he does not recognise me, when surely he'd sooner plunge a dagger into my heart.'

'We have our own problems to worry about,' muttered Tiera.

249

'So what, then? Maintain a truce until we part, so that he might seek vengeance later, at a time of his choosing?'

'That's about the size of it,' said Tiera. 'But if you're thinking of ending him first, be aware he's not the one you should be worried about.'

Sur Loyne swallowed, for Tiera had let her peasant-girl persona slip, revealing a hard edge that gave him plenty to think about.

'As for him recognising you ... he won't,' said Tiera, who'd decided to toy with the knight. 'I put a powerful spell on him.'

'That's why you were in the cells,' whispered Sur Loyne. 'Witchcraft and magic!'

'I'm not denying it.' Tiera stood up to put some more branches on the fire. As she picked up one of the sticks she waved it quickly, making it swish through the air, and Sur Loyne pushed his chair back so fast he toppled over to land with a crash on the floor. Tiera turned to face him, stick in one hand, the tip describing a figure-of-eight. Sur Loyne's terrified expression was so funny she almost burst out laughing, but instead she turned her back and threw the stick on the fire.

Sur Loyne recovered, his face red, while Sur Pryze stared at the pair of them as though they'd been telling off-colour jokes in Elvish. Wisely, he didn't ask why.

At that moment Thonn returned, and he wordlessly passed a fragment of white plaster to Sur Loyne. 'That's the biggest,' he said. 'I hope it meets with your approval?'

'Er, y-yes,' said Sur Loyne quickly. 'Excellent job, young man. Truly excellent.'

The rest of the evening passed quickly, and before long they retired for the night. As Tiera lay on the hard wooden pallet, trying to get comfortable, she thought of the strange twists and turns life kept dishing out to her. Instead of a quite life in Branche, she was now embroiled in a quest to find this Tyniwon character. And then, if they managed to get their hands on him, they were supposed to spirit him out of the Bark kingdom before his involvement in King Larch's death was uncovered.

If he was involved, she thought, but that was something they'd worry about after they found him.

29

Clunk and Millie had almost made their way around the lake. They were keeping one eye on the sky in case the dragon came back, and another on the base of the cliffs in case they spotted a cave. They hadn't met up with Father M and Hurm yet, which meant the other two must have found shelter. Or, thought Clunk, perhaps the dragon had eaten the pair of them first. He decided not to mention this disconcerting thought to Millie, since it was obvious she was keen on Hurm.

Finally, they reached a cave mouth, where they both stopped to stare at the ground in horror. Right there, outside the cave, was a large area covered in bloodstains. They would have been even more horrified if the blood had been red, but instead it was a greenish colour.

'Do you think mighty Hurm wounded the dragon?'

Clunk doubted it very much. As far as he was concerned, attacking the dragon with a sword was like trying to kill a blue whale with a thumb tack, and about a thousand times more dangerous. Then he heard voices, and he crouched and faced the cave. 'Hush,' he whispered. 'I think our companions are within.'

'So why the hush?'

'It may be someone else.'

Millie ducked down as well, and they approached the cave cautiously, bent double. When they got there they crouched behind a boulder, then raised their heads to look inside. What they saw was troubling ... very troubling indeed.

Father M and Hurm were sitting on the earthen floor, just beyond a merry campfire. Facing them, standing with their backs to Clunk and Millie, were three very odd figures. One was short and squat, wearing full plate armour, with a huge axe over one shoulder. Another was a tall, slender male with long blond hair and greenish clothing. There was a bow over his shoulder, and when Clunk noticed the pointed ears he realised it had to be an elf. Finally, there was a short creature in a much-mended jerkin, with dark green skin and short, cropped hair.

'They've been captured,' whispered Millie.

The elf heard her, and he unslung his bow and turned in one fluid motion. Clunk pulled Millie down behind the rock just as an arrow sped through the space where her head had been. It splashed in the water, fifty yards beyond, and then Clunk heard shouting.

'Stay hidden,' he hissed at Millie, and then he leapt up and ran towards the cave. The elf fired two more shots, even as Father M and Hurm struggled to their feet, but the arrows ricocheted off Clunk's metal skin. Meanwhile, the dwarf had taken a fighting stance, his axe ready to meet the advancing robot.

Clunk covered the space in the blink of an eye, his feet throwing up plumes of sand as he raced towards the cave. On the way, he analysed the three enemies, paying no attention to Father M or Hurm. He decided to tackle the dwarf first, because the axe would certainly damage him if a blow landed. On the other hand, the elf's arrows were pinpricks, and the little green fellow didn't appear to be armed.

Clunk was three paces from the dwarf when he saw Father M raise both hands, fingers outstretched. He'd seen the wizard performing spells before, and he expected a huge sheet of flame, or a chilling frost, or some kind of clumsiness curse.

Instead, Father M shouted at the three attackers in Clunk's sights. 'Don't shoot! He's on our side! Don't shoot!'

Clunk evaluated the situation in a split second. Far from three enemies holding Hurm and Father M captive, it seemed the odd-looking newcomers were friends and allies. Unfortunately, by now Clunk was moving so fast there was no way he was going to stop. Instead of crashing into the trio, he sprang into the air, flying over the elf's head and narrowly missing the low-hanging roof of the cave. He described a graceful somersault in mid-air, landed on his hands and rolled in the dirt, before using his legs like pistons against the back wall to bring himself to a halt.

Clunk stood up, dusting himself down, and Father M introduced him. Stonesmasher the dwarf and Slimbough the elf shook his hand gingerly, both of them stunned into silence by his polished metal body and human-like appearance. Splodge, meanwhile, seemed very casual.

'What a wonderful creature,' breathed Slimbough, his elven superiority slipping.

'With a warrior such as this nobody could lose a battle,' said Stonesmasher.

'He's not all that,' said Splodge. 'What?' he added, when the others looked at him in disbelief. 'I grew up around huge dragons. What's a metal man to that?'

Meanwhile, Millie had left her hiding place, and she now entered the cave. Slimbough and Stonesmasher nodded a greeting, while Splodge smiled at her. 'Is everyone safe?' she asked. 'Were you troubled by the dragon?'

'A mere dragon couldn't trouble us,' said Father M heartily. 'Why, in my experience–'

'Good, I'm happy,' said Millie, cutting him off. Then she eyed Splodge. 'Are you a gorblin?'

'Yes ma'am.' Splodge bowed. 'A pleasure to meet you.'

'Where did you spring from?'

'There's a secret door at the rear of the cave.' Splodge looked around the large gathering. 'Well, it used to be secret, at least. We live underground, if you can call it living.'

'Splodge will accompany us,' said Father M, ignoring Stonesmasher's frown of disapproval. 'His local knowledge will be invaluable. Go on, Splodge. Tell them something useful.'

Put on the spot, Splodge just stood there, racking his brains. Then his face cleared. 'Hey, there's something I can tell you about dragons!'

'Go ahead, we're listening,' said Father M pompously.

'Well, did you know they only breed once every 100 years?'

'Like Father M,' said Hurm, and Millie snorted with laughter. All that impressive muscle, and funny too! Little did she know the fighter wasn't actually joking, he was merely exaggerating a little.

'Once a hundred years!' exclaimed Stonesmasher. 'No wonder the beast was so cranky.'

Encouraged, Splodge continued. 'Their young take forty years to hatch, making dragonlings the rarest of creatures.' He glanced at Father M. 'It's just as well you've given up on your foolish quest to snatch one of their offspring, for your chances of success were zero.'

'Hurm not give up,' said the fighter, with the air of one

who would not be swayed by deft, convincing arguments nor imminent, painful death.

'He's right,' sighed Father M. 'We've still got to catch one. It's not just his knighthood, there are huge riches involved, and fame everlasting, and–'

'You had me at huge riches,' said Stonesmasher, and he exchanged a glance with Slim. 'What about you? Your people await news of the latest shipment of building materials.'

'They can whistle for their bricks,' said Slim. 'After all, a home isn't built in a day. Yes, I am indeed in, as you put it.'

They all looked at Splodge, who shrugged. 'I would have died young and alone in the gorblin tunnels. Dying young with a group of friends? Sure, count me in too.'

Father M rubbed his hands together vigorously. 'Now this is what I call a party,' he said, much happier now there were several lines of defence between himself and any danger. 'Why, with our combined talents I'm sure we'll be able to snatch a dragonling, escape the vengeful parents and present it to Queen Therstie!'

The others all nodded and murmured their assent, bar Clunk and Millie. The former had seen humans imbibing alcoholic drinks on one or two occasions, and he knew it rendered them bold and prone to major errors of judgement. He couldn't smell any alcohol in the cave, but if they thought taking a baby dragon would be easy, they had to be blind drunk.

And Millie, having seen her parents struck down by bandits only months earlier, was not in a hurry to join another group, only to watch them suffer the same fate at the hands of angry dragons. 'I just want to go home,' she said quietly. 'Clunk?'

Slowly, reluctantly, he shook his head. 'I'm sorry, I know it's dangerous, but this quest is vital if I'm ever to return home.'

'What about me?' demanded Millie. 'I cannot stay here

alone, dying of starvation, trapped between gorblins and dragons. Must I therefore accompany you on this foolish, nay, suicidal errand?'

Silently, Hurm pushed his way through the others and took Millie in his thick, muscled arms, cradling her head to his chest. 'Hurm protect,' he said quietly.

'Count me in,' said Millie, her voice muffled by his rock-like pecs.

With everyone now happy to proceed, the newly-formed party settled around the campfire to craft an elaborate plan.

'We find the nearest baby dragon, grab the thing and run like hell,' said Father M.

Everyone nodded, for it was a wise plan indeed, and with the matter settled they spread out to feast on Hurm's freshly-cooked rabbits. They all felt it was a poor substitute for freshly-killed dragon, but on the other hand rabbits didn't chew giant rocks nor spew huge geysers of fire.

Clunk could see one or two holes in Father M's rather threadbare plan, but he decided not to voice his concerns. Instead, he went to the mouth of the cave to keep an eye out for huge, hungry dragons. As he stood there, gazing across the lake which had almost drowned his companions, eying the remains of the rockfall which had almost crushed Millie, he wondered whether his personal quest might be putting the others in a little too much danger. Should he give up trying to leave this planet? Slowly, he turned his gaze on the bright blue sky. Beyond that sky, he knew, were countless stars and inhabited worlds. Which one was his?

And then he managed to isolate a thought which had been troubling him for several days now.

Someone out there must realise he was gone. So why hadn't they come looking for him?

A huge patch of burnt wreckage lay on the surface of the ocean, and seagulls bickered and screamed as they hunted for scraps amongst the charred timbers and twisted, blackened ropes.

'Urgh!'

Half a dozen seagulls took flight as a piece of 'wreckage' moved, and they kept their distance as the lone survivor raised a shaking hand to his forehead. It just wasn't his day, the man knew that now, but at least he'd survived the inferno which had consumed the warship, and the huge explosion which had decimated the remains.

The man had a lean, tanned face and a shock of dark hair, although it was hard to tell exactly what he looked like, because his hair was plastered onto his face and his face was smeared with soot and grease. He was clinging to a small barrel, which was the only thing keeping him from joining his ex-crewmates at the bottom of the sea. Actually, he'd seen several triangular fins cutting through the wreckage, and he suspected few members of the crew had made it as far as the ocean floor. Indeed, the sharks had jumped most of them the second they hit the water, putting an end to many a promising career.

The man was thirsty, and tired, and dazed, and as he bobbed on the ocean waves, surrounded by screaming gulls, he pondered the exciting turn of events which had deposited him in that place, at that very moment. All in all, it had been a strange couple of days.

First, he'd been rescued from the ocean by a magnificent sailing vessel. They'd found him treading water, and they'd taken him on board, dried him off and fed him. The big wooden ship was a Methusian man o' war, and the captain explained, over a delicious dinner, that they were hunting an enemy ship which had been spotted in the area. Apparently the evil Stalyans were bent on attacking innocent merchants, trying to disrupt supplies by killing civilians and sinking their ships.

The captain and crew had treated him with courtesy and good humour, and he'd just been getting to know them all when an enemy ship had been sighted. Not half an hour later, the Methusian ship, her captain, and the entire crew had been blown sky-high.

The man would have died with them, only he'd been blasted overboard by an earlier explosion, and had been watching his new friends sailing away from him when they'd all been blown up.

And so he'd survived, but for how long? The man tried to swallow, but his throat was parched and his tongue was swollen. He'd lost track of time, but he was pretty sure it had been a whole day and night since the explosion, and he was starting to experience hallucinations.

He held the barrel tight and closed his eyes, and immediately had a weird vision. He was sitting in a small capsule, buffeted by an ear-shattering roar, and he could see fire tearing past the outside of a small round window nearby. Then a massive jolt, and the next thing he knew he was treading water.

He realised his mind, confused and dazed, was mixing up real events with imaginary ones. An explosion followed by a ducking ... that was real. Fire? definitely. But the capsule and the little round window? Pure fantasy.

With a jolt, the man grabbed at the barrel. He'd almost let go, and that would have been the end. Willing his eyes open, he scanned the horizon for any sign of help. Then, more slowly, he scanned one region again. There was a vague shadow on the water, like the faintest mist, but he knew with stone cold certainty it was land.

Real land, or imaginary?

Well, there was only one way to find out. Still gripping the barrel under one arm, the man paddled with his free hand. Inch by inch he moved through the burnt timbers, floating planks and frayed pieces of rope, and once he was clear he started paddling in earnest, a stubborn set to his manly jaw.

'You've seen off bigger challenges than this,' the man told himself sternly, his voice thick and almost unrecognisable. 'I'm going to survive this bundle of laughs too ... or my name's not Hal Spacejock.'

Sur Rhyff's Plea

Now that you've reached the end of this tome
You should purchase book three and give it a home.
Yes, it's a fantasy series, and we know what that means
There are so many words. Like . . . reams and reams!
(c) Sur Rhyff

The story continues in **A Pair of Nuts on the Throne** . . .

If you enjoyed this book, please leave a brief review at your online bookseller of choice. Thanks!

About the Author

Simon Haynes was born in England and grew up in Spain. His family moved to Australia when he was 16.

In addition to novels, Simon writes computer software. In fact, he writes computer software to help him write novels faster, which leaves him more time to improve his writing software. And write novels faster. (www.spacejock.com/yWriter.html)

Simon's goal is to write fifteen novels before someone takes his keyboard away.

Update 2018: goal achieved and I still have my keyboard!

New goal: write thirty novels.

Simon's website is spacejock.com.au

Stay in touch!

Author's newsletter:
spacejock.com.au/ML.html

facebook.com/halspacejock
twitter.com/spacejock

Acknowledgements

Ian, Dennis, Darla, Emmery, Tony, Peter, Paul Franco, Shane,
Mike, Ray, Ren?, Corey, Olaf, Paul, Lance, Maurice, Alison,
Trevor, Kathy, Simon, Calvert, Don, John, Diane, Kathy, Neil,
Liana, Olivier ... and anyone whose name slipped through
during the frantic proofing period,
thanks for the awesome help and support!

The Hal Spacejock series by Simon Haynes

1. A ROBOT NAMED CLUNK

Deep in debt and with his life on the line, Hal takes on a dodgy cargo job ... and an equally dodgy co-pilot.

2. SECOND COURSE

When Hal finds an alien teleporter network he does the sensible thing and pushes Clunk the robot in first.

3. JUST DESSERTS

Gun-crazed mercenaries have Hal in their sights, and a secret agent is pulling the strings. One wrong step and three planets go to war!

4. NO FREE LUNCH

Everyone thinks Peace Force trainee Harriet Walsh is paranoid and deluded, but Hal stands at her side. That would be the handcuffs.

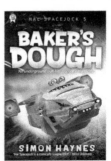

5. BAKER'S DOUGH

When you stand to inherit a fortune, good body-guards are essential. If you're really desperate, call Hal and Clunk. Baker's Dough features intense rivalry, sublime double-crosses and more greed than a free buffet.

6. SAFE ART

Valuable artworks and a tight deadline ... you'd be mad to hire Hal for that one, but who said the art world was sane?

7. BIG BANG

A house clearance job sounds like easy money, but rising floodwaters, an unstable landscape and a surprise find are going to make life very difficult for Hal and Clunk.

8. DOUBLE TROUBLE

Hal Spacejock dons a flash suit, hypershades and a curly earpiece for a stint as a secret agent, while a pair of Clunk's most rusted friends invite him to a 'unique business opportunity'.

9. MAX DAMAGE

Hal and Clunk answer a distress call, and they discover a fellow pilot stranded deep inside an asteroid field. Clunk is busy at the controls so Hal dons a spacesuit and sets off on a heroic rescue mission.

10. Cold Boots

Coming 2019

Ebook and Trade Paperback

The Secret War Series
Set in the Hal Spacejock universe

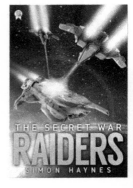

Everyone is touched by the war, and Sam Willet is no exception.

Sam wants to train as a fighter pilot, but instead she's assigned to Tactical Operations. It's vital work, but it's still a desk job, far from the front line.

Then, terrible news: Sam's older brother is killed in combat.

Sam is given leave to attend his memorial service, but she's barely boarded the transport when the enemy launches a surprise attack, striking far behind friendly lines as they try to take the entire sector.

Desperately short of pilots, the Commander asks Sam to step up.

Now, at last, she has the chance to prove herself.

But will that chance end in death... or glory?

Ebook and Trade Paperback

The Harriet Walsh series

Harriet's boss is a huge robot with failing batteries, the patrol car is driving her up the wall and her first big case will probably kill her.

So why did she join the Peace Force?

When an intergalactic crime-fighting organisation offers Harriet Walsh a job, she's convinced it's a mistake. She dislikes puzzles, has never read a detective mystery, and hates wearing uniforms. It makes no sense ... why would the Peace Force choose her?

Who cares? Harriet needs the money, and as long as they keep paying her, she's happy to go along with the training.

She'd better dig out some of those detective mysteries though, because she's about to embark on her first real mission ...

The Peace Force has a new recruit, and she's driving everyone crazy.

From disobeying orders to handling unauthorised cases, nothing is off-limits. Worse, Harriet Walsh is forced to team up with the newbie, because the recruit's shady past has just caught up with her.

Meanwhile, a dignitary wants to complain about rogue officers working out of the station. She insists on meeting the station's commanding officer ... and they don't have one.

All up, it's another typical day in the Peace Force!

Dismolle is supposed to be a peaceful retirement planet. So what's with all the gunfire?

A criminal gang has moved into Chirless, planet Dismolle's second major city. Elderly residents are fed up with all the loud music, noisy cars and late night parties, not to mention the hold-ups, muggings and the occasional gunfight.

There's no Peace Force in Chirless, so they call on Harriet Walsh of the Dismolle City branch for help. That puts Harriet right in the firing line, and now she's supposed to round up an entire gang with only her training pistol and a few old allies as backup.

And her allies aren't just old, they're positively ancient!

Ebook and Trade Paperback

The Hal Junior Series
Set in the Hal Spacejock universe

Spot the crossover characters, references and in-jokes!

Hal Junior lives aboard a futuristic space station. His mum is chief scientist, his dad cleans air filters and his best mate is Stephen 'Stinky' Binn. As for Hal ... he's a bit of a trouble magnet. He means well, but his wild schemes and crazy plans never turn out as expected!

Hal Junior: The Secret Signal features mayhem and laughs, daring and intrigue ... plus a home-made space cannon!

200 pages, illustrated, ISBN 978-1-877034-07-7

"A thoroughly enjoyable read for 10-year-olds and adults alike"
The West Australian

'I've heard of food going off
    ... but this is ridiculous!'

Space Station Oberon is expecting an important visitor, and everyone is on their best behaviour. Even Hal Junior is doing his best to stay out of trouble!

From multi-coloured smoke bombs to exploding space rations, Hal Junior proves ... ***trouble is what he's best at!***

200 pages, illustrated, ISBN 978-1-877034-25-1

Imagine a whole week of fishing, swimming, sleeping in tents and running wild!
Unfortunately, the boys crash land in the middle of a forest, and there's little chance of rescue. Is this the end of the camping trip ... or the start of a thrilling new adventure?

200 pages, illustrated, ISBN 978-1-877034-24-4

Space Station Oberon is on high alert, because a comet is about to whizz past the nearby planet of Gyris. All the scientists are preparing for the exciting event, and all the kids are planning on watching.

All the kids except Hal Junior, who's been given detention...

165 pages, illustrated, ISBN 978-1-877034-38-1

Ebook and Trade Paperback

New from Simon Haynes
The Robot vs Dragons series

"Laugh after laugh, dark in places but the humour punches through. One of the best books I've read in 2018 so far. Amazing, 5*"

Welcome to the Old Kingdom!

It's a wonderful time to visit! There's lots to do and plenty to see!
What are you waiting for? Dive into the Old Kingdom right now!

Clunk, an elderly robot, does exactly that. He's just plunged into the sea off the coast of the Old Kingdom, and if he knew what was coming next he'd sit down on the ocean floor and wait for rescue.

Dragged from the ocean, coughing up seaweed, salty water and stray pieces of jellyfish, he's taken to the nearby city of Chatter's Reach, where he's given a sword and told to fight the Queen's Champion, Sur Loyne.

As if that wasn't bad enough, the Old Kingdom still thinks the wheel is a pretty nifty idea, and Clunk's chances of finding spare parts - or his missing memory modules - are nil.

Still, Clunk is an optimist, and it's not long before he's embarking on a quest to find his way home.

Unfortunately it's going to be a very tough ask, given the lack of charging points in the medieval kingdom...

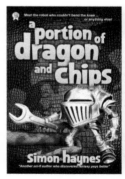  

Ebook and Trade Paperback